She had almost been his wife,

Marcy thought. But almost didn't count. The cold hard fact was that they weren't married, they'd never even been engaged. They shared a child and a past—that was it. Cruz didn't belong to her any longer, and hadn't for a very long time. She had no right to be angry because he'd gone on with his life—and the sooner she got that straight, the sooner she would stop making a fool of herself.

She thought of how he'd looked at her just now and felt her heart ram hard against her rib cage. She could almost convince herself she'd seen something in his eyes, could almost fool herself into believing there had been some emotion there, some...love.

Dear Reader,

Merry Christmas, Happy Holidays of all sorts and welcome to another fabulous month's worth of books here at Intimate Moments. And here's a wonderful holiday gift for you: *Captive Star*, the newest book from bestselling, award-winning and just plain incredibly talented author Nora Roberts. The next of THE STARS OF MITHRA miniseries, this book has Nora's signature sizzle and spark, all wrapped up in a compellingly suspenseful plot about a couple on the run—handcuffed together!

We've got another miniseries "jewel" for you, too: *The Taming of Reid Donovan*, the latest in Marilyn Pappano's SOUTHERN KNIGHTS series. There's a twist in this one that I think will really catch you by surprise. Susan Sizemore debuts at Silhouette with *Stranger by Her Side*, a book as hot and steamy as its setting.

And then there are our Christmas books, three tantalizing tales of holiday romance. *One Christmas Knight*, by Kathleen Creighton, features one of the most memorable casts of characters I've ever met. Take one gentlemanly Southern trucker, one about-to-deliver single mom, the biggest snowstorm in a generation, put them together and what do you get? How about a book you won't be able to put down? Rebecca Daniels is back with *Yuletide Bride*, a secret child story line with a Christmas motif. And finally, welcome brand-new author Rina Naiman, whose *A Family for Christmas* is a warm and wonderful holiday debut.

Enjoy—and the very happiest of holidays to you and yours.

Leslie J. Wainger
Senior Editor and Editorial Coordinator

Please address questions and book requests to:
Silhouette Reader Service
U.S.: 3010 Walden Ave., P.O. Box 1325, Buffalo, NY 14269
Canadian: P.O. Box 609, Fort Erie, Ont. L2A 5X3

YULETIDE BRIDE

REBECCA DANIELS

Silhouette®
INTIMATE MOMENTS®

Published by Silhouette Books

America's Publisher of Contemporary Romance

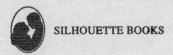

SILHOUETTE BOOKS

ISBN 0-373-07827-7

YULETIDE BRIDE

Copyright © 1997 by Ann Marie Fattarsi

Printed in U.S.A.

REBECCA DANIELS

will never forget the first time she read a Silhouette novel. "I was at my sister's house, sitting by the pool and trying without much success to get interested in the book I'd brought from home. Everything seemed to distract me—the kids splashing around, the seagulls squawking, the dog barking. Finally, my sister plucked the book from my hands, told me she was going to give me something I wouldn't be able to put down and handed me my first Silhouette novel. Guess what? She was right! For that lazy afternoon by her pool, I will forever be grateful." That was years ago, and Rebecca has been writing romance novels ever since.

Born in the Midwest but raised in Southern California, she now resides in Northern California's San Joaquin Valley with her husband and two sons. She is a lifelong poet and song lyricist who enjoys early-morning walks, an occasional round of golf, scouring California's Mother Lode region for antiques and traveling.

TYVMFE!—for Lippy,
for having wiped away an ocean of tears.

Chapter 1

"I don't mind telling you I appreciate your coming right down."

Cruz Martinez tossed his keys and wallet onto the top shelf of the small locker in the doctors' lounge. "Why, Nurse Burns, did you miss me?"

Carrie Burns snorted inelegantly. "Oh, yes, I missed you like I miss trouble."

"Oh, no, you don't, I'm onto you," Cruz said with a wink, pulling off his faded yellow polo shirt and hanging it on a hook in the locker. He reached for the starch-stiff surgical shirt and slipped it over his head. "You love trouble. I've heard about you and those wild bingo games in the basement of the Methodist Church on Wednesday nights. Things get a little rowdy down there, from what I understand."

"Well, you've found me out, Dr. Martinez. What can I say?" Carrie commented dryly, letting the heavy door of the doctors' lounge swing shut behind her short, solid frame. "I'm a loose woman—I admit it. But in spite of that animal magnetism of yours and irresistible charm, what I want from you right at the moment is your medical expertise. It's been crazy around here tonight, and that young resident they sent over from Sparks seems a whole lot more interested in cornering my student nurses in the supply closet than treating the patients."

Cruz immodestly unzipped the fly of his jeans and stepped out of them, then pulled the surgical greens over his boxer shorts. "Doug's okay. He's just young. Besides, you know how hard it is to get any one to agree to come out here to work, so cut him some slack. Outside of the hospital—and your student nurses—there isn't a whole lot for him to do in Mesa Ridge."

"There isn't a lot for anyone to do in Mesa Ridge," Carrie said. "But that doesn't give him the right to harass my girls."

Cruz laughed, tightening the drawstring around his waist. "How do you know your Brownie troop wasn't harassing him?"

"Brownie troop," Carrie muttered, giving her head a shake and planting a firm hand on one of her solid hips. "Aren't you the clever one? And don't you start in on my student nurses. They volunteer their time around here, which is a whole lot more than I can say for your rambunctious Dr. Wheeler, and we'd be hard-pressed to run this place without them."

Cruz held up his hands in a sign of surrender. "Okay, okay, I give up, wave a white flag, throw in the towel, whatever you want. Just don't start lecturing me about your angels of mercy from the junior college again. Why don't you tell me what's been going on around here, instead?"

Carrie sighed. "Like I said, it's been crazy."

"Crazy crazy or just crazy normal?" Cruz asked, slipping on a pair of soft-soled running shoes and lacing them tight.

"Crazy crazy," Carrie told him, gesturing to the chart she held in her hand. "But that's not why I called. There was an accident out on highway 56 a couple of hours ago. A bad one. Hit-and-run. A woman and a young child were brought in. The little girl had a sore wrist, a few cuts and bruises—nothing serious. But her mother...she wasn't so lucky. She was in pretty bad shape when they got her here." Carrie lowered her voice, giving her head a jerk. "I think Dr. Wheeler got a little scared—wanted to just get her to a point where you could see her in the morning. He gave her a quick look, called the injury a puncture wound and stitched her up."

"I gather you thought it was something else?"

Carrie sighed deeply. "To be honest? I don't know. Maybe he was right. But something just doesn't feel right to me."

"How's she doing now?" Cruz asked, taking the chart she offered him.

"She's stable, but barely," Carrie said, turning for the door. "She's lost a lot of blood, and she's also still unconscious and not responding the way she should."

"I'll have a look," Cruz assured her, slipping the chart under his arm.

"I appreciate it," Carrie said. She turned and reached for the door, pulling it open. "And don't say anything to young Dr. Kildare just yet—about my calling you in, I mean. He thinks I'm a bossy old busybody as it is."

"You are a bossy old busybody," Cruz assured her. "But don't worry, I'll keep your secret."

"Thanks." Carrie smiled. "Oh, and by the way, nice boxers."

"Think so?" Cruz asked, a smile tugging at the corners of his mouth as he followed her out the door and down the hospital corridor. "I wore them just for you."

Carrie looked him over carefully. "Hmm," she mused, arching one brow. "You know, you might think about coming down to the church some Wednesday night. We could use some new blood around there."

Cruz laughed. "Oh, Nurse Burns, what would the ladies in the hospital auxiliary say if they heard you talking like that?"

"Dr. Martinez? Oh, thank goodness, Dr. Martinez!"

Cruz glanced up, spotting a student nurse running down the hall toward him. He walked to meet her. "Yeah, what is it?"

"This way, Dr. Martinez. Please hurry," she said, motioning to him as she skittered to a stop and quickly reversed directions. "This way. The patient in R-1—she's calling for you, and she's bleeding, Doctor. Please hurry."

"I had a feeling this was going to happen," Carrie said, tapping the chart she carried as she ran with him down the hall. "It's the woman from the accident. She's hemorrhaging."

Cruz pushed through the door, issuing orders in his wake. He turned to the student nurse behind him. "Page Dr. Wheeler. I want his butt down here stat."

"Right away, Dr. Martinez," she said, rushing back out the door.

Cruz was halfway across the room before he actually saw her, before he actually looked into the eyes of the woman lying on the gurney, and even then it didn't register. An entire instant passed, one whole millisecond of time, before recognition kicked in, before feelings were activated and any acknowledgment was made. But when the realization came, it hit him like a freight train running headlong into a brick wall. Memories assaulted him, and his heart came to a dead stop along with his feet.

"C-Cruz," she murmured, lifting her head from the pillow and holding out a shaky hand to him. "Help me, Cruz. Keep her safe. Don't let anything happen to her. P-please, Cruz. *Please* keep her safe."

"Marcy?" he whispered, feeling the floor list beneath his feet. "My God, Marcy."

Her lips moved again as she tried to push words out, but the struggle proved too much. Soundlessly, her head dropped to the pillow and her eyelids fluttered closed as she slipped into unconsciousness once more.

Somehow he'd managed to move to her side, even though his legs felt watery and useless beneath him. Reaching out, he brushed her cheek with the back of his fingers, needing the contact, needing to prove what his eyes were seeing was real—that she was real.

At the touch of his skin to hers, he was catapulted back to a time when he'd believed in dreams, when he'd thought they could come true and that love really did conquer all. But as it always did, reality had a way of rearing its ugly head, bursting bubbles and putting everyone in their places, and his hadn't been with her.

Four years ago he'd been forced to let her go; he'd had to walk out of her life and never look back. Position and circumstance had given him no other choice. Yet a day hadn't passed that he hadn't thought of her, that he hadn't wished it all could have been different and just this once the dreams could have come true.

"Dr. Martinez? Cruz?"

He heard Carrie talking, or at least he thought she was talking. For the moment, his plane of existence had narrowed to the woman lying before him and the avalanche of memories crashing down around him.

"Cruz," Carrie said again. "What is it? Are you okay?"

It was the alarm in her voice that finally cut through the haze of memories and recollections like a beam of light through a long, dark tunnel. He turned and looked at her, seeing her familiar face and again feeling the wrath of reality as it settled in around him.

Carrie leaned close. "You look awful. What is it?"

"Nothing," he mumbled, shaking off the shock. It didn't matter that this was a woman from his past. She was his patient now, and he had a job to do. "Forget it. Grab that sponge. Let's get this bleeding stopped."

He went into a kind of overdrive, checking his feelings at the door and going through the motions of doctor and patient without letting emotion or memories enter in.

"You were right," he said to Carrie after he'd removed the sodden bandages and inspected the wound. "This doesn't look good."

"Is she...okay?" Carrie asked hesitantly, taking the soiled wrappings from him.

He shook his head, ignoring the hard knotting in his stomach. "I don't know."

He applied himself with an ease and a skill that came only from years of experience. With speed and efficiency, he worked to control the bleeding, calling out concise commands to Carrie. The interaction between doctor and nurse was practiced and carefully choreographed, a ballet of motion and form. It was only as he began to cut away the ruptured stitches that his hands suddenly fumbled, only when his eye caught sight of something glinting against the light that his blood turned to ice.

"What is it?" Carrie asked.

Cruz shook his head. "Something's not right here."

"Did you want me, Dr. Martinez?"

Cruz gazed at the nervous-looking resident standing in the doorway. "Dr. Wheeler, your patient is hemorrhaging."

"I—I didn't know," he stammered, visibly shaken. "I thought I'd managed to get the bleeding stopped."

"Did you even examine this wound before you stitched it up?"

"Of course I did," he said, indignant. "Small, deep perforation of the abdominal wall."

"Any idea how it happened?"

"It was an auto accident. With a significant impact, any number of things in the interior of a car could cause a puncture wound like that."

"No." Cruz shook his head, gently probing the torn flesh. "There's only one thing that makes a puncture wound like this," he said, gesturing for the doctor to observe what he was doing. "And that's a bullet. This woman's been shot."

"What?" The young doctor stared down at the damaged tissue, seeing the small copper object imbedded deep within.

Cruz ignored his startled gasp, pressing a gauze pad over the laceration and pushing the gurney toward the door. "Call the OR," he said to Carrie as he passed her. "Tell them I'm on my way up."

Cruz, help me, Cruz.

Cruz dried his hands, pulled off the cotton surgical cap that covered his hair and tossed it into the bin with the rest of his soiled surgical greens. Those words had replayed themselves over and over again in his brain during the surgery.

Swiping the damp towel across his forehead, he tossed it, too, into the bin, on top of the cap. The truth was he was having a hard time understanding any of this: the fact that Marcy Fitzgerald—*his* Marcy—was in Nevada, in Mesa Ridge, that she was his patient, in his OR, and she wanted his help. Four years ago, he wouldn't have thought she would want anything from him ever again.

He considered the surgery and the bullet that had torn through her soft flesh. It had miraculously missed all vital organs and there had been no serious internal damage, but she had lost a lot of blood—too much, in fact—and that made her vulnerable to complications. Someone had shot her. How could that have happened?

Cruz, help me, Cruz.

What kind of trouble was she in? Who would want to hurt her? This whole thing was like a crazy dream, mixed up and confused.

Cruz, help me, Cruz. Keep her safe. Don't let anything happen to her. Please, Cruz…please. Keep her safe.

And who was it she wanted him to protect? Whose safety was she so concerned about?

He was mulling those questions over, still trying to make sense of this whole crazy thing, when he pushed through the doors out of the OR and started down the corridor toward the elevator. But he'd taken only a few steps before he was brought up short as one large piece of the puzzle suddenly slipped into place.

"This is Annie," Carrie said, gesturing to the little girl standing beside her. "And she refuses to stay in her room and go to sleep until she sees her mommy."

Cruz stared down at the little girl, a strange, sinking feeling in his stomach. He suddenly remembered Carrie's saying something about a child having been brought in, a child injured in the accident. The resemblance was unmistakable, and he knew in that instant this was Marcy's child. This was who she'd wanted him to protect, who she had been worrying about despite a bullet wound to the stomach.

"Hi, An—" His voice gave out, and he cleared his throat loudly. "Hi, Annie."

Carrie turned to the child, giving her a pat on the head. "Annie, this is Dr. Martinez, the man I told you about. He's the doctor who is going to help your mommy get all better."

Annie looked up. "Hi," she said in a small voice.

He knelt, gazing into brown eyes so sweet and so filled with fear they had his throat tightening with emotion. She had her mother's eyes and her mother's lush auburn hair color. She was a beautiful child, barely more than a toddler, and she seemed completely lost and alone.

The knot in his stomach that had started to form the moment he'd seen Marcy in the Recovery Room tightened even more at the sight of her daughter. He had no claim on her, had no right to judge or to question. He'd given all that up the day he'd walked out of her life. But looking at Annie, at her child, he couldn't help wondering who it was Marcy had turned to. Who was the man who had given her the child that should have been his?

"I want my mommy," Annie said in a small voice.

"I know you do," he acknowledged softly, automatically reaching up and pushing a curl back from her forehead. "This has been quite a night for you, I bet."

Annie nodded, but wouldn't be dissuaded. "Is she still…sick?"

Cruz saw the fear in her big brown eyes, and the exhaustion, and he found himself responding. "Well, you know, she got hurt pretty bad in the accident," he quietly explained. "She's going to be all right, but it might take a little while before she feels better. I don't want you to worry, though. She's going to be fine."

"Is she coming now to get me?"

Cruz felt an uncomfortable tightness in his chest. "Not for a little while. We need to let her rest right now."

"But I want my mommy," Annie whimpered.

Cruz exchanged a quick look with Carrie. "Tell you what, if you promise to be very quiet, I'll take you in to see her for a few minutes." He watched her face light up, and her little smile caused his chest to constrict even more. "But you also have to promise me you'll go back to your room with Nurse Burns after that and go to sleep. We got a deal?"

Annie beamed and nodded, sending auburn curls flying in all directions. "Okay."

Cruz's smile suddenly faded. "First, there's something I want to ask you about how your mommy got hurt. Do you remember anything about how it happened?"

Annie nodded again. "The car crashed." She lifted her arm to show him her bandaged wrist. "And Mommy got hurt, and me, too."

"That's right, the car did crash," Cruz said. "But do you remember anything else that might have happened? Before the accident, maybe? Something that might have hurt your mommy?"

Annie thought for a moment. "The other car."

Cruz exchanged a glance with Carrie. "The other car?"

"The other car—the yellow car."

"Yellow car," he repeated, thinking of the sound a bullet might make crashing through the window of a car. "Annie, did you hear anything—a bang or something hitting the car, anything like that?"

Annie shook her head impatiently. "But the yellow car made me scared, and it made Mommy scream." She gave his sleeve an impatient tug. "Can I see my mommy now?"

"Sure," Cruz said, but his frown grew deeper. He

slowly rose to his feet, taking her tiny hand in his. "Come on, let's go." He turned to Carrie as they passed, lowering his voice. "See that the sheriff is notified. Joe Mountain needs to know about this."

"Do you realize it's nearly dawn?"

At the sound of Carrie's hushed voice, Cruz lifted his head from the cradle of his hands. "How is it out there?"

"Quiet," she said, stepping inside the darkened room and letting the door gently swing closed behind her. "Nothing Dr. Wheeler can't handle." Crossing the room, she looked down at the woman sleeping peacefully on the hospital bed between them. "How was her night?"

Cruz followed her gaze to Marcy's beautiful face. "Quiet, too. She hasn't moved."

"Good," Carrie whispered, straightening the linens on the bed. "She needs the rest." Turning her head, Carrie motioned to a dark corner of the room. "How about the little girl?"

Cruz glanced at the cot where Annie lay sleeping. After he'd brought her in to see Marcy following the surgery, he hadn't had the heart to make her leave, so he'd arranged for a cot to be delivered and had put her to bed. It had made Annie feel much better, and he imagined Marcy wouldn't mind waking up and seeing her daughter close by. Also, given the circumstances of the accident and the questions he had, he felt better having them together where he could keep an eye on them both.

"I think she was asleep before her head hit the pillow," he said in a low voice.

"Poor little thing. What a nightmare. She must have been exhausted," Carrie lamented. She stopped and looked back at Cruz, assessing him with a keen eye. "How about you? It's been a long night for you, too. They'll be bringing the breakfast trays around soon. Want me to snag you a cup of coffee?''

"Better watch it, Mrs. Burns, with all this special attention," he said in an attempt to lighten the mood. Despite her good intentions, Cruz felt uncomfortable under her scrutiny and hoped to distract her with a joke. "People are going to start talking."

"Good," Carrie said in a stage whisper. She reached for the plastic water jug on the table beside the bed. "It's about time the people in this town had something to talk about." She carried the jug into the small connecting bathroom, the soft rubber of her thick-soled shoes gently squeaking as she moved over the worn linoleum floor. "Other than Harold Lillywhite and Myrna Kowalski dancing the hoochy-kooch down at the Elks Lodge every Saturday night, that is."

Cruz smiled and nodded, but gossip and the hospital grapevine were things he probably should have considered before he'd decided to spent the night watching over Marcy and her little girl.

"Think she's going to need another unit of blood?" Carrie asked, keeping her voice low as she filled the jug with fresh water and carried it back to the bed.

"I don't think so," Cruz said, letting his gaze drift back to Marcy. "Her color is good, and if she gets the rest she needs, it shouldn't take long for her to make up for what she lost."

Carrie tilted her head back, gazing through her bifocals at the IV. "She lost an awful lot," she murmured. "More than she should have, thanks to Dr. Wheeler."

Cruz felt a flare of anger. He understood better than anyone that a mistake could happen in medicine, despite the best of intentions. But the fact that it had happened to Marcy, the fact that she might have bled to death before anyone had discovered it, had him wanting to punch something or someone.

"It happens," he said, shrugging. Displaying no emotion was his only means of controlling those violent feelings roiling inside. "Every once in a while one gets by you."

Carrie peered over the top of her glasses at him. "Would it have gotten past you?"

Cruz shrugged again and slowly shook his head. "No."

"Well, if you ask me, Mrs. Marcy Fitzgerald is one lucky young woman," she remarked, giving the IV a cursory check. "And she owes you her life."

"Oh, no," he said sadly, an icy feeling piercing his heart like a spear. "She doesn't owe me a thing." Sensing Carrie's curious gaze on him again, he looked up at her. "And it was you who spotted the trouble."

Carrie hesitated for a moment. "I got the impression before...well, she did send the student nurse out to find you. I take it the two of you know each other?"

Uncomfortable, Cruz looked away, rising slowly from the chair beside the bed. "Uh, we used to, a long time ago."

He stretched his arms out, easing muscles made tight from sitting too long in one place. News of his staying the night at the bedside of a patient was no doubt all over the hospital already, but there wasn't much he could do about that now. He didn't exactly relish the thought of idle talk and speculation, but in this case it couldn't be helped. He wasn't about to leave Marcy or her little girl alone until he got some answers, until he found who had hurt her— who had *shot* her—and why. He wanted to know about the yellow car and why it had frightened Annie and why it had made Marcy scream. But most of all, he wanted to

know what she was doing in Mesa Ridge and what she
wanted from him.

"Did you get in touch with Joe Mountain?" he asked
suddenly, changing the subject.

Carrie nodded. "I gave Sheriff Mountain a full account-
ing. His office had already made a report on the accident,
but this put things in an entirely different light. He wants
to talk to them both. He said he'd be over sometime this
morning. Of course, I told him he'd have to check with
you first, though." She sighed, giving her head a shake,
and looked down at Marcy. "What's this world coming
to? People shooting at one another. Who would have
wanted to hurt this lovely young woman, and with a precious little girl in the seat next to her? You know, it's a
miracle they both weren't killed."

Cruz frowned, anger mingling with fear. He'd spent the
past several hours sitting in the dark, thinking the very
same thing. It didn't seem to matter that he hadn't seen
her in four years, that she no doubt hated him and was no
longer a part of his life. The thought of her being hurt, of
her coming so close to being killed, struck a fear in his
heart he'd never experienced.

His eyes felt scratchy, and he rubbed at them with the
palms of his hands. "They got lucky, all right."

"I'll say." Carrie sighed. She hesitated for a moment.
"I assume it was before."

He stopped, removing his hands from his eyes and giving Carrie a puzzled look. "What was before?"

"Before you came to Mesa Ridge—when the two of
you knew each other."

"Oh," he said, walking slowly to the window and gazing out at the faint light from the sun, which was peeking
over the horizon. He should have known she wouldn't let
him off the hook easily. "Yeah, it was."

"When you lived in L.A.?"

He turned around and shook his head. "Uh, no. In Davis."

"Med school?"

"Yeah."

"She's a doctor?"

"A lawyer."

"Oh," Carrie said, her eyes widening in surprise. "You don't say."

"Yeah." He sighed, turning to look out the window again.

"You must have known her husband then, too."

Cruz reeled. "What?"

"Well...her husband," Carrie said carefully. "You know, Annie's father."

The image of Marcy in a white dress, kneeling at an altar, that flashed through his mind sent such a searing pain through his heart it was all he could do not to wince.

"Uh, no," he mumbled, his throat feeling dry and raw.

Carrie looked down at Marcy again. "I wonder if it was him."

"Him?" Cruz's frown deepened. "What are you talking about?"

"The person who shot her."

Fury pounded at his temples, making his head throb painfully. That very thought had crossed his mind once or twice during the night. Had it been a spurned husband or a jealous boyfriend who had leveled that gun at her, or had it been just another random act of a maniac in a world gone mad?

"Her driver's license said Chevy Chase, Maryland. Isn't that somewhere near Washington, D.C.?" Carrie continued, not waiting for him to answer. "What do you suppose she's doing here in Mesa Ridge? Were you expecting her for a visit?''

Expecting her? He sooner would have expected to see Saint Nicholas himself wheeled into the ER than Marcy Fitzgerald.

"No," he murmured. "I wasn't expecting her."

"Hmm," Carrie mused. "Curious, isn't it? I mean, it's not exactly like Mesa Ridge is the kind of place you'd just happen to be passing through. It sounded like she'd come here to see you."

"Uh, look," he said abruptly, not even wanting to get started down that road. "I, uh, I've got to get out of here. I should go check on Doug. Do me a favor and stay with them until Joe Mountain gets here. I don't want them left alone."

"Touchy subject?" Carrie stepped away from the bed, keeping her voice low. "I didn't mean to upset you,"

"I'm not upset," he said, knowing full well everything about his speech and manner belied that point.

"I didn't realize it was such a sensitive issue with you. I—"

"It's not," he insisted impatiently, cutting her off again, but he sounded defensive and childish even to himself.

"You said yourself I'm a busybody. If you want me to mind my own business, just say so. I was only—"

"All right, I will. Mind your own business."

Carrie immediately stopped and threw her hands up in a sign of surrender. "Okay, you've got it."

Cruz watched as she walked to where he stood, not sure whether to stay his ground or prepare to duck. He hadn't meant to snap. After all, she had no way of knowing how sensitive he was on the subject of Marcy Fitzgerald.

Stopping just in front of him, she placed her hands on

her square hips and looked up at him. "So how about that cup of coffee?"

Cruz gazed into Carrie's weathered face. She could be rough and bossy, and downright nosy at times. But she was also one hell of a nurse and had been a good friend to him since he'd come to Mesa Ridge. None of this was her fault. He was striking merely because she was there.

"I asked her to marry me once," he said in a quiet voice. "I had wanted her to be my wife."

I love you, Mommy. I love you.

Marcy felt herself smiling. She couldn't see Annie, but she could hear her sweet little voice floating through her subconsciousness from somewhere in the outside world. Love swelled in her chest. Annie was her life, her reason for living. Her child was what gave her existence purpose and meaning, and hearing her small voice floating through her head was like feeling the sun after a long, cold night.

Love you, too, baby. Love you, too.

Marcy wasn't sure if she'd actually said the words, wasn't even sure speech was possible in the hazy dream world she found herself in. There were other things she would have liked to say, things she wanted Annie to know. Such as not to worry, that everything was going to be okay now, that they were going to be safe. But she couldn't get the words to come out. They seemed to get lost in the soft vapor of warmth and fatigue that surrounded her, and couldn't find their way clear.

Not to worry, she thought as the mist transformed into a billowy cloud, cushioned beneath her. At the moment she was too sleepy to talk. Her body was drifting on the cloud, and she was too exhausted even to try to open her eyes. Her dreams were so inviting after so many days of running hard and fast, so she allowed herself to surrender to the comfort of sleep. It was okay to rest now, because Annie was safe. They'd made it to Mesa Ridge, and Annie was with her father. There would be time later for talking things out and making explanations. The important thing was Cruz was there, and he'd protect their baby.

Cruz.

The sound of his name echoing through the windy passages of her subconsciousness stirred something strange and forbidden in her. For four years he'd been taboo, and she'd had to work hard to ban him from her thoughts and her dreams, not allow herself to remember. Yet it hadn't been easy. Every time she looked at Annie, every time she caught a glimpse of him in their daughter's sweet little face, she was reminded again of all she'd had and all she'd lost—what could have been, but never would be.

Cruz.

Only, it felt so warm, so safe, drifting on a cloud; what could it hurt to think of him now? She could picture him in her mind—his dark hair, his coal-black eyes, the way he had looked in those early years in Davis when they'd first met. A doctor and a lawyer—they'd been like oil and water at first. She'd been the rich girl with the private-school education; he'd been a poor kid in school on a scholarship, struggling to make a better life for himself. They'd come from completely different backgrounds, had grown up in completely different worlds, and yet she'd thought their love had erased those differences. It had for her, but she hadn't found out until too late that it hadn't erased anything for him.

Cruz.

Cruz hadn't wanted her, hadn't really wanted her love. He'd been more interested in proving a point, in taking on a society that believed that if you were poor, you weren't allowed to touch fair-skinned rich girls, weren't permitted entry into the world of privilege and power. Getting someone like her to fall in love with him, to agree to marry him, had been his way of proving to himself that those restrictions didn't apply to him.

Pain twisted in her heart, and she felt the sting of betrayal just as freshly as she had four years ago. Why couldn't he have loved her?

"Cruz."

Chapter 2

"I'm right here."

The sound of his voice sent shivers rushing through her system. The soft, fluffy cloud beneath her dissolved, landing her hard against the mattress and leaving her conscious and cognizant.

"Cruz?" She looked up at him, wide-awake now. "W-what happened?" She struggled to sit up. "Where's Annie?" The sudden stabbing sensation in her stomach had her wincing with pain. "Wh-where's my baby? Is she...is she all right?"

"She's fine. Annie's fine," he assured her, quieting her with a hand on the shoulder. "She's asleep." He nodded to the small cot in the corner. "Right there. See?"

Despite the dim lighting in the room, Marcy could make out Annie's tiny form on the cot and her auburn curls spilling out against the stark white hospital sheets.

"She was exhausted," Cruz said. "But she wouldn't go to sleep until she made sure you were okay."

"Thank God." She sighed, sinking back against the pillows. Her eyes stung with tears, and she squeezed them tight. "Thank God." After a moment she opened her lids and looked up at Cruz. "The accident—she wasn't hurt?"

"A sore wrist, a few bumps and bruises, nothing serious," he assured her. He reached down and gently rested a hand over the bandage on her abdomen. "Not like this."

Marcy felt the dull throb beneath his touch and remembered the piercing pain that had left her breathless and faint. "Am I going to be all right?"

"You're going to feel pretty lousy for a while, weak and exhausted," he warned, finding it more difficult than he'd expected to keep the tone of his voice even and unemotional. "But you'll be fine." He paused for a moment, taking a deep breath. "You both got lucky."

"Lucky," Marcy murmured, closing her eyes. She wasn't so sure. Grateful, certainly. She had no doubt about that. She was *very* grateful Annie hadn't been hurt, that the two of them were alive and in Mesa Ridge. She was also grateful she was too tired for reality to sink in...the reality that she was lying there talking with Cruz Martinez as if he were merely the doctor who had treated her in an emergency and not the man who had deserted her just days before she was to become his wife. Grateful, yes. Lucky? Knowing the truth and knowing she was going to have to tell him, she didn't exactly feel lucky.

"My throat," she mumbled. "It's so dry."

"It's from the anesthesia," he said, reaching for the water bottle. Cradling her head, he held the bottle while she took several sips through the straw.

"What time is it?" she asked, leaning back on the pillow.

Cruz set the water bottle down on the stand beside the bed and made a cursory check of his watch. "Almost six.

Carrie, uh, the nurse, just went to see about your breakfast tray.''

Breakfast. She remembered glancing at the clock on the dashboard just moments before everything happened. It had read 9:49 p.m. She had no memory of anything since then, except that moment in the Recovery Room, that one brief moment when Cruz was there.

"The accident," she said, gingerly pushing herself up against the pillows. "I don't remember much, but there was another car. Do you know what happened?"

The yellow car, Cruz thought darkly. Did she remember that? Did she remember a gunshot or taking a bullet in the stomach? "I don't know any details about the accident," he said, not wanting to press too soon for answers, not when she needed her strength. "I do know the authorities have been notified and they're investigating. Joe Mountain is the sheriff. He wants to talk to you later this morning, but we'll see if you're feeling up to it first."

Marcy watched him as he spoke, marveling at how little he'd changed in the past four years. His eyes were the same, his hair as dark and as thick as she remembered, his shoulders as straight and as broad. It was pure vanity that had her reaching up and brushing a hand through her own tangled mass of hair. After feeling the dry, matted mess, she wished that she hadn't. What did he see when he looked at her—a wreck of a woman, four years older and worse for wear?

She dropped her hand to her side, grateful there wasn't a mirror around, grateful she didn't have to see herself and know exactly how bad she looked.

"Was anyone else hurt in the accident besides Annie and me?" she asked, bringing the sheet up closer to her chin, considering for a moment slipping it over her head. "Anyone else brought to the hospital?"

"No," Cruz said, shaking his head. "From what I understand, it was a hit-and-run."

"Then no one has been around looking for us? No packages arriving with my name on them?"

"Packages?" Cruz regarded her for a moment, brows furrowed. "Marcy, what's all this about?"

"I—I just want to know about the accident," she said evasively, "that's all."

"You want to know about the accident?" he snapped, suddenly annoyed. She was the one who had shown up out of nowhere, the one asking for his help. The least she could do was be honest. "Or about the bullet you took in the stomach?"

Marcy felt another burning stab that had nothing to do with the injury she'd sustained. It was from shock and fear and an overwhelming feeling of helplessness.

A bullet. She squeezed her eyes tight. There was no doubt in her mind now. It was Brad Buck. It had to be. Somehow he had found them, had followed them. But how? How had he known?

Marcy felt the pressure of fury rising in her chest. Buck was either getting desperate or bored, but either way it only made him more dangerous. What was she going to do now?

Looking up at Cruz, she could see the questions in his eyes, and the suspicion. Instead of escaping the nightmare, she'd brought it with her, brought it to him. She had hoped for a little time, had hoped she could ease into the reasons that she'd come and that she'd brought Annie to him, but time had run out. It helped a little that the aftereffects of the anesthesia and pain medication had taken the edge off her nerves and numbed her fear. That made it easier to do what she had to, which was to jump right in and do what she'd been avoiding for four long years: tell him the truth.

"We need to talk," she said.

"We can talk later," he said, taking a step back. "You rest now."

"No," she said, grabbing his hand to stop him and cutting him off. "I can't wait. I have to talk to you. Now, before Annie wakes up and..." She turned her head and looked at Annie, who was sleeping so peacefully just a few feet away. Her voice dropped to a whisper. "And before it's too late." She turned back to him, looking into his eyes and seeing Annie's in them. "I may have waited too long already."

Cruz regarded her, feeling the hairs along the back of his neck start to bristle. "Sounds serious."

"It is," she confessed softly. "And I'm not sure how to start. This is awkward, I know, just showing up like this out of the blue. I'm probably the last person you expected to see."

"Well, maybe not the last," he lied, the corners of his mouth turning up for just a moment in the briefest of smiles. "But pretty close."

Marcy didn't smile. Instead, she turned away, her eyes stinging again and emotion making it difficult for the words to come out. "I'm in trouble, Cruz. I'm in trouble and I need your help."

Cruz wasn't conscious of moving, wasn't sure how it happened, but suddenly he found himself leaning close, holding her small hand in his. "Marcy, you know I'll help any way I can."

"Will you?" she asked, lifting her gaze to his again. "I'm not so sure you'll feel the same way after you hear what I have to say."

The look in her eyes had his entire body growing cold. He'd spent the night wanting answers; now a sense of foreboding had him almost dreading what she might say. He knew it hadn't been mere chance that had brought her all this way. She'd come for a purpose, and from the way she was acting, it was a serious one.

"Why don't you just say it?" he asked in a tight voice.

Marcy drew in a deep breath, thinking back to that day in her office when she'd been assigned the case of Brad Buck. It seemed as though a hundred years had passed since then. She'd had no idea at the time how much the case would change her life, or that it would bring Cruz back into it.

"It has to do with a case I'd worked on," she said. Despite the fatigue, despite the weakness, she launched into the story, telling him about the arrest of Brad Buck, the infamous mailbag bomber, whose unique brand of letter and package bombs had held the nation in terror. His capture and subsequent trial and conviction had made headlines around the country. Having escaped from the authorities, they launched a massive manhunt to bring him in. "You might have heard something about it," she said, lying back against the pillow, feeling more exhausted and weak than she could ever remember. "It was all over the wire services a few weeks ago."

"The mailbag bomber," Cruz murmured, remembering the headlines that had filled the newspapers for weeks. "Of course I've heard. Who hasn't?" He looked down at her, picturing her in a packed courtroom as she gave an impassioned speech to a jury. "I had no idea you were involved in his prosecution."

"Oh, I was involved," she said with a humorless laugh. "And you have no idea how much I regret it."

"Regret it? Why? Because he escaped?"

"Because he's after me now," she whispered, fighting off the fatigue.

"What?" Cruz felt something cold in the pit of his

stomach. The flat, unemotional tone of her voice had his sense of dread building, and the cold began slowly to seep through his body. "You don't mean…" He trailed off and his gaze drifted to the bulky bandage that covered her abdomen. "The accident? It was him? The bomber? Why?"

"Because he's crazy." Marcy closed her eyes and drew in a shaky breath. "Retaliation, revenge, retribution." She opened her eyes and looked up at him again. "Call it whatever you want. For whatever reason, he's fixated on me. He wants to punish me for everything that's happened to him. He wants to even the score by hurting me." She suddenly became aware of moistness on her face as a tear spilled over an eyelid and dropped onto her cheek. "But the worst part is he wants to torment me, to punish me, by hurting…" She reached up, squeezing his hand with both of hers, pulling him close. "Oh, God, Cruz, he'll hurt Annie. Just to get back at me, he'll hurt Annie."

"Oh, my God," Cruz murmured, gathering her into his arms. For that moment there was no past between them, no hurt feelings and painful sacrifices. They were just two people reaching out for comfort, reaching out to each other.

Marcy surrendered to Cruz's embrace, feeling safer than she had with an FBI agent stationed outside her home. Maybe it was her weakened condition, maybe it was shell shock or fatigue, but she didn't want to question why it felt so good to be with him again; it just did. She'd been fighting the battle alone for so long, and for the first time in a very long while, she didn't feel alone anymore.

"H-he must have followed us, but I don't know how," she mumbled against the wrinkled cotton of his surgical shirt. "I didn't tell anyone we were leaving—not my parents, my boss. No one knew about Mesa Ridge or you."

Cruz pulled back, looking down at her. "It was very dangerous taking off by yourselves like that."

The delicious feeling of comfort disappeared, as duty and the truth stared her in the face. "I know. You're right." She nodded, pulling out of his hold. She turned and looked at Annie, who was still asleep on the cot. "I thought that if I got far enough away, he'd never find her. I thought Annie would be safe here with you."

Cruz felt a tight band of emotion squeeze at his heart. "You brought your daughter to me?"

She turned back to him. "To protect her."

The slow, steady rhythm of his heart suddenly jumped, pounding hard and erratic in his throat. "What about you? Who would protect you?"

"I'm concerned about Annie. That's all that's important to me," she told him honestly. She reached out to him again, grabbing at his sleeve. "Please...keep her here with you. What he really wants is me. If I go back to Washington, he'll follow me." She paused, banking a surge of emotion. "I just have to know Annie will be all right, that she'll be safe. Will you help me, Cruz? Will you protect Annie? Please, please tell me you'll protect her."

"Of course I will. You know that," he assured her. "But what about..."

She saw the question in his eyes, the question that was there between them, the obvious question he'd stopped himself from asking. "What?"

He gazed at her. She was frightened and weak, and he'd promised himself he wouldn't rush her, but somehow he couldn't stop himself. "What about Annie's father?"

Marcy forgot about emotions and feeling weak, forgot about Brad Buck and his threat of revenge. She had spent years praying this moment would never come, hoping she could bury the truth, forget it existed and never have to deal with the consequences.

But looking up into Cruz's dark eyes, she realized how foolish she'd been. Truth always had a way of coming out, of exposing the shadows in life and correcting the distortions. This truth wasn't going to stay buried anymore, and this moment had been a long time in coming.

"Cruz—" Her throat was so tight she choked on the words. "I don't suppose there's any easy way to say this...."

Tension had every muscle in his body growing rigid as he watched her struggle for words. "Just say it," he said after a moment.

She looked up at him. "It's...it's about Annie."

"What about her?"

Her hands squeezed into tight fists as she braced herself. "Annie is, uh, she's...Annie is my child and..." She gazed into his coal-black eyes and saw recognition hit. "And yours."

Cruz stared at her, the ringing in his ears becoming a cacophony of noise and confusion. It really hadn't been necessary for Marcy to actually say it; he'd known even before the words were out. Realization had struck him like a meteor racing through the atmosphere and slamming into the Earth. It was as though something in him had sensed it, some intuitive ability had enabled him to perceive what belonged to him—and Annie Fitzgerald did.

"Mine," he murmured, turning to the child sleeping on the cot. His legs felt wooden as he crossed the room and looked at her. He'd seen her before, had talked with her, even held her little hand. But he knew she was his now, knew his blood ran in her veins, and it was as though he were seeing her for the very first time.

He knelt, reaching out a careful hand and twisting one

of her small curls around his finger. She was so much like
her mother, with her fair skin and auburn hair, but he could
see traces of her Latino heritage. They seemed so obvious
to him now. Why hadn't he seen them before?

Marcy watched him, the sight of father and daughter
causing the breath to stall in her lungs. It was something
she'd thought she'd never see, a meeting she'd been determined would never happen. And yet it was happening,
and it had tears welling in her eyes and her heart filling
with emotion.

Cruz Martinez. He had used her and tossed her aside as
though her life had meant nothing to him at all. Yet watching him now, watching him study Annie with a father's
awe and pride, had her feeling guilty and ashamed.

"I—I know it's a shock," she said, but the words
sounded hollow and inadequate.

"A shock." He looked up, his dark eyes piercing the
gloom. He stood up and walked back to the bed. "How
could you do this?" he demanded in a harsh whisper, his
gaze accusing now. "How could you not tell me?"

"What do you mean?" she asked, feeling all her defenses go up. "You know how it was between us. You
walked out on me, or have you forgotten?"

He deflected the accusation like a boxer avoiding a body
punch. "But to keep my child from me? How could you
do that?"

The look of hurt and betrayal in his eyes had the tears
spilling down her cheeks. She didn't want to feel regret,
didn't want to be remorseful or feel sorry for him. She was
the injured party here, not him. *Not him.*

"You'd taken off. I was alone. What was I supposed to
do?"

"You could have told me."

His voice really hadn't risen that loud, not by ordinary

standards, but in the quiet room it boomed like thunder. Swearing under his breath, he shot an anxious glance at Annie.

The little girl stirred on the cot, giving her nose a rub and making a funny little coughing sound. Slipping a thumb into her mouth, she rolled onto her side. After a moment, a tiny hand reached out from under the covers, grabbed one of her long curls and twisted it around a finger.

Cruz watched, waiting until she'd fallen asleep again, then glared at Marcy. "You didn't think I had a right to know?"

"We weren't together any longer," she said in a whisper. "You'd packed your things and gone. You didn't seem concerned about what you'd left behind."

Frustrated, he ran a hand through his hair. "This isn't high school, Marcy. It wasn't as though I'd left my class ring behind," he said, not bothering to hide the sarcasm in his voice. "We're talking about a child—*my* child."

"*My* child," she corrected. "You left me. You made your choice. How was I supposed to know you would care? You didn't want me. Was I just to assume you would want my baby?"

He was a doctor. He knew the kind of trauma her body had sustained, knew she needed her strength to recuperate. But he wasn't exactly thinking like a doctor right now. He was thinking like a man—a man who'd just discovered he was a father and a man who'd been denied his child. He wanted to strike out, to rage and smash his fists into walls.

Only, he didn't, but not out of any sense of medical ethics or consideration for her frail condition. He didn't because of the small voice that called out, cutting through his anger and fury like a beacon shining through the fog.

"Mommy?"

Marcy made an attempt to brush her tears away, but the sound of Annie's voice brought even more flowing down her cheeks. Struggling, she reached out a hand toward the cot where her daughter lay. "Hi, baby."

"Mommy," Annie said again, her voice hoarse from long hours of sleep. She sat up on the cot, pushing the covers aside, then ran across the smooth linoleum toward her mother's bed, giving Cruz a wide berth as she passed.

Marcy opened her arms, and Annie scrambled up the side of the high hospital bed and into her embrace. It didn't seem to matter that Annie's knee brushed over her bandaged middle, or that her arms were weak with exhaustion and her whole body throbbed with pain. What mattered was that her daughter was with her and the little girl was safe.

"We got hurt, Mommy," Annie murmured sleepily against her mother's hospital gown.

"We sure did, baby," Marcy said, her voice cracking with emotion. She didn't dare look up at Cruz, didn't want to see the censure and rebuke, the anger and the disappointment, in his eyes. She knew they needed to talk, that they would have to sort through the hard feelings and decide where to go from here, but not now. "They told me you hurt your wrist."

She nodded, pulling back just far enough to show her mother the Ace bandage wrapped around her arm. "Hurts."

"I'll bet it does," Marcy said.

Annie turned and rested a hand on Marcy's bandaged wound. "You had a oppa...a oppa...oppasion."

Marcy smiled. "An operation."

"He did it," she whispered, pointing behind her in Cruz's general direction.

"He? That's Dr. Martinez," Marcy said, watching Annie's cheeks flush. "Can you say good morning?"

Annie buried her head in the crook of her mother's neck again and shook her head. But after a moment, she reached a hand out behind her and gave him a small wave.

Cruz looked at Marcy. Annie's silly, innocent little gesture had managed to crack the tension wide-open and they both laughed, despite the anger, despite the accusations, despite the past.

Cruz forgot about exacting explanations and making demands. He was too captivated by this child—*his* child. He was overwhelmed by the fact that this precious little girl was his flesh and blood. She fascinated him, intrigued him, and he couldn't seem to take his eyes off her. He wanted to watch her, listen to her, hear her laugh and learn everything there was to learn about her. He didn't know how things were going to work out, how he and Marcy would feel about each other or get past their differences, but at that moment it didn't really matter. This was his daughter, and he was never going to let her go.

Annie sat up again. "He let—"

Marcy stopped her. "He?"

Annie's cheeks reddened again, and she gave Cruz a quick look. "Dr. Mar-teen-ezz," she said shyly. "He let me come in to see you last night and he made the nurse bring that." She pointed to the cot in the corner. "And he put a new bandage on my arm and he gave me some milk and he let me sleep over there."

"He did?" Marcy inquired, glancing up at Cruz. She could read nothing in his expression now, nothing that would tell her what he was thinking or how he felt. He'd been thoughtful to Annie, and for that she was grateful. "That was nice," she said, turning back to her daughter. "I liked waking up and seeing you close by."

Annie's smile faded. "I was scared."

"I know you were," Marcy said, not wanting to think about how it must have been for her or how much danger she'd been in. The ordeal of the crash, the paramedics, the ambulance—she must have been terrified.

Marcy glanced up at Cruz again. He'd behaved like a protective parent, soothing Annie, caring for her, putting her to bed. He might very well hate Marcy for having kept the truth from him, but there wasn't a doubt in her mind that Cruz wouldn't let his feelings get in the way of protecting Annie.

"The yellow car scared me."

Marcy looked back at Annie. "I know. It scared me, too."

"Why did it hurt us, Mommy?"

"Oh, sweetheart." She sighed. The tense, emotional scene was beginning to take its toll, and she fought off a wave of fatigue. "I'm not sure."

"Will it come back? Like the bad person, will it come back to hurt us?"

Cruz heard the quiver in her tiny voice, and suddenly the terrifying tale Marcy had told became all too real.

"No, Annie," he said in a firm voice. "I don't want you to worry about that." Marcy and Annie had the same surprised expression when they looked up at him. "No one's going to hurt you as long as I'm around."

"Good morning. Breakfast time." A student nurse pushed through the door with two trays stacked one on top of the other. She gave the three of them a bright smile. "Is everybody happy?"

Chapter 3

"Mrs. Fitzgerald?"

Marcy looked up, surprised to see a tall man standing in the open doorway of her room. "Yes? And it's *Miss* Fitzgerald."

"Sorry," he said, slipping off his cowboy hat as he stepped inside. "I'm Joe Mountain." He reached inside his sheepskin jacket and pulled out a badge. "Mesa County sheriff. I'd like to ask you a few questions if you're feeling up to it."

Marcy's eyes widened. Sheriff Joe Mountain wasn't exactly what she'd expected. With a strong, handsome face and long black hair, the Native American officer looked like something out of a fantasy Western.

"Yes, of course, Sheriff," she said, touching the remote control on the bed and moving herself up into a sitting position. Actually, compared with this morning, she was feeling almost human again. She had some food in her now and had taken a long nap, and while she didn't exactly feel

like swinging from the chandeliers, she did feel stronger.
"I've been expecting you."

"I came by earlier," he said, walking across the room,
"but you were resting and Cruz—I mean, Dr. Martinez—didn't want you disturbed. Just so you'll know,
though, my deputy has been outside the door since the
investigation began, and we've notified the federal authorities."

"You called the FBI?" Marcy asked.

"Brad Buck is a fugitive from justice," he reminded
her. "If he's in this area, if indeed he's responsible for
running you and your daughter off the road last night, then
I want the manpower to bring him in." He took out a small
spiral-topped notepad from the breast pocket of his shirt
and flipped it open. "Of course, the federal agents are
going to want to talk to you, but I wonder if you would
mind answering a few questions for me in the meantime."

"I don't mind," she said. She gestured to the chair beside the bed as she reached for the call button. "I'd just
like to check on my daughter first. The nurses were watching her while I rested. I just want to make sure she's
okay." She shrugged, giving him a helpless look. "I get
a little nervous when she's away from me for too long."

"That's understandable, given the circumstances," Joe
said, rejecting her invitation to sit with a shake of his head.
He took several steps closer, however, and slipped his
badge back inside his jacket. "But your daughter is fine.
She's down on the first floor with my deputy and Cruz."

"Cruz?" Marcy jerked up her head. "What were they
doing?"

He fumbled through his pocket until he found a pen,
then pulled it out and clicked it open. "I think it was
supposed to be a visit from Santa to the pediatrics ward,
but somehow it ended up in gurney races up and down the

aisle.'' He stopped and peered over the top of the notepad. ''And I think our team is winning.''

''O-our team?'' Marcy stammered.

''When I left, Annie and my deputy had a gurney length on Cruz and somebody dressed in an elf costume.''

Joe Mountain's deadpan expression never wavered, but Marcy thought she'd seen something flash in his dark eyes, something wry and amusing.

''Oh,'' she said, leaning back against the pillows. ''I keep forgetting Christmas is just a few days away.''

''I suppose our winters are a little different from what you're used to in D.C.''

''I suppose they are,'' Marcy murmured, automatically looking out the window at the afternoon sun streaming into the room. Driving cross-country, they'd encountered a variety of weather, from snow and sleet to the dry heat of the desert, but she'd barely noticed the changes.

''Cruz tells me the two of you are old friends.''

She glanced back at the sheriff. What else had Cruz told him about her? ''Well…something like that.''

Joe Mountain's pen paused on the notepad and he looked up. ''Something like that? You mean you're not old friends?''

''Not exactly. I mean yes, we were—*are*. I mean—'' She forced herself to stop and draw in a deep breath. ''We know each other.''

''Stayed in touch all this time?''

''No, not really,'' she said, realizing how strange this must be sounding to him.

''Not really,'' he repeated slowly in a skeptical voice. He considered this for a moment, regarding her. ''You're a long way from home, Miss Fitzgerald. You've come quite a distance to see someone who's not exactly a friend.''

Marcy sighed, wondering what it was about cops and their questions that automatically made a person act guilty. "I guess what I meant, Sheriff, was yes, Cruz and I were friends once, a long time ago."

"I see. So you came here to look him up, ask for his help?"

"Yes, that's right. I wanted to get Annie out of Washington."

"I see," he repeated thoughtfully. "And from what I understand you elected not to share this information with the federal authorities in D.C."

"That's right."

"Do you mind telling me why?"

Marcy sighed and shook her head. "Look, Sheriff, I realize this might not make a lot of sense to you, but believe me, the past several months have been a nightmare for me. I was only thinking of Annie, trying my best to protect her."

"I can understand that," he said. "I just think the FBI would argue they were trying to do the same thing."

"Maybe they were," she conceded. "But all I know is that Brad Buck showed up at my daughter's preschool. I don't know how he found her or what he intended to do, but I wasn't about to trust anyone after that."

"No one except Cruz, that is," he reminded her.

Marcy looked away, feeling her cheeks grow warm. "Like I said, I want Annie out of Washington—until Buck is caught."

He nodded, making a notation in his notepad. "They seem to get along pretty well."

"Who?"

"Cruz and your daughter."

Marcy frowned. The thought of Cruz and Annie laughing and having fun together had the tension building in the

back of her neck. It was unreasonable, of course, but she
expected Cruz to *protect* Annie, not develop a relationship
with her. Despite the gratitude she felt, she wasn't exactly
ready to share her daughter with him.

"From what Cruz told me," Joe said, glancing up from
his notes, "you never actually saw the driver of the other
car, is that correct?"

"Hmm—w-what?" Marcy stammered, the question
sending the unpleasant thoughts scattering. "Oh, yes,
that's right. The windows were tinted—too dark to see."

"So really, you can't say for certain it was Buck behind
the wheel?"

"No," Marcy admitted. "But believe me, Sheriff, I
know it was him."

"You sound pretty sure," he stated, lowering the pad.

"I am sure. I know this guy, Sheriff Mountain. I spent
the last year and a half of my life putting together a case
against him. I know what he wants and how he thinks.
And believe me, I know it was him in that car last night.
I *know* it."

One corner of Joe Mountain's mouth lifted in the
slightest half smile. "I believe you."

Marcy smiled, suddenly liking the sheriff very much.
"Thank you."

"So tell me about this yellow car," he said, looking
down at his notepad again. "Remember anything unusual
about?"

"Actually, I'd seen the car earlier in the day."

He looked up again. "Oh?"

"Yesterday morning, as we were leaving the motel."
She told him about seeing the car then, and later that eve-
ning at the restaurant. "The gaudy shade of yellow, bright-
red flames on the hood, tinted windows—it was hard to
miss."

"I can imagine," Joe commented, making a notation. "There were traces of yellow and red paint along the side of your car."

Marcy leaned her head back against the pillows. "I thought I'd been so careful, so cautious," she said, sighing heavily. "Checking who was behind me, making note of who had the rooms next to us in the motels we stayed at, who sat in the booths next to us in the restaurants. When I first spotted the yellow car outside the motel, I didn't think too much of it. I mean it was so conspicuous—you couldn't miss it." She sighed again. "I didn't even think of getting a license number."

Joe stepped away from the bed, walking to the window and staring out across the crowded parking lot. "Yellow car with red flames. Not exactly the car you'd pick if you were trying to fade into the background."

"Of course not," Marcy said, raising her head off the pillow. "My God, I've been so stupid." She turned to Joe Mountain. "Don't you see? He knew I wouldn't be looking for him in some gaudy-looking car like that." She sank back against the pillows, her hands curling into fists. "Hide in plain sight—it's exactly the kind of thing this guy does best and..." She pounded her fists on the mattress. "I should have seen it coming."

"But he took a shot at you this time."

Marcy pressed a hand along her tender abdomen. "I know," she mumbled. Her voice became emotional. "Which only means I underestimated him, Sheriff Mountain. I can't afford to do it again, not when it means Annie could get hurt."

Joe turned, regarding her for a moment, then crossed the room to the bed again. "He's not going to get close to anyone," he assured her. "Not as long as I'm sheriff in this county."

Marcy looked up at him. She'd worked with a lot of law enforcement officers in the past—federal, state, and local officials—but there was something about this tall, quiet man that had her believing he could do exactly what he said.

"Mommy, I won. I won, Mommy."

Marcy jumped, startled at the sudden burst of sound. As she turned toward the door, her breath caught in her throat. Annie beamed down at her mother from her perch high on the hip of Santa Claus, who was standing there as big as life in his red suit and black boots and big, round belly.

"What? You won?" Marcy asked, her voice sounding faint because of the ringing in her ears.

"The race," Annie announced proudly. "I beat Santa."

Marcy stared at the looming figure holding her daughter. "Santa?"

"It's not really Santa." Annie giggled, pulling at the cap on Santa's head. "It's just pretend. It's really Coos."

"Cruz?" Marcy murmured, suddenly recognizing the dark eyes peering at her over the thick white beard. Sheriff Mountain had mentioned a visit from Santa, but she'd never imagined this. "You mean Dr. Martinez."

"Too hard," Annie said, scrambling up onto the bed. "And Coos said friends call each other by first names." She looked back at him, giving him a wave. "And he's my friend, Mommy." She turned back to her mother, not even stopping for a breath. "And so is Ryan. He's a policeman, and I got to ride on the top of the gurney, and Ryan pushed me really, really hard and we went so fast."

Marcy gazed into Annie's big brown eyes and felt completely overwhelmed. "It, uh, sounds like you had quite a time."

"Uh-huh," Annie said, nodding. "And I got to be Santa's helper and pass out the presents."

Marcy turned to Cruz, watching as he pulled off the white wig and beard. His gaze was dark and hostile when it met hers, and she felt her defenses going up.

"Is that right," she said stiffly, turning back to Annie. "I wondered where you were when I woke up." She glared at Cruz. "Perhaps your friend will tell me next time so I won't have to ring for the nurse to find out where you are."

"You needed your rest," Cruz said, tossing the wig and beard onto a chair in a heap. "I didn't want you disturbed." He addressed Joe. "Which is why you've got about two more seconds to finish up here."

"One thing I hate," Joe said with a sigh, flipping his notepad closed. "Santa Claus with an attitude." He put the pad and pen in his pocket. "I've got what I came for. I'm outta here." He turned to Marcy. "Thank you Mrs.—sorry, Miss Fitzgerald. If you need me for anything, my deputy's name is Ryan Samsun and he'll be right outside. He'll know how to reach me."

Marcy reached out a hand. "Thank you, Sheriff."

Joe took her hand. "Promise me you won't give him the slip."

Marcy smiled. "I'll try not to."

"And you," Joe said, giving Annie's curls a tousle. "You take care of your mom. Make her rest, and don't let her be out there racing those gurneys."

"I won't." Annie giggled.

Joe walked over to Cruz. "Your patient, Doc, she's a hell of a lady."

"Yeah," Cruz muttered, his dark eyes narrowing.

He'd known Joe Mountain for four years, ever since he'd come to Mesa Ridge, and had enormous respect for him. They'd become friends—good friends—both understanding what it was to be judged not on your worth but by the color of your skin. They backpacked together, fished together, confided in each other, but watching Joe with Marcy just now, watching the two of them talking, interacting, seeing the way Marcy looked at Joe and the way Joe looked at Marcy, had his system flooding with heat.

"Dr. Martinez? A Christmas present arrived for you."

Cruz looked at the student nurse standing in the open doorway. "A present?"

"Isn't it wrapped beautifully?" the young woman asked, holding up the small square box "It was at the nurses' station with a note saying I should deliver it to you in room 311." She pointed to the festive holiday gift tag attached to the bow. "See?"

Cruz's heart lurched. Maybe it was the shape of the package, or the thin wire inside the bow that glinted in the light, he wasn't sure. He just knew without a doubt that was no present; it was death, all wrapped up in a pretty package.

He looked back at Marcy and Annie on the hospital bed and felt his blood turn to ice.

"Oh, no," Marcy murmured, his silent communication relaying itself to her. She stared at the package, its bright, colorful paper suddenly grotesque. The holiday wrapping didn't fool her. She'd seen packages like that before, packages that were filled with terror and death. "God, no. He's after you now."

"Get them out of here," Cruz said to Joe, gesturing with a nod. He walked cautiously to the young nurse, speaking in as calm a voice as he could. "I don't want you to move."

"But why? What did I do?"

"Nothing," Cruz assured her. "Please, just don't move, and very carefully hand me the package."

"I don't understand," she said, putting the package in his outstretched hands.

"You don't have to," he said, staring down at the parcel. "Just get the hell out of here and tell the supervising nurse to start moving people out of this wing."

The student nurse turned and bolted for the door.

"Annie, I want you to stay up there with your mom," Joe said, rushing to the hospital bed and kicking the brakes on the wheels free. "We're going for a little ride."

"Oh, boy," Annie said, as he wheeled them toward the door.

"Cruz?" Marcy began, reaching out a hand to him as Joe wheeled her by. "Cruz?"

His eyes were dark and full of emotion, and in one clarifying instant, she realized no matter what had happened in the past, she couldn't bear the thought of his being hurt.

"He's got to get out of there," she said, turning to Sheriff Mountain and hearing the panic in her own voice. "You've got to help him. Get him out of there."

"Don't worry about it, Miss Fitzgerald," Joe said, motioning for his deputy. "He'll be all right."

Joe began shouting orders, directing the startled medical staff to start evacuating patients from the surrounding rooms. Marcy watched in horror the confusion unfolding around her. She clutched Annie to her, praying Joe was right, praying Cruz would be okay. She watched as the frantic staff scrambled to get people out; heard cries and gasps of frightened patients and saw the torn and broken holiday decorations. She'd done this; she'd brought this chaos, this terror. She'd unleashed Brad Buck onto the innocent people of Mesa Ridge and onto Cruz, and the nightmare had become atrocity.

"And no one saw him?"

Joe shook his head, resting his elbows on the Formica

tabletop. The doctors' lounge of Mesa Ridge Hospital was quiet and deserted, in stark contrast to the way things had been several hours ago. "Looks that way."

Cruz shook his head, running a shaky hand through his hair. He'd been as steady as a rock when he'd carried the bomb out of the hospital, but he'd been trembling ever since. The thought of how close that maniac had come to Marcy and Annie had shaken him to his core.

"You mean a guy can just walk in here, set a bomb on the counter at the third-floor nurses' station, and nobody notices?" he scoffed cynically. "Nobody sees anything?"

Joe shrugged, fingering what remained of a dozen doughnuts in an open box on the table. "I didn't say that."

"But you just said—"

"I said no one saw Buck."

"Well, if they didn't see Buck, what did they see?"

"Some clown in a Santa suit," he said, popping a stale piece of doughnut into his mouth. "They thought it was you."

Cruz swore under his breath, staring down at the coffee in his cup. It was dark and murky and had gone stale several hours ago. "So what about the FBI?"

Joe nodded. "Several of their field agents have arrived. They're in the process of transferring Mrs. Fitzgerald and her daughter to the safe house now."

"Miss."

Joe looked up. "What?"

"It's 'Miss,'" Cruz corrected, taking a hesitant gulp of coffee. "Not Mrs. *Miss* Fitzgerald."

Joe regarded his friend for a moment, then smiled. "Yeah, imagine that."

Cruz studied him, his dark eyes narrowing. He remembered the way Joe and Marcy had talked together, how they'd smiled at each other. "What the hell is that supposed to mean?"

"Nothing," Joe said, shrugging innocently, but his smile grew wider. "Just imagine that."

Cruz scowled and swallowed the rest of his coffee. It didn't matter that it was bitter and icy cold. It suited him right now, and his disposition.

"CNN called the office earlier," Joe informed him. "Apparently, they picked up on the story when the FBI responded."

Cruz groaned. "Oh, great."

"Yeah," Joe said, popping the last of the stale doughnut into his mouth. "They wanted to know what we did when we discovered the bomb."

"What did you tell them?"

Joe shrugged again, dusting powdered sugar off his hands. "The truth. We evacuated the hospital and called our bomb squad to deactivate the device."

"Bomb squad?" Cruz asked skeptically. "That would be you and me dumping the thing out in the desert and letting it blow?"

Joe drained his coffee cup and pushed himself away from the table. "You got it, buddy." He crushed the foam cup he held and tossed it into the wastebasket. "Things are liable to get a little crazy around here."

"Great. That's just what we need in this hospital—a couple million reporters hanging around, getting underfoot."

Joe looked back at him. "Lucky break you won't be around to have to deal with them, then."

"What are you talking about?" Cruz asked.

"The safe house."

"What about it?"

"Well, let's just say you'll be calling it home for a while, too."

"*What?*"

"Just until we bring this creep in," Joe said reasonably.

"Oh, no," Cruz said, shaking his head and rising to his feet. "This place you and the feds have arranged for is for Marcy and Annie. I'm not the one in danger. What the hell makes you think I'd go to a safe house?"

"You mean other than the fact that the bomb had your name on it?" Joe asked, serious now. "That little package that arrived today wasn't meant as a warning. It was meant to kill. It was the real McCoy—a *real* bomb, with explosives and a detonator. I'd say that's a pretty good indication this guy's made you a target."

"But I can't go," Cruz insisted. "I can't leave. I've got patients to see and a hospital to run. What is this town supposed to do without a doctor?"

"Carrie said you've got some doctor in from Sparks helping out now," Joe said. "Sounds like that problem's solved."

"He's a resident," Cruz said, his voice getting louder. "And not even a very good one."

"Then let's hope there's a sudden outbreak of healthiness in Mesa Ridge," he said, his voice just as loud. "Because like it or not, Doc, you're outta here."

"I don't like it," Cruz stated stubbornly.

"Well, right now, what you like and don't like just isn't a real high priority."

"Then it had better become a priority," he insisted, feeling more overwhelmed than angry. "Because short of arresting me, I'm not going anywhere."

"Ever hear of something called protective custody?"

Cruz glared at him. "You wouldn't dare."

"Oh, I dare," Joe assured him, reaching down and picking up another broken piece of doughnut and popping it into his mouth. "And I'd hate to have to arrest you. Especially since you still owe me fifty bucks."

"This is outrageous," Cruz muttered, sinking onto the chair again. He knew the futility of fighting the inevitable, knew his back was against the wall.

"Did you think having a nutcase trying to blow you up would be fun?"

"Then how come I'm the one who feels like a prisoner?"

"Come on, it won't be that bad," Joe coaxed. "Besides, I don't know what you're complaining about."

"You mean other than putting my life on hold, having to go into hiding just because some homicidal maniac took a course in basic chemistry and has decided he'd like to see me in a couple hundred pieces on my office wall?"

"No, I mean being stuck in a secluded spot with a woman like Marcy Fitzgerald—*Miss* Marcy Fitzgerald." Joe smiled. "Some men might not find that too hard to take."

"Oh, right, real cozy," Cruz snorted, but the thought had something stirring deep inside him. "Just me and her and FBI agents crawling all over the place."

"Actually, there'll just be two agents with you at all times—one inside, one out," Joe amended. "But there is her daughter to consider."

Her daughter. Cruz scowled. His daughter. Annie was his, too, which made the idea of the three of them being confined alone together all the more impossible.

"Look, why don't I just agree to stay here at the hospital? I can sleep in the lounge, continue to see my patients. The feds can assign me an agent if they want."

"You mean this hospital? The one where any crackpot

can walk in and hand-deliver a little love note of TNT?"
Joe shook his head. "I don't think so."

"Then arrange for me to stay somewhere else—anywhere."

Joe's smile faded. "What the hell is this all about? I'm
just talking about a few days here, not a permanent ar-
rangement. A few days, what's that?"

Cruz drew in a tired breath. Joe was right. What were
a few days? And even though being with Marcy would be
difficult, could he really feel comfortable trusting her
safety and the safety of their daughter to strangers?

Their daughter. He thought of Annie, of her big brown
eyes and bright smile. He didn't want that monster anywhere near her. Marcy had overcome her anger long
enough to ask for his help; he could at least overcome his
for the sake of Annie's security.

He looked at Joe and drew in a deep breath. "Okay."

"Good," Joe said, slapping him on the shoulder.
"Come on, I'll drive you by your place to pick up a few
things."

"Yeah," Cruz muttered, following Joe to the door.

"And look at it this way. There are going to be so many
federal agents, state troopers, highway patrol and National
Guard in this area within the next twenty-four hours that
Brad Buck isn't going to be able to go to the bathroom,
let alone start planting bombs, without running into a
badge. You're not going to have to stay tucked away for
very long."

They walked out into the hospital corridor, where they
turned a corner and headed down the narrow hall toward
the parking lot. "Marcy...she's still very weak. They need
to be careful moving her."

"Don't worry," Joe assured him, pushing through the
glass doors and stepping outside. "We're not going to let

anything happen to the lady." He unlocked the front passenger-side door of his four-wheel-drive squad car and pulled it open. "And she'll have her doctor right there to take care of her. Climb in," he said with a nod. He rounded the car to the driver's side and slipped in behind the wheel. "In the meantime, why don't you just relax and tell me what the real story is with you and *Miss* Fitzgerald."

Chapter 4

"How's that feel?"

Marcy eased herself back against the pillows. The ride from the hospital to the small, secluded house had been a long and uncomfortable one for her. What little energy she'd had from her nap earlier was long since gone, and the stitches along her incision felt raw and irritated. Still, she understood the necessity of the FBI's elaborate process of transporting her to the safe house they'd arranged for with Sheriff Mountain's help.

They'd followed a convoluted route from the hospital, advancing and backtracking along streets and roads, changing vehicles one after the other and turning and twisting, until she'd lost all sense of direction. It had been an arduous journey that had used up what was left of the afternoon and very well could have moved her miles from their starting point—or mere blocks, for all she knew. Still, after realizing how close Brad Buck had gotten—again—she wasn't sure too much care could be taken.

"Wonderful," she said, looking up into the kind face of the bulky FBI agent and smiling. "Thanks."

"There's a room down the hall for your daughter, but Dr. Martinez said you'd probably prefer having her in here with you," he said, picking up a clipboard and reading down his checklist.

Dr. Martinez. Marcy thought of Cruz and how he had looked in her hospital room with that bomb in his hands. She'd been assured any number of times in the past several hours that he was all right, that the bomb had been removed and no one had gotten hurt, but she was still uneasy.

She couldn't think about the fear, couldn't let it enter her thoughts or infiltrate her consciousness, or she never would make it. Instead, she concentrated on the anger, on her outrage and loathing of Brad Buck. The whole nightmare only seemed to get worse. There didn't seem to be any place she could go that he couldn't find her, and everywhere she went, everyone she touched became ensnared in Buck's web of terror and death.

"I can have them bring another bed in here," the agent continued, "if you'd like."

"Yes," Marcy said, pushing the disturbing thoughts from her mind. "Yes, please, I'd like that."

He shouted orders to several of the agents roaming the hall outside the small bedroom. "There are also instructions that you should take a pain pill in about..." The agent checked his wristwatch. "About ten minutes." He rummaged through a leather satchel on the chest of drawers and pulled out a vial. "I'll put it here on the nightstand and get you a glass of water. That way it will be all ready for you."

"My daughter?" Marcy asked, shifting on the narrow

bed. The throbbing in her abdomen had turned to fire, and she winced as she moved.

"She's on her way, and she's fine," he assured her, checking his list again. "We're in continuous radio contact with the car. It shouldn't be more than five or ten minutes." He looked up, slipping the clipboard under his arm. "It appears we're set. Agents Varela and Brown will be outside if you need anything."

"Okay," she said, retrieving the medication vial from the nightstand. "There's only one pill in here."

The agent looked at her in anticipation, as though waiting for her to make her point. "Yes?"

"Well, they're only good for a few hours," she said, feeling her whole body throb. "What happens then? How do I get more medication?"

"Oh, don't worry about that," the agent said, making a dismissive gesture with his hand. He picked up his leather satchel and started for the door. "Your doctor will be able to give you more."

The vial slipped from her hand and fell soundlessly onto the bed beside her. "My doctor?"

"Dr. Martinez." He lifted a hand to the tiny radio receiver almost hidden in his ear and listened. "As a matter of fact, the van has just pulled up outside."

"You mean he's here?"

"That's right."

"You mean you'll have to bring him by every time I want a pill?"

"Oh, no," the agent said, shaking his head. "Dr. Martinez will be staying. He'll be in the room at the end of the hall."

"Isn't this 'Mad-Hattie' Crawford's place," Cruz asked, peering out the darkened window of the unmarked van at the weathered wood-framed house perched on a small knoll overlooking the center of town.

"Sure is," Joe said, pulling off the road and maneuvering the wide van down the narrow drive.

He turned back to Joe. "You mean this is it? This is the safe house?"

"Yeah, what were you expecting?"

Cruz stared at the house. He wasn't sure what he'd expected, but this tired-looking place, with its sagging roof and heavy wisteria trailing across the front, wasn't it. "I don't know, but not this."

"It's close to town, and yet there aren't any curious neighbors to come poking around," Joe replied. "It's secluded from the street by the trees and shrubbery, and yet the perimeter of the house is clear, easier to patrol." He brought the van to a stop and turned the key to quiet the engine. "It was either this or the Dew Drop Inn." When Cruz spun around and glared at him at the mention of the rundown motel and notorious bar on the outskirts of town, Joe smiled. "It was a joke. I'm joking."

Cruz gave him a killing look, then glanced back at the house. "What about Hattie?"

"Down in Vegas with a sister of hers."

"Thank goodness for that," Cruz muttered, breathing a sigh of relief and picturing "Mad-Hattie" in her feather boa and combat boots. She was without a doubt Mesa Ridge's resident eccentric, who drove around town in her dilapidated pickup, toting a double-barreled shotgun as she delivered baked goods to local residents and merchants. He'd treated her a couple of times last winter for arthritis, which she referred to as "lumbago," and she had rewarded him with giant plates full of cookies. Still, quirkiness and a few stiff, creaking joints aside, the seventy-three-year-old was as sound as a dollar. "I'm not sure I could have handled it if she'd started baking."

"You mean you don't like her oatmeal cookies?"

Cruz caught sight of movement in the shadows of the porch and squinted. "Is that what they are?"

"Yeah, at least I think so," Joe said, opening the van door. "Except down at the station we use them for door-stops and to get prisoners to confess." He stopped a moment and laughed. "You know, you'd be amazed at what some people are willing to confess to avoid having to eat one of Mad-Hattie's disagreeable little delicacies."

"Who's that on the porch?" Cruz ignored Joe's joking.

Joe peered into the shadows. "One of your baby-sitters."

"One?"

"I told you there would be two, one outside and one inside," Joe said, stepping out onto the drive. "Just like bookends. Come on, I don't want you standing out here."

Muttering, Cruz pushed open the van's door. Grabbing his crammed duffel bag and his doctor's black bag from the seat, he got out, rounded the van and followed Joe up the porch steps.

The agent at the door nodded in a solemn greeting. "Sheriff Mountain, Dr. Martinez." He opened the front door, motioning to them. "Inside, please."

Cruz shot Joe a hesitant look, then stepped through the open doorway and into a small living room. With the shades drawn, it seemed dark, and it took several moments for his eyes to adjust. When they finally did, the old, worn furnishings and tired Christmas decorations only made the place seem that much drearier.

"Hello, Dr. Martinez."

Cruz turned at the sound of the voice, finding a tall, powerfully built man stepping into the room.

"I'm Field Agent Varela," he said, extending his hand.

"Agent Varela," Cruz mumbled.

"Sheriff Mountain? Don Varela, FBI," he said, turning to Joe. "We spoke over the radio."

Cruz wandered around the living room while the two law enforcement officers talked. Despite the gloomy atmosphere and unconventional feel of the place, Hattie's living room was surprisingly neat and tidy. It was more the idea of being crowded together with Marcy that made him uneasy with the closeness of the house.

"Can you think of anything else you might need, Dr. Martinez? Do you have any questions?"

"Nothing really," Cruz muttered.

"Okay, then," Varela said. "Just remember to keep the shades drawn at all times, stay out of any open doorways and don't go wandering around outside. Other than that, relax and make yourself at home."

Cruz nodded, thinking relaxing was about the last thing he felt like doing. He held up his duffel bag and his doctor's black bag. "Someplace I can put these?"

"Sure. You're in the room at the end of the hall," Varela said. "If you'd like, I can show you."

Cruz shook his head, starting across the room. "That's okay. I can find it."

"Mrs. Fitzgerald is resting."

"Miss."

Like stereo speakers on either side of the agent, Cruz and Joe corrected his mistake in unison. Surprised, Varela looked from one to the other. "Excuse me?"

"It's 'Miss,'" Cruz explained, feeling stupid. "Miss Fitzgerald. She's...not married."

"I see," Varela said, nodding as though trying to figure out the relevance of that particular bit of information but unable to. "Okay, then, *Miss* Fitzgerald—your patient—

she's in the first room on the right if you want to check on her.''

"Yeah, I guess I should," Cruz said, almost to himself. "What about Annie?"

Varela put a hand to the tiny radio receiver in his ear, listening for a moment. "They're about a mile up the road."

Cruz nodded, grabbing the black bag and heading down the hall. The small corridor felt more like an emotional gauntlet than a passage, but he ignored the apprehension he felt at seeing Marcy again. She was still his patient, no matter how many secrets she'd kept from him, and he couldn't let his feelings get in the way of that.

"Come in."

She responded almost immediately to his knock, dashing any hope he'd had that she might be sleeping and he'd have an excuse to put off having to face her again. He paused with his hand on the knob for just a second longer than he should have, just long enough for him to remember the expression on her face when she'd seen him with that bomb in his hands. There had been sheer terror in her eyes, and she'd looked at him almost…almost as if she cared.

Only, he knew that was impossible. Whatever feelings she'd once had for him, whatever love had filled her heart, had died long ago—so long ago she felt it was okay to keep him from his child.

Steeling himself, he pushed the picture of her panic-stricken face and terrified eyes from his mind. It was difficult enough to see her and be with her without responding to feelings and emotions that simply weren't there. Turning the knob, he slowly pushed the door open.

"Hi," he said, stepping into the room.

"Hi," she replied, her eyes opening wide in surprise.

"I…I just got here," he said, feeling stupid. He'd never

had much talent for small talk, and his nerves were making it even worse. "I'm, uh, down the hall."

"Yes," Marcy said in a quiet voice. "The agent told me."

"How are you feeling?"

"Fine—" She started to sit up, but a sudden painful stitch in her abdomen had her wincing and falling back against the pillow. "Fine, I'm fine."

"Incision bothering you?"

"A little," she said, gingerly shifting her weight along the mattress and letting out a breath. "It stings."

He walked over to the bed, then lifted the sheet and pushed aside her hospital gown and panties. But as he peeled back the bandage and began to inspect the fresh stitches, he found himself fumbling, his hands clumsy.

Attending a patient was something he did dozens of times during a day, but she wasn't just any ordinary patient, and going about the routine motions of examining her weren't ordinary, either. The bedroom, with its drawn curtains and dark mahogany furniture, had none of the cold sterility, none of the detached professionalism of a hospital room. It had a personality, a warmth and a feeling, and it gave feeling to what he was doing, as well. He struggled to maintain his doctor's impartiality, but he couldn't quite forget the fact that they were alone in a bedroom, and the intimacy was not lost on him.

"How was the ride from the hospital?" he asked, hoping his bedside manner hadn't deserted him completely.

"Long," she said, flinching at the feel of his hand along the sensitive skin.

The bed was low, causing him to bend close, and he made the mistake of turning his head just enough to see her looking up. Suddenly he wasn't touching an incision left from an operation he'd performed. He was touching skin—Marcy's skin.

His mind suddenly flashed back, pictures coming alive. Almost involuntarily his fingers spread across her, and he thought of his seed in her, thought of her belly growing round with his child, round with Annie. Marcy had cheated him of that, of seeing and experiencing the earliest moments of his child's life.

"Yeah, well, I guess it was necessary," he said stiffly, snatching his hand away. He hurriedly replaced the bandage and stepped awkwardly away. "At least that's what they tell me."

"Right," she said, quickly pulling her gown back into place and covering up with the sheet. "That's what they tell me, too."

He stood looking down at her for a moment, feeling awkward and stupid. He'd thought he could be with her, thought he could touch her and treat her just as he would any other patient, but he realized that was impossible to do. He couldn't forget the fact that this was the woman he'd loved, the woman he'd wanted for his wife. He couldn't look at her, couldn't talk to her, couldn't touch her, without being aware of that.

"The incision looks fine," he said, wondering if she could feel his tension. "No ruptured stitches, no sign of infection."

"Then how come it hurts so much?" she asked, attempting to shift her weight to find a more comfortable position.

"The bullet went deep, cutting a pretty good path through the muscle and tissue of your abdomen. It was necessary to repair that damage," he explained. Talking about something as neutral—and as familiar—as medicine had him relaxing a little. He welcomed the opportunity to get ahold of his emotions, to try to regain his composure and attempt to start thinking rationally again. "The abdominal muscles are ones you use a lot, walking, bending, sitting, even lying down. When they are hurt or injured, you can bet you're going to feel it. Just ask any woman who's ever had a C-section."

Cruz heard the words, but couldn't believe they'd actually come out of his mouth. Had he lost his mind? What had he been thinking, bringing up the subject of childbirth with her? Had he been *thinking* at all?

"Uh, look, I'm, uh, sorry," he stammered. "I didn't mean to talk about…"

"About what? C-sections?" she asked, scooting up on the bed. "I didn't have one, if that's what you're wondering."

"That wasn't what I was wondering," he said with a tired sigh. "I'd figured that out for myself."

"Oh?"

He nodded toward her tummy. "No scar."

Marcy let out a long breath and smiled sadly. "This is so awkward."

He nodded in agreement, feeling the tension in the room slowly begin to crumble. "I know."

"This whole thing just keeps getting worse." She looked up at him, forgetting the discomfort and awkwardness. "The accident, blurting all that out about Annie, and now…now Brad Buck." She paused for a moment, her chest rising and falling with emotion. "You've got to know, Cruz, you've got to believe I never meant…when I brought Annie here, this thing this morning…I never meant for you—"

"No, Marcy, don't," he said, shaking his head. "You were concerned for your daughter." He stopped, taking a deep breath. "For our daughter. You wanted her safe." He paused, emotion making the words difficult. "It...it meant a lot that you brought her to me, that you'd trust me with her." He cleared his throat and looked away. "You had no way of knowing that maniac would follow you."

"Except now I've put you in danger, too."

"There's an army of police and FBI out there looking for that creep." He took a slow step forward. "They're going to find him. I've got no doubts about that. There's a lot we need to talk about, things we need to settle, but what's important right now is keeping Annie safe and just getting through all this. I think we can both agree on that."

"You're right," she said, closing her eyes and feeling her head begin to throb. "You're right." She opened her eyes and looked up at him. "I guess I'm just having trouble thinking straight right now."

"That's because you're exhausted. You need to lie down and get some rest, and as your doctor, I'm ordering you to do just that," he stated. "I can give you something to help you sleep if you'd like."

"No, that's okay," she said, gingerly settling back. "They told me Annie will be coming in a few minutes. I'll feel better once I see her, then I'll take a nap."

He turned and slowly crossed the room. At the door he stopped to look back at her. "Natural childbirth?"

Marcy nodded. "Eighteen miserable hours."

Somehow they bonded in that moment, something that communicated father to mother, man to woman. Cruz stepped into the hall and closed the door behind him. He thought of Marcy and the long hours of labor. As a doctor, he'd witnessed the miracle of birth many times, had seen the valiant struggle of a mother enduring all she could for her child. Had Marcy struggled alone? Had there been no one to sit with her, hold her hand and comfort her when the pain became unbearable?

"Coos! Coos!"

Cruz barely had time to turn before Annie came running down the hall toward him, dragging her worn teddy bear by the arm.

"Well, look who's here," he said, kneeling. Her long, dark-auburn curls danced with every move, and her eyes were bright and alive with excitement.

She giggled, yanking her bear into her arms. "And we had fun."

He watched her as she told him all about her ride from the hospital, studying her as he would a fine piece of art. She was so much like her mother—the way she laughed, her expressions, the set of her chin—and yet for the first time he recognized his offering. He could see delicate hints and subtle similarities to his mother and his sisters...and himself. The shape of her mouth, the angle of her cheek, the richness of her skin—they spoke of who she was and the bloodline she carried.

Watching her, he felt a fierce wave of paternal pride engulf him. He was no longer just a man; he was a parent, a father—Annie's father. In the space of a day his whole life had changed, and he knew he would never look at things the same way ever again.

"And then we got in a car," she continued, growing more animated as she went. "But it wasn't like Mommy's car. It was big and had lots of seats in it like the bus at preschool, but it was different, and we drived a really long time till we got to another car, and then we got in that car, but I didn't like it too much 'cause it was just a regular old car, and we drived to a truck that had all this writing on it." She paused just long enough to take a breath, but she couldn't help the giggle that bubbled out. "Coos, it was fun."

"It sounds fun." Cruz laughed, thinking only a child

could find something enjoyable about the elaborate method the FBI had devised to transport them.

"And now me and Mommy get to stay here," she said, laughing with him. "With you. It's going to be fun, too."

"Sure," Cruz said, looking into her innocent face and suddenly feeling very tired himself. "We're going to have a lot of fun. You and I are really going to have a chance to get to know each other."

"And Mommy, too."

Cruz's smile stiffened. Given the circumstances and the conversation he'd just had with Marcy, he wasn't sure it was possible to find anything "fun" about the situation. It was no doubt going to be just as awkward and difficult as he'd imagined. But at least they'd agreed on one thing—keeping Annie as safe and as happy as possible.

"Of course your mommy, too," he said after a moment. "But remember, she's still very weak and is going to need a lot of rest."

"'Cause of the oppa-ration, huh?" Annie added solemnly.

Cruz smiled. "Right, because of the operation. But we're going to take care of her."

"'Cause you're a doctor, huh?"

"Right, and maybe you can be my nurse, help me take care of my patient. How does that sound?"

"Fun," she said, squeezing her bear tight. "And Mommy will get all better."

"I'll say she will," he said, rising to his feet. "Now, why don't you go in and tell her all about the big car?" He reached for the doorknob and gave it a turn. "And see if you can get her to take a nap while you're at it."

He watched just long enough to see the little girl run across the room and into her mother's arms. No doubt having Annie bounce against her stitches didn't feel too pleasant, but from the look on Marcy's face, she didn't seem to mind. She was thinking about her child right now, not her own discomfort, and oddly enough he found he could relate—something he wouldn't have been able to do twenty-four hours ago.

"What the—?" Feeling something in the small of his back, Cruz turned and checked the sofa. Something peeked out of the crack between the cushion and the back. He slipped a hand between them and yanked it free.

"They're socks."

Cruz looked at Joe, who was leaning against a wall in the small archway between the living room and dining room, then back at the tangled clump in his hand. "They're what?"

"Socks," he repeated with a shrug. "Hattie stuffed her couch with them."

"With…"

"With socks," Joe said when Cruz trailed off.

"Good Lord," Cruz mumbled, holding up the knotted wad. He recognized them now. They were indeed socks. Brown, black, blue, even argyles.

"Yeah, well." Joe smiled at Cruz's shocked reaction, pushing himself away from the wall and walking farther into the room. "It was a few years back. Must have been before you took over at Mesa General. The whole town was talking about it."

"But why socks?"

Joe chuckled. "You know how when you do your laundry and you somehow always end up with an extra sock, one without a mate?" His smile broadened as Cruz nodded. "Well, I guess it happened once too often to Hattie. She decided to find a good use for those socks. She went all over town collecting everybody's mismatched ones."

"You're pulling my leg."

"I swear." Joe laughed, holding up a hand. "I'm not kidding. She had bags of them."

"Socks," Cruz muttered again.

"Of course, they had to be clean," Joe added.

Cruz gave him a skeptical look. "I don't believe you."

Joe laughed more. "I'm telling you the truth. Ask Ryan or Carrie if you don't believe me."

Cruz shook his head. "I will."

Cruz's bewildered expression had Joe laughing harder. "Last I heard, she was starting to collect them again."

"You're lying."

Joe took a deep breath, forcing the smile from his lips. "I'm not. She wants to sew them together."

"Sew them together? What for?"

The corners of Joe's mouth started to twitch again. "She's got plans to reupholster the chair." When Cruz looked up at him, they both started laughing. "And the ottoman."

They were helpless after that, one spasm of laughter seizing them after another. It felt good to laugh, good to forget for a moment about mail bombs and secrets kept, and ease the strain of a day spent tense and uncertain.

"Remind me," Cruz said finally, falling back against the sock-filled sofa and wiping at the tears in his eyes, "to call for a CAT scan next time she's in. I want to see what's going on in that woman's head."

"Hey, tell me something," Joe said, taking a deep breath to calm himself. He reached for the ottoman, pulling it close to the sofa, and sat down opposite Cruz.

"What do you want to know?" Cruz said with a relaxed sigh.

"What's really going on between you and Marcy Fitzgerald," he said, leaning forward and resting his elbows on his knees. "Tell me the rest of it."

Chapter 5

"The rest of what?" Cruz lifted his head, the good mood from the laughter suddenly disappearing.

"Come on," Joe said, leaning back. "You know what I'm talking about. The reason you've been tied up in knots since *Miss* Marcy Fitzgerald was brought into the ER, the reason you can't talk about the woman or even get near her without breaking out in a cold sweat."

Cruz rested his head against the sofa and closed his eyes. "Don't, Joe. I don't want to talk about this—not now."

Joe regarded him for a moment, then nodded in concession. "Okay, maybe you're right," he said, depositing his empty cup on the coffee table. "They're just down the hall, and we really can't talk. It's just…"

"Just what? Morbid curiosity?"

"You know me better than that," Joe insisted.

Cruz nodded. "You're right. I'm sorry."

Joe smiled sadly "When I saw you earlier, you and Annie together." The smile on his lips faded and he looked away. "I'm not interested in poking my nose where it doesn't belong. What happened between you and the lady is none of my business. But you and I—we're friends, we've been through a lot together." He paused for a moment, sighing heavily. "You were there for me when my life took a dive. There was a time after Karen walked out that I didn't care what happened to me. If it hadn't been for you and those fishing trips in the boonies, I'm not sure I would have made it."

"The boonies," Cruz murmured, thinking of Joe's remote cabin high in the mountains, where they would go when pressures got too great. "What I'd give to be there now. Kick back, drop a line in the water—just forget all this."

"Things are going to be close around here," Joe reminded him. "You, the woman, the child. It could get rough for you."

"I'm going to be fine."

"You sure about that?"

"Look," Cruz said, suddenly sitting up. He appreciated Joe's concern, he really did. He just didn't want to talk about this, didn't want to think about it. "I told you she's an old friend. Don't make something more out of this than there is."

"Friends." Joe nodded, standing up and walking to the chair where he'd tossed down his sheepskin jacket. "And I suppose it was because of your *friendship* that the little girl ended up resembling you."

Cruz's gaze shot up. "How— W-what...what are you talking about?"

"Doc, come on, this is me you're talking to. You only have to see your face whenever you look at the child or her mother," Joe said in a low voice, shrugging into his coat. "That woman in there was more than your friend, and that child Annie, she's yours."

Cruz slowly rose to his feet. "Is it that obvious?"

"Maybe not to everyone, but not everyone knows you the way I do."

Cruz ran a shaky hand through his hair. "I didn't know about Annie until yesterday. Marcy never told me."

Joe swore under his breath, crossing the room to where Cruz stood. "Look, I don't know everything that's going on here, but I can take a pretty good guess," he said, his voice barely above a whisper. "I admit, I suspected that maybe you and Marcy…well, that the two of you had been a little more than friends, but it wasn't until just now, until I saw you and Annie together, until I realized—" He stopped and drew in a deep breath. "Believe me, if I'd known, if I'd suspected, I never would have pushed you about staying here with her. I'd have found another way."

Cruz rubbed a hand along the back of his neck. "I'm not going to lie to you. It's not going to be easy. I mean, Marcy and I, well, it didn't end too good between us. And now this, finding out about Annie." He shook his head, breathing out a small laugh. "Well, let's just say it hasn't helped the situation. But we're both adults, and we both agreed that whatever happened between us, whatever problems there were, are in the past. What's important now is Annie, and keeping her safe."

"I'm glad to hear you say that," Joe said, supportively resting a hand on Cruz's shoulder. "Because this Brad Buck is one dangerous bastard. There's no telling what he's capable of." He walked several steps toward the front door, buttoning up the front of his jacket. "Keep on your toes, Doc. It could mean your life and the life of your little girl."

Your little girl. Joe's words hung in the room long after

he'd left, reverberating through Cruz's mind like an echo
through a canyon. Annie was his little girl, his own flesh
and blood. He'd only just discovered the truth about her,
but already he was willing to do anything to protect her.
He'd give his life to protect her—and Marcy.

Marcy. He'd walked out on her four years ago, had purposely hurt her, but not because he hadn't loved her, not
because he hadn't wanted to share his life with her. He'd
left because he'd cared so much, because he'd loved her
enough to give her back to the world he knew she belonged in. He'd spent the past four years telling himself
he'd done the right thing, he'd done the only thing he
could. Only, now he wasn't so sure.

If he hadn't left, they would be married now. Marcy
would be his wife, and he would have been there when
she'd discovered she was pregnant, would have been there
to share her joy and watch her belly grow. He would have
held her hand during those grueling hours of labor, would
have supported and comforted her, and he would have
been there to hold Annie after her birth.

Cruz closed his eyes and rubbed at them with the palms
of his hands. The truth stared him in the face, harsh and
bleak—a truth he didn't want to face, a truth that said no
matter how noble his design, no matter how selfless and
good his intentions had been, the fact remained that if he
hadn't left that day, if he'd stayed and their wedding had
gone on as planned, none of this would have happened.
The mailbag bomber would only have been a name in the
news, not a threat to their lives, and Brad Buck would
never have gotten anywhere near them.

"Mommy!" Annie shrieked, jumping up from the floor
and heading across the living room toward her. "You're
up. You're up!"

Marcy reached out to rest a hand along the doorjamb for support. She was up, all right, but just barely. The tenderness in her abdomen caused her to walk hunched over, but after nearly twelve hours of uninterrupted sleep last night, a long, restful day and a good dinner, she felt better than she had since waking up in the Recovery Room to discover the nightmare had followed them to Nevada.

She had stood in the doorway between the living room and the hall just long enough to take in Cruz and Annie together, talking and teasing each other, laughing and playing. They were sitting side by side on the carpet, legs crossed in front, and leaning back against the lumpy sofa.

They made quite a picture. With their heads close, they looked every bit the father and daughter, and something tightened in the pit of her stomach, something that had nothing to do with stitches and bullet wounds. Annie and Cruz had been together almost constantly in the past twenty-four hours. He seemed to delight in his daughter, and Annie responded in kind. It was almost as if the child knew there was something more going on, almost as if she sensed the connection between them.

"I'm up," Marcy said, gesturing at her hunched position. "Sort of."

Cruz rose to his feet and crossed the room to where she stood. "You're determined to rip out those stitches, aren't you?"

"I'm not trying to," she replied innocently, hearing the disapproval in his voice. "I'm not used to sitting still, that's all."

"Well, if you needed something, you should have called," he said, not bothering to hide the irritation in his tone.

"I don't need anything," she insisted, feeling her defenses start to rise. "I was just getting bored in there all by myself."

She felt his hand at her waist and did her best not to jump. Instead, she took the arm he offered, letting him slowly lead her to the sofa. She wouldn't have felt so awkward if he'd smiled or something, but he didn't. He merely looked at her as though she were an interloper, as though she were interrupting, as though she didn't belong.

"You shouldn't be up," he said in a low voice, leaning close as he helped her ease onto the cushions. "It's too soon."

He was so near that their cheeks could have brushed, so near that, for a flash, she almost thought she could remember what it had felt like when he'd kissed her.

"Look at you," he said, running a hand along her forehead to her pulse at her neck. "You feel warm and your heart is racing. If you're not careful, you could end up with an infection."

"I don't have an infection," she said, knocking his hand away. She told herself the heat crawling up her neck was from anger, and not because he stood so close. "And my heart is racing only because walking with your back like a pretzel can be a little tiring."

"It's tiring because it's too soon for you to be up and around."

She glared at him, making a face. "All right, then, Doctor, sue me."

"Mommy, Coos helped me make a new list for Santa, and we put it in an envelope and he said I could use a kiss for a stamp and I showed him my Barney book, and we colored pictures and played Candyland," Annie rattled on, scrambling up onto the sofa, next to her mother. "And Coos said he'd make the sheriff bring me the Winnie the Pooh movie so we could watch it on tellabision."

"My goodness," Marcy said, turning to Annie. From the corner of her eye, she watched Cruz walk back across the room and sit down on a cracked vinyl ottoman.

"And we made popcorn," Annie went on, scurrying down off the sofa to the large stainless-steel bowl lying on the carpet where she and Cruz had been sitting. She picked it up with both hands and carried it to her mother. "Want some?"

"Oh, no, not popcorn," Marcy said, reaching into the bowl and grabbing a handful. "I love popcorn." She tossed several pieces into her mouth and smiled down at Annie. "Yum, good."

"Me and Coos made it," Annie announced proudly. "He held me up and let me pour it in the pan, but I hadda be careful. Know why?"

Marcy looked from Annie to Cruz, then back again. "Why?"

"'Cause it's *hot!*" she said with a giggle.

"Do you want something more to eat?" Cruz asked then. "I'm sure there's something in the kitchen if you're hungry."

Marcy shook her head, reaching for another handful. "No, this is great." She rested her back against the lumpy sofa. "Actually, the soup and sandwich at dinner were plenty."

"Coos let me pick out the soup."

Marcy thought of the bowl of clam chowder on her dinner tray along with a turkey sandwich. "Well, no wonder we had chowder." She laughed, giving Annie's nose a tweak. "Your favorite." She turned to Cruz, her smile falling just a little. "So, you've been doing the cooking."

Cruz shrugged nonchalantly, feeling foolish now as he remembered the care he'd taken with the trays he'd prepared for her. "They stocked the pantry. It's just a matter of opening a few cans."

Marcy nodded and reached for another handful of popcorn, but she was thinking about the neatly folded napkin and carefully placed flatware on her dinner tray. She was shocked now to realize how little thought she'd given to the actual mechanics of their day-to-day existence. It hadn't even occurred to her until now who might be preparing the food she ate or who cleaned up after she was finished. The FBI had provided them protection, not room service. Of course it had to be Cruz. There was no one else.

Still, she couldn't help feeling just a little strange. There was such an intimacy associated with food, and intimacy had died between them a very long time ago.

"Are you sure you're not still hungry?" he asked again.

"Positive," she said, lifting a piece of popcorn to her mouth and popping it in. "Just snacking."

Cruz quickly looked away, feeling a little as though he'd taken a punch in the stomach. No doubt she'd forgotten, but he remembered the times they had raided the icebox together, the midnight snacks they would carry back to bed and feast on until desire took over.

"Where are agents Varela and...what was the other one's name? Brown?"

"Yeah, Brown," Cruz said, watching her pop a large piece of popcorn into Annie's mouth and listening to both of them giggle. "Brown's outside somewhere. Varela's in the kitchen. Did you need him for something?"

She shook her head, yawning. "No, just asking." She shifted gingerly along the cushion. "I just wondered if there'd been any word about...well—" she glanced at Annie, then back to Cruz "—you know."

"Yeah," Cruz said, following her drift. She didn't have

to verbalize her concerns or her curiosity about the status of the manhunt for Brad Buck. He understood them all too well. "Unfortunately, there's no news."

"Too bad," she said, laying her head back and fighting off another yawn. She grimaced as she shifted her weight again in an effort to get comfortable.

"Stitches still bothering you?"

"A little," she said, shifting once more. "But not as much as this sofa." She pressed at the cushions. "What is with this thing? It's so lumpy."

"That's 'cause of the socks," Annie said matter-of-factly, stuffing another handful of popcorn into her mouth.

"The what?" Marcy inquired with a puzzled laugh.

"The socks," Annie repeated, her mouth full. "They're in the sofa."

"What are you talking about, socks in the sofa?"

"That's what's in there," Annie said, punching the cushion with her small fist. "Coos says there's a whole lotta socks inside." She leaned closer, her voice lowering. "That's how come we sit on the floor." She made a face, holding her nose and giggling. "Don't want to sit on stinky socks."

Marcy turned to Cruz. Surely she had misunderstood them. "There are socks in the sofa?"

"I'm afraid so."

"*Socks,*" she said again, enunciating precisely. "*S-o-c-k-s?*"

"Socks," he repeated. With hands on his knees, he pushed himself up off the ottoman.

"Inside?"

"It's complicated."

"But—"

He raised a hand as he walked back to the sofa, stopping her. "Don't ask. It's a long story." Without any hesitation, he bent down, scooped Marcy up in his arms and gently lifted her. "And no story for you tonight." He turned and headed for the hall. "You look exhausted. It's bedtime."

"No, I'm okay," she insisted.

"You're exhausted. I can see it in your face."

"Well, thank you very much," she muttered dryly. "Why don't you just come right out and say I look lousy?"

Cruz ignored her sarcasm. In reality, she looked anything but lousy. In fact, she looked so good he found himself wanting some space, wanting to be as far away from her as the small house would allow.

"Stop arguing," he said, ignoring her struggle. "I'm bigger than you. Besides, just consider it doctor's orders." He glanced down at Annie and winked. "Right, Nurse?"

"Right!" Annie agreed, running along in front of them. "Bedtime, Mommy. Nurse's orders, too."

"Well, okay," Marcy said, surrendering to the inevitable. "If you're going to gang up on me."

She didn't struggle as he carried her down the narrow hall and into her room. The truth was, she really was tired; she just didn't like admitting it to him. She was so tired, in fact, that she didn't even fight being in his arms.

"There," he said, settling her on the narrow bed. "At least it's more comfortable than the sofa."

"I guess." She sighed, falling back against the pillows. She gazed at him and forgot about being defensive for a moment. "I hate this," she confessed as he pulled the quilt up around her. "Feeling tired and weak all the time."

"It's not going to be forever," he assured her, straightening. "Give it some time."

"Time," she said wearily. "I do seem to have time on my hands these days."

"Then it shouldn't be a problem to rest and take it easy."

She rolled her eyes, muttering, "If I don't go stir-crazy first."

Annie rummaged through the large suitcase beside the bed, pulling out several oversized books. "Okay, Mommy, time for your bedtime story."

Cruz looked at Marcy and lowered his voice. "Although how you say you have time on your hands with *somebody* around..."

"I guess you're right." Marcy laughed, scooting to one side as Annie climbed up beside her. "You know," she said after a moment, serious now, "I really do appreciate everything you're doing—the meals and everything." She reached up and gave one of Annie's long curls a tug. "And keeping 'The Pest' occupied."

"I'm not a pest," Annie insisted, basking in the attention of the two adults. "I'm a nurse. Right, Coos?"

"You're my best nurse," he said, giving Annie a wink. He glanced back at Marcy, shrugging one shoulder. "I confess, I'm not crazy about the cooking part. But this character..." He reached out and tweaked the tip of Annie's nose. "I kind of think she's growing on me."

Marcy watched him as he walked back across the room toward the door. "For what it's worth," she said as he reached for the knob, "I think the feeling's mutual."

Cruz stopped and turned around. "It's worth a lot."

It was there again—that feeling arcing between them, that connection that would always exist because of the child they shared.

"Okay, Nurse," he said after a moment, shifting his gaze to Annie. "One story for the patient, then lights out. Got it?"

"Got it," Annie answered with a giggle.

Cruz looked at Marcy again, hesitating for just a moment. "Good night."

"Good night," she whispered, watching the door close behind him.

She was suddenly very depressed, and she felt like bursting into tears. Except this wasn't the time for tears. Not here, and not now. Now she had to be strong, for Annie's sake and for the sake of her own sanity. But someday, when all this was over, when Brad Buck was behind bars and Annie was safe, when Cruz Martinez was just a memory in her life once more, she was going to cry herself a river—again.

"Okay, *Nurse*," she said, quickly blinking the tears away and forcing the emotion out of her voice. "What's the story going to be tonight?"

"Mommy? Mommy, wake up."

Annie's voice cut through her subconscious like a light through a tunnel and she was awake instantly. "Annie?"

"Mommy, I'm scared."

With the shades drawn tight, the room was black, making it impossible to see. Fumbling about, Marcy found the small lamp on the nightstand and turned the switch. A glow cut through the thick darkness.

"What is it, baby?" she asked, reaching out to Annie, who was sitting up in her bed just a few feet away. "Come here."

Annie pushed the covers aside and ran to her mother's bed. "Th-there was this big monster," she stammered, climbing up onto the mattress. "And—and he was trying to get under the covers to get me."

Marcy pulled Annie close, feeling the little girl's heart beating wildly. She wasn't surprised after all that had happened and all they'd been through that Annie would have bad dreams.

"A monster?" she asked, making it a point to look back at the bed, shaking her head. "I don't see a monster."

Annie stared at her empty bed. "H-he disappeared when you turned on the light."

Marcy ran a soothing hand along Annie's forehead, pushing a curl away from her face. "You know what I think happened? I think maybe you had a bad dream and the monster *disappeared* when you woke up."

Annie looked up at her mother, then back at the bed. "Maybe...maybe he's under the bed."

"Maybe," Marcy said. "But he'd have to be an awfully skinny monster. It's pretty small under there." She pulled back just a little, looking down at Annie. "And I don't think I've ever seen skinny monsters, have you?"

Annie thought for a moment, then shook her head. "Monsters are big and hairy, and they have great big teeth."

"Well, I don't think anyone too big or too hairy could fit under there," Marcy offered.

Annie shot another uneasy look at the bed, then turned to her mother again. "Can I stay here? With you?"

Marcy smiled, snuggling them down into the covers. "Sure," she said, reaching for the light and switching it off. "Just be careful. My tummy still hurts."

"Okay," Annie whispered, cuddling. She lay still for a moment, then pulled back. "He'll protect us—you and me. He told me."

"He? You mean Agent Varela?"

"No," Annie said, yawning as she shook her head. "Coos. He said no one was going to hurt us, not while he's around."

"Oh?"

"I like Coos a whole bunch, Mommy."

"That's nice, sweetheart," Marcy mumbled, feeling an old wound opening inside her, a wound much more painful than the one caused by Brad Buck's bullet. She tucked the covers around them tight. "Go to sleep."

Marcy lay awake in the darkness for a long time, long after Annie's breathing had become deep and even. She stared up at the ceiling, thinking about Cruz and the exchange they'd had in the living room earlier.

They had been considerate and polite with each other. He'd shown sincere concern for her condition; she'd expressed her gratitude for his help with Annie. There hadn't been any accusations, no angry outbursts; the whole thing had been very modern, very adult, very civilized. So why wasn't she satisfied?

She had expected him to be upset when he'd learned the truth about Annie, when he'd learned she'd kept him from his child, from even knowing he was a father. She'd assumed he would hate her for what she'd done, no matter how justified she believed herself to be. But she'd also known he would make an effort to put his feelings aside because of Annie, to concentrate on making the best of an impossible situation.

And he'd done that. He'd put his anger and his hostility aside, put his feelings on hold for the greater good, just as she'd hoped. Only, he'd gone much further than she'd anticipated, succeeded far beyond her wildest expectations.

She thought of the way he'd looked at her, of his detachment and nonchalance. He'd looked at her as he would have looked at anyone, as if she were just another stranger, another of his patients, instead of the mother of his child.

Marcy closed her eyes, the darkness in the room not black enough to block out the image of his remote, unemotional expression from her memory. There had been a time when she thought she knew him, when she thought she understood who he was and what he wanted. Unfortunately, she'd had to learn the hard way just how wrong she had been. Still, she knew him well enough to know that he was a passionate man, one who felt things deeply and sincerely, and it was obvious he felt nothing when he looked at her.

Indifference. That was what she'd seen in his eyes. For four years she'd wondered why he had hurt her, had tried to figure out what had happened to make him walk out on her, why he'd left. Now she had her answer. It wasn't a question of whether he loved her. It wasn't even a question of whether he hated her. The raw, unvarnished truth was she simply didn't matter to him, and that, she was finding, was more painful than being left at the altar.

Annie mumbled something in her sleep and shifted positions. Marcy waited for the child to get comfortable, then gathered her close again. She thought of how Cruz had laughed and teased Annie, of the care he'd given her, and the attention. There was nothing indifferent in the way he looked at her. Every time they were together, every time he talked about her or said her name, the emotion—the passion—was there.

It had been strange to see the two of them together. It had been a little like putting two lost pieces of a puzzle together—father and daughter. For four years she'd allowed hurt and anger to convince her he had no place in *her* daughter's life, that there was nothing connecting him to *her* little girl.

But watching the two of them together made her realize she'd been fooling herself. She could ignore it; she could refuse to acknowledge it; but she couldn't change history, couldn't alter fact—and the fact was Annie was Cruz's daughter, too. It was impossible to look at her and not see

him, too. The connection was there, in the dark eyes they
shared, in expressions and mannerisms, and in a hundred
other small, subtle ways she'd refused to acknowledge for
the past three years.

I like Coos a whole bunch, Mommy, don't you?

Marcy felt the sting of tears behind her closed lids. She
had spent the past four years trying very hard to hate Cruz
Martinez, trying to put him out of her memory and out of
her heart. She wanted to forget what it had been like to
have him hold her, how safe and protected she had felt in
his arms. Now she realized how miserably she'd failed.
She'd forgotten nothing, except how painful the memories
could be.

She'd believed him when he'd said he would protect
her. He'd protect her because she was Annie's mother. But
he couldn't protect her from everything that would
hurt—he couldn't protect her heart.

Chapter 6

"You don't look hungry."

Marcy glanced up from her full plate of food. "Oh, really?" She put her napkin down and rested her elbows on the table. "Tell me, Doctor, how does hungry look? I'm curious. Exactly how does one *not look* hungry?"

Cruz drew in a deep breath, shooting an uneasy glance in Annie's direction. "If you don't like the hamburger, maybe I could fix you something else."

Marcy felt anger and frustration gathering in her like pressure building in a volcano. "I don't want you to fix me anything else." She pushed herself away from the table and rose to her feet. "In fact, I don't want you to do anything for me."

"Marcy, sit down," he said in a low voice.

"Yeah, Mommy," Annie said, biting into her hamburger. "You haven't eaten your dinner."

"I'm not hungry," she said in a tight voice, struggling for control. She slid her chair back and stood up, then started around the table. "I think I'll go lie down for a while."

"You haven't eaten anything all day," Cruz said accusingly, catching her by the arm as she passed. "You need to keep up your strength."

"Well, thank you, Doctor," she said in a sarcastic voice, yanking her arm away. "I appreciate your concern."

She stalked off down the hall, stomping into her room and slamming the door.

It had been four days—four endlessly long, tedious days—since they'd taken up residence in the safe house, and four long days of Cruz's placid bedside manner and detached concern. Her recovery was moving along wonderfully. She felt stronger, rested and much less vulnerable. She'd even begun getting dressed every morning, sitting at the table for her meals, even helping in the kitchen a little. Her incision was healing, and Cruz had informed her only this morning the stitches were nearly ready to come out. Physically, she was doing great; emotionally, however, she was walking a tightrope.

She restlessly paced back and forth between the narrow strip of carpet separating her bed from Annie's, back and forth, back and forth, the room feeling more cramped and more confining with each sweep she made. She'd acted like an idiot just now, she knew that. Irritable and unreasonable, lashing out like some kind of shrew. She just couldn't seem to help it.

Frustrated, she flounced down on the bed, forgetting about her stitches for a moment and wincing with surprise at the sharp pain that radiated up her belly like a hot iron.

"Ouch," she groaned, holding her stomach and falling back across the mattress. She sank her hands into her hair, considering for a moment pulling it out, but squeezed her eyes tight, instead. "What's the matter with me? What's the matter with me?"

She groaned again, trying desperately to push the image of Cruz from her mind. His cool eyes and patronizing smile were enough to make her scream; this was worse than some exotic form of torture. He was killing her with kindness—doing all the right things, being thoughtful and considerate. Only this kindness, this consideration, didn't come from his heart; it came from his sense of duty, his desire to do the right thing. He didn't care about her; he was going through the motions, doing the right thing for Annie's sake and the sake of their situation.

She should be grateful, she knew. She should just accept his indifference, appreciate the fact that he'd let her off the hook so easily, that there had been no messy scenes or angry accusations. He was good to Annie. Wasn't that all that was really important? Wasn't that what she wanted, what she'd hoped would happen?

Then why was she feeling so lousy? Why would she have gone stark, raving mad had she sat at the dining-room table for one moment longer?

The past four days had been the longest in her life, longer than the lengthy days of Brad Buck's trial, longer than the endless days spent driving cross-country. It didn't seem to matter what she did, what she said or how she acted; Cruz hadn't so much as raised his voice to her. In fact, outside of the narrow parameters of her recovery, he'd barely spoken to her at all. Apart from being his patient, it was as if she didn't exist for him—and that, she was finding, was driving her crazy.

"Would you like to talk about it?"

She jumped when she realized he had quietly opened her door and stepped into the room.

"Did it ever occur to you to knock?" she demanded, struggling to sit up.

"I'm sorry," he said in a low voice. "I thought it might disturb you."

"*You* disturb me," she snapped, bracing her stomach with a hand as she slowly stood. "What are you doing here?"

"You were upset," he said quietly. "I thought maybe you'd want to talk about it."

She turned away, shaking her head. "Well, you were wrong. I don't feel like talking about it." She looked back at him. "And I sure as hell don't feel like talking about it with you."

He glanced down at the carpet, shifting his weight to his other foot. "I just thought it would help."

There wasn't so much as a hint of emotion in his voice, and it only fueled her anger. She wasn't in the mood for his plastic concern and patronizing manner. "Help what?"

"Help us avoid what just happened," he said, taking several steps farther into the room. "That was quite a performance you put on in there."

"Performance? What are you talking about?"

"I'm talking about the scene you created at the dinner table. It upset Annie. I'd like to see that it doesn't happen again."

Of course he was right. She had created a scene. And it probably hadn't been too wise to behave that way in front of Annie. But to have him point it out to her was infuriating.

"Where is Annie?" she asked, starting for the door. "I want to see her."

"I don't think this is a good time."

"*You* don't think," she said with a sarcastic laugh. She

reached an arm out to push past him. "Frankly, Dr. Martinez, I don't give a damn what you think."

"Well, normally, Miss Fitzgerald, I'd say that was just fine with me," Cruz said.

He caught her by the arm, bringing her to an abrupt halt, and gazed down at her, his cold eyes a stark contrast to his low, sedate monotone.

"However, when it comes to Annie, what I think is going to matter from now on."

"Let go of me," she insisted, struggling unsuccessfully against his grasp. "I want to see Annie. I want to know she's okay. Where is she?"

"She's fine," he said, his hold around her arm tightening just a fraction. "She's in the kitchen with Agent Varela, and I don't want you talking to her until you calm down a little."

Fury burst in her like fireworks shattering the night sky with a million tiny lights. "Who the hell do you think you are, telling me when I can see my daughter and when I can't?"

"I'm her father, that's who," he said, his voice not quite as controlled now. "Something you conveniently keep forgetting."

"I haven't forgotten anything," she said, trying to yank her hand away. "Including how to feel—which is more than I can say for you."

"What?" he said, releasing her arm. "You don't think I have any feelings?"

"I know you don't," she muttered, rubbing at the spot where he'd grabbed her.

He put his hands on his hips. "And how did you come to that conclusion?"

She stared at him. "What conclusion? It's the truth. Look at you. You walk around her like a...like a zombie."

"Zombie?" Stepping back, he regarded her. "Are you sure you're feeling all right?"

Marcy felt the anger simmering in her start to boil. "Don't you dare be condescending to me," she said, glaring up at him. "Walking around here with your superior attitude and phony concern. You don't think I can see right through that placid bedside manner of yours?"

"Would it make you feel better if I flounced around here making demands, stomping my feet and acting like a spoiled brat?" he asked caustically, his eyes narrowing. "Would that make you feel better?"

She stalked closer, balling her hands into fists. "At least I'd know you were still human."

He shook his head, making no effort to hide his disdain. "You're being ridiculous."

"Why? Because I'm showing some emotions?" she countered, seeing something flash in the murky blackness of his eyes. "At least I have some. At least I still know how to feel."

"I feel," he insisted in a low voice.

"Is that so?" She folded her arms across her chest. "Tell me, Cruz, what do you feel?"

He stared at her for a moment, then shook his head. "I don't believe you. What do you want from me? I've tried treating you with courtesy, have been cooperative, considerate, and you're acting as if that's some kind of crime."

"Cooperative and considerate—is that what you call it?"

"Actually, I call it behaving like an adult," he said, his voice just a little louder. "Something you obviously know nothing about."

She reared back as if he'd slapped her. "You're calling me childish?"

"That's how you're acting."

"Well, thank you for your diagnosis, Doctor," she said, her voice low and mocking. "But then, what I do and how I act is really none of your business now, is it?"

"It is when it upsets my daughter."

Marcy saw something flash in his eyes, something hot and predatory. "Look, maybe we should get something straight right here, right now. You might have fathered that little girl in there, but she's *my* daughter, do you understand?"

"Oh, I understand, all right," he said in a low, dangerous voice. "I understand you only decided to tell me the truth because you needed something from me, because I could be of some use to you." The rapid rising and falling of his chest was the only outward evidence of his growing anger. "What do you think is going to happen once all this is over, Marcy? Am I just to fade into the background again, disappear? Forget I have a daughter?"

"No," she said, but her voice faltered just a little.

"Good," he said, taking a step forward. "Because I can tell you, that's not going to happen."

"You mean you're not going to walk out on Annie the way you did me?"

Marcy could feel the rage in him. It radiated from him like heat from a fire. Yet she wasn't daunted. She found it familiar, and curiously comforting. After so many days of patient indulgence, she welcomed the emotion, welcomed the signs of life.

"I thought," he said, enunciating carefully as he struggled for control, "we were going to try to put our feelings aside on all this, for Annie's sake. I thought we had an agreement."

"Agreements get broken. You of all people know that," she said, her voice purposely challenging. She knew what she was doing, knew just what tone to use and which buttons to push to ensure a reaction from him. "We had an agreement four years ago, but you didn't seem to have any trouble breaking that one."

"I don't want to get into that now."

"No, I don't imagine you would. After all, there aren't a lot of excuses you can offer, are there?" She took a step forward, her voice biting and sarcastic. "So what was it, Cruz? What made you change your mind? You never did tell me."

"Stop it, Marcy."

"Cold feet? Second thoughts? What?"

"Don't do this."

"Were you lying when you said you loved me?"

"Marcy, I said stop," he told her, his voice thundering now.

"Don't like hearing the truth?"

"You want to talk truth, Marcy?" He took another step forward, glaring down at her. "Yes, I walked out, and, yes, I hurt you. But you got your revenge, didn't you?"

"Get out," she said, pointing toward the door.

"Don't you think denying me my child evens the score?"

Marcy staggered back a step, his words hitting her like a blow to the stomach, leaving her breathless and dizzy. "How dare you!"

"You're the one who wanted to talk truth."

She looked up, feeling the sting of tears in her eyes. "I hate you."

He didn't doubt that for one moment. She did hate him. He could see it in her eyes and feel it in his heart. She had been brutal with him, striking exactly where she knew it would hurt the most. She'd poked and prodded, goading him with her accusations and inciting him with her reproach. She'd said he had no feelings, believed if she wounded him he wouldn't bleed, but she'd been wrong. He *did* feel—too much. Her words had cut like a knife, and, like a street fighter, he'd struck back, low and dirty.

The raw look of pain in her eyes made him start to hate, too. He hated that he'd hurt her again, hated the mistakes they'd made and the tangle their lives had become. Something snapped in him; some fine, thin line that had been holding him together for the past four days; some final, delicately fragile thread of control. He grabbed at her, catching her by the upper arms and hauling her to him.

"Then hate this," he growled, pressing his mouth to hers in a crushing kiss. He wanted to punish her for pushing him, wanted to punish himself for being as low and as vile as she believed him to be. Only, something happened when his lips touched hers, something that changed the anger in his blood to fire and left him breathless and desperate for her. "You think I have no feelings, that I'm made of stone?" he whispered, pulling his lips from hers and gasping for breath. "Don't you know that every time I see you, every time I hear your voice or look into your eyes, I remember?" His hands kneaded the flesh of her arms, and his voice became coarse with emotion. "I have no feelings, but I remember what it felt like to be with you, to have you beneath me, to have your hands on me, to move together." His lips brushed hers, inhaling her breath. "I remember what it felt like to be in you."

He lowered his lips to hers again, for a kiss that was no less powerful, no less intense, than before. He forgot all about behaving responsibly and honoring agreements. Her taste was invading him, exploding through his system like one of Brad Buck's bombs erupting full force. For the moment, there was no right or wrong, no past or present and no looking back. There was just the woman in his arms and a desire he'd denied for far too long.

"If you think I have no feelings," he said, pulling his mouth from hers with a groan, looking down into her huge brown eyes, feeling the need pounding in his system, "think again."

Then he stalked out of the room, slamming the door behind him.

Marcy stood in the middle of the room, listening to the sound of her breath rushing in and out of her lungs and feeling her heart pulse furiously in her neck. She stared at the shut door, waiting for the world to take shape around her.

She had known Cruz was a passionate man, that he was capable of intense emotions and powerful desires—which was exactly why she'd found his indifference to her so hard to take. Still, she'd never seen him like this—so wild, so unleashed—not even when they'd been together.

Closing her eyes, she thought of his fury, of the anger that had twisted his face and distorted his features. He'd been furious with her, full of rage. But there had been no anger in his kiss, and fury had turned to desire.

Opening her eyes again, she shivered at the small thrill of exhilaration that darted down her spine. Staggering back, she put a shaky hand out, feeling her way to the edge of the bed, then collapsing onto the mattress. The incision in her abdomen pinched under the strain of her movements, but she was only vaguely aware of discomfort. Adrenaline was pumping through her system at such a frenzied rate she would have been hard-pressed to feel any-thing—anything other than the fire pulsing through her system.

"Cruz," she murmured, her raspy whisper cutting through the silence of the room. She ran her fingertips over her lips, the sound and the feel of his name causing another shiver to migrate down her spine. She'd accused him of being indifferent, of not caring. What a fool she had been! There had been nothing indifferent in the way he'd kissed her, nothing thoughtless or unfeeling in the things he'd said.

She rolled onto her back and stared up at the ceiling, letting her mind drift. Being in his arms had been like waking up after a deep sleep, like feeling the sun after a long, cold winter. Like a blossom in the spring, she'd come alive. All the feelings she'd buried, all the needs she'd ignored, stirred from their slumber and sprang to life. She remembered what it was to feel like a woman again, and what it was to want a man—to want Cruz.

With a sudden horror, she opened her eyes and sat up. She wanted Cruz. After all this time, after all that had happened, she still wanted him. How could that be?

"Oh, no. Oh, no," she groaned, covering her mouth with her hand. "What have I done?"

Like Pandora, she had cracked the lid on a box that should have remained tightly shut. She'd looked at a truth she'd kept hidden for years, a truth she'd let escape and could ignore no longer. For better or for worse, for richer or for poorer, she was still in love with Cruz Martinez— in spite of everything. She could accept or reject it; she just couldn't deny it.

"What am I going to do now?"

"You mean you've got nothing?"

"I mean that everything that can be done is being done." Joe Mountain took off his cowboy hat and tossed it onto the ottoman. "There are roadblocks in place, every airport, train station, bus depot, car-rental agency, used-car lot and motorcycle shop has been put on alert. Hell, they've even notified bicycle shops to be on the lookout.

There have been hundreds of reported sightings, and each one of those is being checked out.'' He leaned his head back against the worn brocade of the chair's high back. ''I wouldn't call that 'nothing.''

Cruz sat on the floor, reclining against the sock-stuffed sofa. His knees were bent, and his elbows rested against them. Worrying the pencil he held in his hand, he looked up at Joe, cocking his head. ''Have you got Buck?''

''No,'' Joe admitted.

''Then you've got nothing.''

Joe closed his eyes and rubbed at them with the palms of his hands. ''You're right,'' he said with a tired sigh, lifting his booted foot onto the ottoman alongside his hat. ''We've got nothing.''

Cruz swore to himself, snapping the pencil in half. ''He couldn't have just disappeared into thin air. What happened to him? Where the hell is the son of a bitch?''

''Yeah, well, I'm a little curious about that myself,'' Joe muttered dryly. ''An army of FBI, the entire state police force and two units from the National Guard have covered practically every square inch of the state of Nevada. If this guy has found a hole to crawl into that we haven't found yet, I'd like to know where it is.''

With another low curse, Cruz threw the broken halves of the pencil across the room and rose to his feet. ''You'd think after four days you'd have something.''

Joe opened his eyes. ''I told you, we've got leads— hundreds of them—and one of them is going to direct us to him. It's just going to take some time, that's all.''

''Oh, just some time,'' Cruz snapped sarcastically, pacing back and forth across the room. ''And what the hell am I supposed to do in the meantime?''

Joe sat up, his frown deepening. ''You'll do what you have been doing, the only thing you can right now.''

Cruz wheeled around. "What do you mean the only thing I can? I can't do anything. I can't work. I can't leave. I can't even go outside. I'm going stir-crazy in here, stuck inside day in and day out with...with..."

Joe lifted his foot off the ottoman and slowly stood. "With Marcy? With your daughter?"

Swearing violently beneath his breath, Cruz kicked at a stack of newspapers piled by the front door, sending them cascading across the carpet. Bending, he made a half-hearted attempt to pick up the mess, but abandoned the effort after a few tries.

"Annie's incredible," he said in a quiet voice, calm now. "I still can hardly believe—" He stopped, drawing in a deep breath and putting his head down. "Seeing her, being with her every day, all day—it has almost made all this other garbage worth it."

"And Marcy?"

Cruz looked up. "I'm losing it, Joe. I thought I could handle this—you know, for Annie's sake." He stopped, shaking his head. "Now I'm not so sure."

Joe hesitated for a moment. "Something happen? Between you two, I mean."

Cruz smiled, but sadness had it coming out more like a grimace. "Only that I did something stupid." The smile faded, and he turned away. "*Really* stupid."

"You didn't, uh, you know..." Joe began.

Cruz breathed out a laugh and shook his head. "God, no. Believe me, I think the woman would rather have my head on a platter about now than take me to bed."

"Sounds like Miss Fitzgerald isn't too happy with you."

"No, she's not."

"You two have an argument or something?"

Cruz thought of Marcy and how she had looked standing in that tiny bedroom, hair flying, cheeks flushed with color and eyes fiery hot with anger. He'd never seen her in a courtroom, but he didn't doubt she would be formidable in front of a jury, especially when she was arguing something she felt passionate about.

Passionate. That didn't even begin to describe what he'd felt when he'd grabbed her to him and kissed her. He'd also felt anger and desperation, and a desire so strong it gnawed at his insides. Passionate. What was it that Marcy felt? Was it possible after all that had happened between them that she had been fired up and passionate about him?

"Something," he mumbled, turning back to Joe. "She was feeling—" He stopped, shaking his head. "Oh, hell, I don't know what she was feeling. Bored, I guess. Or restless. All I know is before I realized it, she was screaming at me, accusing me of all sorts of things and telling me I had no feelings and..."

"And what?" Joe prompted when Cruz trailed off.

"And I just sort of lost it."

Joe picked up his hat and fiddled with the brim, mulling over Cruz's words, then carelessly tossed it onto the seat of the chair. "What did you do?"

Cruz swallowed, tasting her in his mouth. "I kissed her."

Joe raised a brow. "Oh."

Cruz looked up, feeling embarrassed. "Yeah, *oh.*"

Joe shrugged. "Sounds like you both were pretty angry. People do all sorts of crazy things in the heat of anger. It doesn't help that you're stuck here together day in and day out. Maybe it was good that you had a chance to mix it up, blow off a little steam. Maybe it will help clear the air."

"Maybe," Cruz grumbled, not convinced.

"Get a good night's sleep," Joe suggested. "Give yourselves a chance to cool off a little. I'll bet this will all blow over by morning.''

Cruz let out a heavy sigh. "Maybe, but I wouldn't hold my breath.''

"You don't know how the lady is feeling.''

"She hates me. She said so,'' Cruz told him, shooting a glance down the hall. "She accused me of being cold.''

"Maybe you should tell her she's wrong.''

He looked back at Joe. "It's not that simple. She has reason to hate me, Joe. You don't know what I did to her.''

"I know that was in the past,'' Joe said. "And I know hate can't exist without love—''

"Don't, Joe,'' Cruz said, cutting him off.

"Don't what?''

"Don't romanticize this. It's over between Marcy and me. It's been over for years. I had my chance and I blew it. I hurt her so bad she'll never forgive me. One kiss isn't going to change anything.''

"No?''

"No.''

Joe shrugged, reaching over and snatching up his hat from the chair. "Tell me something, Doc. When you were kissing her, what was she doing?''

"What do you mean what was she doing?''

"What was she doing? Struggling? Kicking? Biting? What?''

Cruz thought of Marcy's soft lips and the feel of her breath against his cheek. "No.''

"Okay,'' Joe said, slipping his hat on over his long hair. "So it sounds like the lady was kissing you back.''

Chapter 7

"**Y**ou're not going to open it?"

Marcy nodded. "Yeah, I am. Eventually."

Don Varela dropped several heaping teaspoons of sugar into his coffee and gave it a lazy stir. "I guess one of Sheriff Mountain's men brought it out during the night. He left it with my partner, and he gave it to me when he woke me up for the night watch."

Marcy gazed at the thick manila envelope in her hands and felt her heart stumble. "I don't think I will ever be able to look at something like this again without wondering if it's going to blow up in my face."

"Ah, yes, the legacy of Brad Buck," Varela said thoughtfully, blowing gently into the steaming mug. "It has no doubt left its mark on a lot of people's lives." He gingerly took a sip from the cup, then made a face. "But you don't have to worry about this delivery," he said, nodding to the envelope she held. "It came directly from D.C. The man himself, your boss."

But despite Varela's assurance, Marcy wasn't convinced. She didn't make assumptions when it came to Brad Buck. Carefully feeling the pouch, she cautiously slipped a finger under the flap and tore it open.

Seeing the neat stack of legal-sized folders inside, Marcy breathed a sigh of relief, her whole body relaxing. She thought of U.S. Attorney General Randall Crane, with his perfectly styled gray hair and camera-ready smile. He'd been a fixture in her life far longer than the four years she'd worked in his office. Thirty years ago, he'd been her father's roommate at Stanford, and the two men had remained close friends. Of course, he'd just been ''Uncle Randy'' back then, not the country's top law enforcement official, and certainly not her boss. When he'd offered her the position on his staff in Washington, she knew many had said the offer smacked of nepotism, but not many would say that now. She'd worked damn hard since she'd taken the job, even though a career as a high-powered, high-profile prosecutor wasn't exactly the career she'd wanted. Still, she'd given it all she had, because after Cruz had walked out, it had been all she'd had left until Annie was born.

Cruz. Marcy closed her eyes. She'd barely slept last night. She'd been too restless to settle down, too agitated and uneasy. She'd tossed and turned for hours after Annie had drifted off, thinking about what had happened, about Cruz and that kiss, driving herself crazy. Finally, not able to stand it any longer, she'd gotten up. With the house dark, she'd wrapped herself in a bulky terry-cloth robe and found her way to the kitchen, and she'd been sitting at the small Formica table with Agent Varela ever since, talking and sharing several pots of coffee. Between his periodic patrol of the house and grounds, she'd learned Agent Varela had married his high-school sweetheart, had a grown

son, a teenage daughter, and could hold more coffee than
any person she'd seen in her life.

Looking up, she peered at the window above the sink.
Outside, the sun was just beginning to peek over the horizon. It would be daylight soon. Cruz would be getting
up and she was going to have to face him.

Marcy glanced away from the window, feeling a fluttering in her chest. She couldn't tell if it was the result of
nerves or just a side effect from all the caffeine she'd in-
gested in the past couple of hours.

"I take it you know what it is."

Marcy's thoughts scattered, and she turned to Agent
Varela. "What's that?"

"The envelope. I take it you know what's inside."

"I have a pretty good idea," she said, glancing down
at the envelope in her hands again. She recognized the size
and the shape of a case file and understood what it meant.
There would no doubt be a message inside, a handwritten
note from Randall asking her to look the file over and be
ready to move on it when she returned to work.

Marcy smiled. She was sure her parents were making
his life miserable. They would be frantic with worry about
Annie and her and pestering him constantly for updates on
how they were. But Randall was like a shepherd with his
flock; he would be worried, too. Sending her a case to
study was his way of reaching out, his way of giving her
a light at the end of the tunnel, of reminding her she had
a life and a career waiting when all this was over.

Marcy turned the envelope over and started to peel back
the flap, then stopped. She appreciated the gesture and she
appreciated the care and the concern behind it; she just
wasn't in the mood for another case. She didn't know if
she had the strength or the energy to think about starting
another one, didn't know if she wanted to.

"Change your mind?" Varela asked, reaching for the coffeepot and freshening her cup.

Marcy smiled. "You know what? I think I have—about a lot of things. To hell with it," she said, tossing the envelope onto the center of the table and reaching for her cup. "To hell with cases and courtrooms and the whole damn legal system."

Varela chuckled. "To hell with night shifts and stakeouts and stale doughnuts."

Marcy looked at him and laughed, too. "And to hell with working."

Varela laughed harder, toasting her with his coffee cup. "Amen to that."

"What's so funny?"

As Marcy heard Cruz's voice, the smile on her face turned brittle. With a shaky hand, she lowered her coffee cup to the table, fearful she might spill it, and looked up at him. He stood in the kitchen doorway, dressed in jeans and a T-shirt, his feet bare and his tall frame swallowing up almost all the free space.

"Just a couple of hardworking civil servants complaining about our jobs," Varela said, reaching around behind him and slipping another mug off the hook beneath the kitchen cupboard. He poured the cup full and offered it to Cruz. "We all can't be as rich as you doctors."

Cruz's gaze slid to Marcy. "Oh, I'll bet some of us can," he murmured. He looked back at Varela, taking the cup the agent offered. "What's everyone doing up so early?"

"I pulled night patrol." Varela shrugged, holding back a yawn. "And my fellow hardworking friend here is suffering from a little insomnia."

Cruz looked back at Marcy again. "You feeling all right?"

"I feel fine," she said, the erratic rhythm of her heart having nothing to do with the caffeine this time. "I just wasn't very sleepy."

"You need your rest," he reminded her, giving her a closer look. "You've still got a ways to go before you're back to normal."

"I know," she said, feeling awkward and uncomfortable under his dark gaze. "I'm fine, really."

"There you go," Varela said, tapping the manila envelope as he pushed his chair out from the table and stood. "The perfect excuse. 'Sorry, Boss, I couldn't do any work—doctor's orders.'" He carried his empty coffee mug to the sink and rinsed it out. "Time for me to take a look outside." He glanced at his wristwatch, comparing the time on it with the one on the clock on the kitchen stove. "Unfortunately, the good doctor has said nothing about me getting any rest," he said, pulling his handheld two-way radio from his pocket. "And my boss is expecting me to check in pretty soon." He walked to the back door and pulled it open, his eyes alert despite his casual manner. "If you need me for anything, remember—" He stopped and pointed to the back-porch light switch, which had been rigged to a dull buzzer. "Don't open the door. Just signal."

Cruz waited until the door closed, then turned to Marcy. "You sure you're all right?"

"I'm fine," she insisted, pushing herself away from the table and walking to the sink. "I just couldn't sleep, that's all."

"I could give you something," he said, watching as she washed out her cup and reached for a dish towel.

"You mean a sleeping pill?"

"You'll rest," he said reasonably, pulling out a chair and sitting down.

She shook her head, drying the cup and hanging it back on a hook. "No, thanks. I'll take it easy today."

"Was Varela serious about this?" he asked, pointing to the envelope on the table. "You've got work to do?"

Marcy turned and glanced at the file as she reached for the empty coffeepot and began rinsing it out. "Not really. I suspect it was meant more to give me something to do, something to keep my mind occupied."

Cruz nodded, thinking of the career she'd carved for herself and feeling just a little intimidated. "Will it?"

"Keep me occupied?" She shrugged, glancing back at him and then to the envelope on the table, trying to summon some enthusiasm. "Maybe."

Cruz pushed his hair back from his face and sipped at his coffee, watching her as she gathered what few dirty dishes there were and began washing them, too. "I can get those things later."

"That's okay," she said with a casual wave of her hand, inadvertently sprinkling water all along the counter. "I hardly do anything around here anyway."

He took another drink of coffee, watching her wipe at the counter. "Hungry? I could start breakfast."

"No, thanks, really," she said stiffly, suddenly aware of the bulky robe and the tangles in her hair. She quickly finished washing and drying the remaining dishes, then tossed the towel over the rack and started across the kitchen toward the door. "I'll check on Annie, maybe have something with her later."

"Was it because of last night?" he asked as she reached the door.

Marcy skittered to a stop. "What?"

"The insomnia? Couldn't sleep because of what happened last night?"

"No," she insisted with a laugh that sounded forced and

silly even to her own ears. "I just couldn't sleep, that's all."

"Maybe we should talk about it anyhow."

"Why?"

Cruz set his coffee mug down and swiped at his hair again. "Because maybe it didn't keep you up last night, but it did me."

Marcy swallowed, looking down into his dark eyes and feeling her heart rate start to speed up again. How was she going to do this, stand there and talk to him as though last night meant nothing, as though that Pandora's box in her heart hadn't been opened and sent emotion and desire scattering in all directions?

"There's nothing to talk about," she said with a careless shrug. "We were both upset. We both said a lot of stupid things. Why don't we just forget it?"

Cruz pushed himself away from the table and stood. "Are you going to be able to do that?"

"Sure," she said, with a careless wave, hoping that she sounded more convincing to him than she did to herself. "Why not?"

"Why not?" he asked skeptically. He walked around the table to where she stood. "Marcy, you felt something last night. I know because I felt it, too."

Marcy closed her eyes and turned away. "You're wrong."

"Am I?"

"Yes, you are." She turned back around. "Look, Cruz, I don't want to argue anymore. I really don't. If last night showed me one thing it's that we both have a lot of anger, justified or not." She walked back to the counter, folding her arms around herself. "And you were right. This isn't the time to hash all this out between us. Our lives are in turmoil. Brad Buck on the loose, being confined together in this tiny house—we're on edge. I was out of line yesterday, I admit it. I had no right striking out at you. You've been decent through all of this. Considerate, kind. I had no right pushing you like that.'' Looking up at him, she hugged the robe to her tight and felt a flush start to crawl up her neck toward her cheeks. ''What happened last night, between us…it was anger. That's what you felt, Cruz— anger. It would be wrong to confuse it with anything else. I was angry. You were angry. And that's the only reason what happened last night…happened.''

Cruz watched the color rise in her cheeks, replacing the pallor of a night with too little sleep. ''What about now?''

''What about now?''

''Are you still angry?''

Guarded, Marcy studied him for a moment. ''Are you?''

''About Annie, yeah.''

She considered this briefly, then nodded in acceptance. ''Okay, that's honest, and I can understand it.''

Cruz took a step forward. ''Now you be honest.''

She loosened the hold on her robe and folded her arms across her chest. ''I spent four years telling myself I hated you. How's that for honesty?''

He stared down at her. ''Do you?''

She looked up at him, feeling the breath catch in her throat. It wasn't so much what she saw his eyes that had her forgetting about the long, restless night she'd spent; it was more what she didn't see. Gone was that cool, professional scrutiny, the indulgent sneer and detached indifference. He looked different than he had the past several days. While she could see the signs of his anger, the traces of his annoyance and frustration, she could also see an accessibility, a vulnerability, that hadn't been there before.

''You're Annie's father. I can't forget that.''

''That's no answer.''

"Maybe not," she said, stepping around him and starting for the dining room. "But I'm not sure I know what the answer is."

Cruz reached out as she moved past him, halting her with a hand on her arm. "I'm sorry."

"For what? For being honest or for not loving me enough to marry me?"

"It wasn't—" Cruz stopped, drawing in a deep breath and slowly releasing his hold on her arm. "I'm sorry you were hurt."

Marcy saw something move across his face, some fleeting emotion, some passing thought, but it was there for only a moment before it was gone. Still, she felt the sincerity in his words and appreciated the honesty behind them.

"I've got Annie," she said. "That's all that matters now."

Cruz watched her as she continued across the worn linoleum floor toward the dining room and disappeared around the corner. He felt winded and weak, a little as though he'd just finished running a marathon or taken a blow to the stomach.

He slid down onto a kitchen chair, resting an elbow on the hard table and cradling his bowed head in his hand. He'd very nearly done something stupid—again. He'd almost blurted out the truth, almost confessed the reason he'd walked out on her four years ago. But that would have been a mistake. It was too late for explanations, too late to try to untangle the mess he'd made of all their lives. It was better just to let her think what she would, to let her continue to hate him if it helped her get on with her life.

He looked down at the thick envelope on the table. Her work. Despite the special circumstances that had ensued with Brad Buck, her work was meaningful. It was the kind of work that changed people's lives and made the world a better place.

He picked up the package, imagining her poring over the contents, assessing tactics and plotting strategy. She was brilliant at what she did and would have shriveled up and died in a place like Mesa Ridge. Marrying her and bringing her here would have been a waste of her talents, and she would only have been miserable in the end.

In the distance he heard the muffled sounds of Annie and Marcy as they greeted each other. Annie would be bright and bouncy after a long night's rest, ready to tell him about the dreams she'd had or a story she'd heard.

Cruz closed his eyes, and he felt a heavy tug on his heart. He had to keep telling himself he'd done the right thing, he'd made the right choice for everyone, because if he allowed himself to doubt, if he let himself think for even a moment that he might have made a mistake...

He tossed the envelope down and pushed himself away from the table with such force the steel legs of the chair scraped noisily along the old linoleum. No, he wouldn't do that, wouldn't fall into the trap of second guesses and doubts. He couldn't allow himself to think about what might have been, what kind of life the three of them might have had if circumstances had been different.

"Coos."

Cruz looked up just as Annie raced across the kitchen and made a flying leap into his lap.

"Good morning," he said, clearing his throat and blinking away the stinging sensation in his eyes.

"I'm hungry."

"Oh, yeah?" he queried, lifting her with him as he rose to his feet. After setting her down on the counter, he opened the cupboard door. "What would you say about some French toast?"

"Yum," she replied, rubbing her tummy.

Cruz turned around, glancing at the empty archway between the kitchen and the dining room. "How about your mom?"

"She was sleepy," Annie said, setting her stuffed bear down on the counter beside her. "She's gone to lie down."

"Well," Cruz said, turning back to Annie and reaching for a bowl from the shelf, "we can take her a tray later."

Cruz went about preparing breakfast while Annie told him all about a dream filled with unicorns and her teddy bear and about a great big mountain made of ice cream, but his mind kept drifting back to Marcy.

He knew where he stood now, and it was better that way. There was nothing she wanted from him, nothing more than his help, and maybe sometimes his understanding. He told himself it was easier like this; he wouldn't have to deal with the pressure of uncertainty or the stress of ambivalence. He wouldn't have to be so afraid of showing any emotion now, wouldn't have to be concerned about revealing too much. There would be no more uncomfortable confrontations, no more awkward encounters or unwanted desire.

He reached for a towel and wrapped it around Annie like an apron. It was all working out, he told himself. They would get through this and straighten out the details about Annie, then go their separate ways. Marcy had her work, he had his work and they'd both have Annie. It was what was best for all of them, what was meant to be.

He looked into Annie's sweet little face and felt a pain travel straight through the center of his heart. It was all working out, he reminded himself again. All he had to do now was convince himself of that.

* * *

"Maybe you should think about calling it a night."

Cruz jumped, his head snapping up and his eyes blinking open. "Hmm, what?" he mumbled, sitting up in the chair and checking his watch. "Wh-what time is it?"

"I didn't mean to startle you." Varela laughed, slipping his arm through the leather strap of his shoulder holster. "But I gotta tell you, you don't look too comfortable sitting up in that chair." He drew out his Glock, giving it a quick check. "Why don't you hit the hay? It's way after midnight."

"Yeah, I guess I should, although I've had more luck sleeping here than on that bed back there," Cruz said, stifling a yawn as he rose slowly to his feet.

"Pretty uncomfortable?"

"Let's just say it makes this chair actually seem comfortable," Cruz said dryly, stretching the stiff muscles in his neck and back. "You pull a night shift again?"

"Yeah," Varela said, slipping the gun back into its holster. "Brown's doing one last check outside before I spell him for the night." He leaned closer, lowering his voice. "He's a lot younger than I am, and damn, it gets cold out there at night."

Cruz smiled and nodded. "Gotta pay your dues."

Varela laughed. "That's what I keep tellin' the kid."

Cruz yawned again. "How about you? You manage to get some sleep?"

"Oh, yeah. I snagged a couple of hours earlier," Varela said with a casual wave of his hand. "Not enough, but in my line of work you get used to it." He reached for a stretched and faded zippered sweatshirt and slipped it on over the holster. "Like doctors, I guess."

"Yeah." Cruz smiled, rubbing at his stiff neck. "But I'm not sure we ever really get used to it."

"I'm heading out to the kitchen to make a pot of coffee," he said as he started through the living room toward the dining room. "You're welcome to join me. I don't imagine you're interested in the caffeine, but I did notice Mrs. Crawford keeps a bottle of whiskey behind the jar of pickles in the pantry. It just might make that rack you're sleeping on feel a little more like a bed."

"It just might," Cruz said, following him through the living room and into the kitchen. It would have been too much to hope that Hattie was a tequila drinker, but he wasn't in the position to be picky. Anything that would numb his senses and help him to stop thinking would do just fine.

It had been a hell of a day—a hell of a day after a long, sleepless night—and he wasn't sure how much more he was going to be able to take. He'd thought that after everything that had happened with Marcy—after all the anger, the striking out, the talking…the kiss—things would have been better between them. He'd hoped that clearing the air would make them more relaxed, more at ease with each other. Instead, it seemed to have done just the reverse. They'd spent a tense day, awkward and uncomfortable around each other, trying very hard to stay out of the other's way.

"I hope I didn't steer you wrong," Varela said, stepping out of the pantry and holding the bottle of amber liquid up to the light. "I don't know about this stuff. I don't think I've ever drunk whiskey that I couldn't see through." He unscrewed the top and hesitantly smelled the contents. "Oh, yeah, this stuff will either put you to sleep or kill you." He took another whiff and his eyes watered. "And after a hit of this, I'm not sure you'd care which."

"What the hell," Cruz said, accepting the bottle from him and glancing down at the label as he pulled open the door of the cupboard. "It's going to take something with a little backbone to make that mattress in there look good.''

"Well, I can tell you that stuff smells like it has backbone, all right," Varela added dryly. "And maybe a fist or two along with it. After enough of that, I don't imagine you'll care where you sleep."

"Sleep," Cruz muttered, grabbing a small glass from the shelf. "I don't think anyone's been sleeping very well around here." He looked at the picture of a popular cartoon character emblazoned on the side of the glass. "Except Annie, maybe."

"That Annie," Varela said with a chuckle. "She's about the sweetest little thing."

"Yeah, she is sweet," Cruz agreed, pouring a shot of whiskey into the glass and wondering if whiskey could help explain some of Hattie's peculiar habits.

"And she would sure keep you on your toes," Varela said, filling the tea kettle with fresh water and placing it over a burner on the stove. "She asked me the other morning why they didn't just make bullets out of ice."

Cruz looked up. "Ice?"

"Yeah, ice bullets." Varela dumped a generous portion of ground coffee into the cone filter. "She said then if you ever got shot, they'd just melt and go away, and you wouldn't need an operation like her mother had." He turned around, giving his head a shake. "Damn, that's pretty good for a three-year-old."

"Out of the mouths of babes," Cruz said in a tight voice, before picking up the glass and pouring it down in one swallow. The amber liquid burned his throat, then landed in his stomach like a ball of fire, smoldering there.

"You got that right," Varela said, watching Cruz's reaction to the alcohol with amusement. "How's that bed lookin' now?"

"Better," Cruz said, barely able to talk, feeling as

though his throat was on fire. However, it was going to take more than one shot of whiskey before he started to feel better about the rest of his life. "But just to be on the safe side..." He picked up the bottle and poured himself another shot, then downed it, too, in one gulp.

"Ouch." Varela laughed, making a face. "Son, you'd better slow down just a little. Rotgut like that in big doses can eat your insides."

Cruz braced himself against the counter, waiting for the fire in his throat to die down. "Ready to live dangerously?" he asked, tilting the bottle toward Varela. "I don't think you'd have to worry about the cold outside."

"Sorry, but not when I'm on duty. Besides, I don't mind telling you I've been known to hold my own when it comes to knocking down shots, but that stuff..." He paused, giving the bottle and Cruz another skeptical appraisal. "That stuff's too nasty even for me." He shook his head, his smile growing broad. "Leave it to those little old ladies."

Cruz looked at the bottle in his hand, feeling the room list just a fraction. "It's nasty, all right," he said, slowly screwing the cap back on. "I just wonder how much of this Hattie had before the idea of stuffing the sofa with socks sounded like a good one."

"Stuffing the sofa with what?" Varela asked as the tea kettle began to rattle and send droplets of water spurting onto the hot burner.

Cruz laughed, feeling more relaxed than he had in the past five days. "Never mind, you don't want to know."

"You're probably right," Varela said, reaching for the kettle and pouring the hot water over the coffee. "And you won't find me arguing with anyone who can throw whiskey down the way you just did. Doctor, sir, my hat's off to you."

Cruz laughed again, vaguely surprised when it came out

sounding more like a giggle than he was comfortable with. Unfortunately, he was feeling anything but sleepy at the moment. But he was just too relaxed to be very concerned. "Well, don't be too impressed. Not yet anyway. I just might have knocked down two shots of Hattie's homemade bug spray."

They both laughed. Varela finished making his coffee, then poured himself a steaming mug and carried it to the kitchen table. "Doesn't look like there was much work done today."

Cruz leaned back against the counter, feeling the warmth of the alcohol in his arms and legs. "Work?"

"Yeah," he said, gesturing to the manila envelope still lying in the middle of the table. "I don't think Mrs. Fitzgerald was exactly in the mood to start in on another case just yet."

"Miss," Cruz mumbled, staring down at the table.

"What was that?" Varela asked, pulling out a chair, then sitting down.

Cruz shook his head. "Nothing, never mind."

"I could tell when I gave it to her—the envelope, I mean." He brought the mug to his lips, blew gently and took a sip. "She kept saying she was going to open it, but between you and me, I think the lady has seen all she wants of a courtroom."

Cruz frowned. "What makes you say that?"

"Would you?" Varela shrugged. "I mean, she finally succeeds in putting this nutcase away, then he busts loose and makes her life a living hell." Varela took another sip of coffee. "No, I don't blame her for being fed up."

Cruz felt a sudden pressure in his chest. "Is she fed up?"

Varela opened his mouth to answer, but the sudden blast had his words dissolving in a cloud of light and sound.

Chapter 8

"**W**hat the—?" Varela wiped at the blood pouring down his forehead and into his eyes, blinding him. Reflex had him drawing his gun, despite the fact he couldn't see.

"Buck," Cruz snarled through gritted teeth. He crawled across the floor, yanked the leg of the table and pulled it over on one side. Then he reached for Varela and dragged him behind the table. "Give me the Glock."

Varela shoved the gun into Cruz's hand. Cruz took aim at the gaudy light fixture in the center of the ceiling and shattered it in one shot.

"Here," Cruz said, grabbing a towel from the counter and handing it to Varela. "Careful wiping your eyes. Just dab."

"The woman—Annie," Varela said, taking the towel and grabbing the gun from his ankle holster.

"I'll get them," Cruz said, moving toward the dining room.

He didn't let himself think, didn't let himself feel too

much or imagine anything. He just moved through the dark house as fast as he could. His mind was focused solely on Marcy and Annie, first getting to them, then keeping them safe.

"Cruz, my God, what was that? What's happened?"

Marcy's frantic whisper in the darkness when he pushed through the door and into her room sent a breaker of relief washing over him equal to a tidal wave. But there was no time for the luxury of reaction. He had to get them out of there, and he had to do it fast.

"Stay down on the floor," he said, the dark room making her little more than a blur. "Where's Annie?"

"I've got her," Marcy murmured.

"Coos?" Annie whimpered, reaching out in the darkness. "Coos, I'm scared."

He felt her little hands on his shirt and gathered her into his arms. She was terrified, too terrified even to weep. "I know, sweetheart. But I'm right here. I'm not going to let anyone hurt you."

"P-promise?"

He tightened his hold on her, praying he could make it so. "I promise."

"Where's the FBI—Varela, Brown?" Marcy asked, reaching them in the darkness.

"Varela's in the kitchen," Cruz said, finding her arm and pulling her to him. "He's injured. I don't know what happened to his partner." He moved his hand up her arm to her cheek. "You okay?"

"We're fine," Marcy said in a shaky voice, finding his hand and grabbing it with both of hers. "What happened?"

"Explosion of some kind," he said, feeling her trembling.

She leaned close, bringing her lips to his ear. "It was him, wasn't it?"

She was so close he could feel her breath against his skin, so close he felt the tremble in her breathing. "I don't know," he said, slipping an arm around her and heading for the door. "But we're not sticking around to find out. Stay down."

He led them out the door and down the hall. Annie clung to him, too frightened to argue or ask questions, and Marcy held tight to his hand. When they reached the living room, Varela was waiting.

"Looks like a bomb. It took off the back porch and a good chunk of the roof," he said, tossing the bloody towel onto the carpet. He crawled to the front window and peered through a crack in the shade. "Front door looks okay, but it might be booby-trapped."

Cruz settled Marcy and Annie in the middle of the room, then grabbed his medical bag from the dining room and crawled to Varela. "Let me take a look at those cuts."

Varela turned around, dried blood streaking his cheeks. "It feels a little scratchy in my left eye."

Cruz reached into his bag and pulled out a penlight. "Small wonder," he murmured, reaching back inside his medical bag. "You've got a sliver of glass in it. Hold still." He motioned to Marcy, handing her the penlight. "Keep this pointed here," he said, positioning her hand just right.

"I—I'm shaking," she whispered. "I'm sorry, I can't stop."

"You're doing fine," he said, repositioning her hand. With a quick, precise move, he plucked the speck of glass from the delicate eye tissue with a pair of tweezers. "This will have to be looked at," he told Varela, tossing the tweezers back into his bag, then pulling out a sterile gauze pad. "But this will have to do in the meantime." Turning to Marcy, he took the penlight from her. Even in the darkness he could feel her fear, and it tugged at something in him. He wanted to hold her close, soothe and comfort her, but there was no time for that. "You did good," he whispered, running a finger along her cheek.

Instinctively, she turned her head to his touch, staring up at him. Then, moving quickly, she slid back, gathering Annie in her arms.

"I'm getting them out of here," he said in a low voice, turning back to Varela.

"How? Where?" the agent demanded.

Cruz thought for a moment. "What about your partner?"

Varela hesitated a second, shooting an uneasy glance at Marcy and Annie. "Dead," he said softly. "There must have been some kind of detonation device on the step, and it blew when he started to come inside."

"The radio?"

"I'm only picking up static. Buck has probably used some sort of jammer, blocking the signal."

"The telephones are useless," Cruz mumbled, his mind scrambling.

Varela strained to check the time on his watch. "If Brown checked in when he was supposed to, it'll be another hour before anyone even starts to get suspicious."

Cruz swore under his breath. "The van—where is it?"

"Out front, but we can't take a chance that crazy son of a bitch hasn't booby-trapped that, too."

Cruz thought for a moment. "Wait a minute. Hattie's got a pickup in the garage," he said, his mind moving in a million different directions at once. "The garage is attached to the house. He doesn't know what's in there. There's a chance he didn't get to it. I can hot-wire it." He stopped for a moment, the idea taking shape. "There's a place I know of." He looked at Marcy and Annie, who were huddled together against the sofa. "They'll be safe there. With your eye, I'll drive."

Varela shook his head. "I'm staying."

Cruz snapped his head around. "What? You can't. This whole place might go."

"He used a gun on her once. He could be out there right now," Varela said in a low monotone.

Cruz looked into the agent's worn face and knew what he was risking.

"You'll need cover—just in case," Varela said, his voice a raw whisper.

"You take this," Cruz said, cramming the Glock back into his hand and keeping the smaller caliber handgun for himself. "Cover us until we're clear of the house." He hesitated for only a moment, then added, "When the others get here, tell Joe I've taken them to the boonies. He'll know where that is."

"The boonies," Varela repeated, nodding. "Got it."

Cruz hesitated a moment longer, reaching out and resting a hand on Varela's shoulder. "Take care of yourself."

"You take care of them," Varela said, gesturing with his chin. "And keep your head down."

Cruz nodded, then crawled across the floor to where Marcy and Annie were. "Come on," he whispered, reaching for Annie. "Stay close and keep your head down."

He led them through the shadows, past the dining room and the kitchen.

"Oh, my God," Marcy gasped, seeing the broken glass and littered floor. "Oh, my God." She pulled out of Cruz's hold, covering her mouth with her hands. "He's going to get us," she said in a half cry, half murmur. The rise and fall of her chest grew more pronounced and more agitated with each breath. "No matter where we go, he's going to find us." Tears glistened in her eyes, then spilled down her lashes onto her cheeks, and she looked wildly from Cruz to Annie, then back again. "He's going to find us—you, me, Annie—and he's going to...he's going to—"

"No," Cruz said in a firm voice, sliding Annie to his side and grabbing Marcy by both arms. "Stop it. Marcy, stop it right now. Look at me," he demanded, giving her a firm shake. "Look at me." When she brought her gaze up, he could see the wild, irrational shock in them and knew if he didn't get her out of there soon, the fear was going to do more damage to her than Buck's bombs had done to the house. "I won't let him hurt you, do you understand? Brad Buck isn't going to get anywhere near you again. Got that?"

"Mommy," Annie whimpered, clutching at her. "Don't cry, Mommy. Please, Mommy."

The sound of Annie's voice had Marcy blinking, had a flicker of recognition and understanding flash in them.

"A-Annie, sweetheart," she stammered, looking down at her daughter and wrapping her arms around her. "I'm sorry. I'm sorry. I'm okay now. I'm sorry."

"Coos will take care of us," Annie said. "He promised, Mama. He said he'd take care of us. 'Member, Mama. 'Member?"

"I remember, sweetie," Marcy said, her voice steady again. She lifted her gaze to Cruz. "I'm sorry. It's okay now."

"You sure? We can rest a minute."

She shook her head. "No, I'm fine. Get us out of here."

Cruz could almost see her push the shock and the fear aside and felt his heart swell. "Follow me."

They made their way to the door connecting the kitchen

and the garage. After leaving them by the door, Cruz made a quick check of the garage and the tired-looking vehicle inside it. He was hardly a demolitions expert, but to his layman's eyes the vehicle appeared undisturbed by Brad Buck's tampering. Besides, he had to chance it—it was their only way out. Returning to the kitchen door, he waved Marcy and Annie down a crooked step and into the cab of Hattie Crawford's rusted old pickup.

"Are you sure this thing will run?" Marcy asked skeptically, eyeing the battered interior. "It looks like it belongs in a junkyard."

"I hope so," Cruz mumbled, struggling to reach under the dashboard. "Hattie still drives it." Something under the steering column gave way with a snap, and he pulled out a snarled wad of wires. "Of course, it might run on socks or something."

"Well, I just wish she had stuffed a few in this seat," Marcy said, pulling Annie onto her lap and shifting off a rusted spring piercing through the torn vinyl. "It could use a little cushioning."

Cruz touched two wires together, causing a spark and the old engine to cough and choke. "Damn," he muttered when the engine died. He crossed the wires and tried again. This time the engine responded, rumbling to life with a furious roar.

"Hurts my ears," Annie said above the noise, her hands on either side of her head.

"Is that the engine or another bomb?" Marcy asked, leaning toward Cruz.

"We're not sticking around to find out," Cruz said, depressing the clutch and grinding the gears into reverse. "Both of you, onto the floor as low as you can—and hang on."

Slamming down hard on the accelerator, Cruz released

the brake and they shot backward—crashing through the garage door and out onto the drive. Shifting again, he furiously turned the wheel, whirling the truck around in a cloud of dust, and headed for the road. A sudden blast had the window beside him shattering.

"He's shooting at us," Marcy said, covering Annie's little body with her own.

"Just stay low," Cruz said, ducking down as far as he could and still see over the wheel. "Varela will cover us."

As Cruz turned onto the road, several thuds hit the side of the truck. But when the pickup reached the tall hedge that lined the road and blocked them from the house, the sounds stopped, and they were swallowed up by the darkness.

"I think you can come up on the seat now," Cruz said as he switched on the headlights. The house had disappeared miles behind them, and there was no sign of anyone following them. "But keep your heads low."

"What do you think?" Marcy asked, carefully lifting Annie up onto the seat and sliding up beside her. She peered around cautiously. "Do you think he's following us?"

Cruz glanced in the rearview mirror, then at Marcy. "I don't think so, but we're not going to take any chances."

She spotted the town lights up ahead and sat up a little further. "Where do we go—to the sheriff's office, back to the hospital?"

"Oh, no," Cruz said, shaking his head. "The FBI, the state police—they've had their chance and Buck still managed to slip past them. It's what the guy loves, what he's best at—sliding in right below your nose." He shook his head again, braking the truck just before Mesa Ridge's main street and veering off onto a side road. "I'm not trusting anyone this time. We're heading for a place no

one knows about, where Buck never will find us." He
looked at Marcy. "No argument?"

Marcy gathered Annie close and shook her head. "Not
from us."

Cruz gazed at them both, cuddled on the seat, and felt
proud. He turned away and stared at the road ahead of
them. She might hate him; after all this was over, she
might never want to see him again. But she trusted him,
and right now, in Hattie's rusty old truck, rumbling down
a lonely road at breakneck speed, that was all that mattered.

"We're here."

Marcy opened her eyes, flustered and confused, and
stared into Cruz's dark eyes. She cleared her throat, her
mouth feeling dry and her tongue thick. "We're here? I
can't—I can't see anything."

"It's the trees," Cruz said with a quick nod. "They'll
hide the truck. I've opened the cabin, so let me take Annie
in and put her down first. You wait here until I get back.
The path is steep, and I don't want you falling."

She suddenly realized he was standing there with the
passenger door open, holding Annie in his arms. She
moved to sit up, to say something, but a sharp, stinging
pain in her neck had her falling back against the seat, instead.

"Do you think he followed us?" she asked, straining to
see through the darkness.

"I think we're okay," he said. "It would be hard to be
behind us on that mountain road without being spotted."

"I can't believe I fell asleep," she said, rubbing at the
stiffness in her neck. She eased herself up.

"You're not the only one," he said, turning so she could
see Annie's sleeping face.

Marcy reached up and lovingly ran a finger along Annie's cheek. "She was so frightened."

"But she was so good," he said. "She did exactly as she was told. Didn't argue, didn't cry. Not all kids would have done that." He looked back at Marcy. "Let me get her to bed. Wait here."

Marcy tried to watch them as Cruz made his way along the path, but it was too dark, and soon they were both swallowed up by the blackness. She rubbed at her neck again, wide-awake now, and slid from the truck onto the ground. It was only then that she realized she was barefoot—and had on only the light cotton pajamas she'd worn to bed. They offered her little protection against the night wind, and a shiver had her hugging herself tight.

"Cold?"

She jumped, looking up as Cruz appeared out of the darkness. "Freezing." She opened her arms, gesturing to her pajamas and bare feet, and his T-shirt and jeans. "None of us is exactly dressed for this."

"There are some clothes in the cabin," Cruz said, slipping a hand on her upper arm. "We can find something in the morning. There's a stove inside and wood in the bin. We'll stay warm tonight. Annie didn't even move when I put her down. She's sound asleep. But in the meantime…" In one smooth motion he swept her off her feet, then closed the truck door behind her.

"Cruz," Marcy gasped, shocked by the sudden move. "You don't need to carry me. I can walk myself."

"Not on this path you can't," he said. "Not barefoot."

"I'm too heavy," she said, trying to wriggle free. "We'll both fall."

"Don't argue," he ordered, moving carefully through the darkness. "The only thing that's going to make me fall is you wiggling."

Marcy gave in, the warmth from his body too inviting to resist, and settled into his strong hold. "You must be tired."

Cruz shook his head, gingerly maneuvering around a large boulder. "Too much adrenaline pumping."

"God knows I've got plenty of that pumping, too, yet I nodded off." She breathed out a small laugh and shook her head. "I still can't believe it. You'd think I had people shooting at me all the time."

Cruz gave her a sidelong glance. "Well, lately…"

She thought of the bullet wound in her abdomen and grimaced, finding no humor in that. "Yeah, I suppose you're right. I worry about Annie, though. I mean, how is all this going to affect her?"

"She'll take her cue from you."

"What do you mean?"

"If you're fine, she'll be fine," he said simply. "After all this is over, you might want to have her talk with someone if she has any fears, any concerns, but I think she'll be just fine."

"Is that your professional opinion, Dr. Martinez, or your personal one?"

Cruz looked down at her. He'd treated literally thousands of patients since he'd begun his medical career, yet until Marcy and Annie were brought into his ER, he'd never treated a patient he had a personal interest in.

"I'm not sure," he said honestly. As they rounded a small outcrop of rocks, the small cabin appeared on the path just ahead of them. Cruz gestured with the tilt of his chin. "Here we are, home sweet home."

With the yellow glow of a lantern inside, the tiny lodge looked inviting. "What did you call it?"

"The boonies."

"Whose place is this anyway?" Marcy asked as Cruz

climbed up the step and carried her across the narrow porch.

"It's Joe's," he said, kicking open the door and lowering Marcy onto the floor. "We come up here to fish— there's a stream just over the ridge."

The raised grains on the wood floor felt sharp against her feet, and she walked gingerly to a narrow cot in the corner, where Annie peacefully slept. "Are we very far from Mesa Ridge?"

"Couple hours," he said, closing the door.

"We drove for two hours?" she gasped, tucking Annie's blanket around her tight. Then she tiptoed to a rugged-looking table with four chairs and sat down.

"We don't call it the 'boonies' for nothing," he said, opening the door of the black potbellied stove.

Without the warmth of Cruz's body, there was nothing to protect her from the night chill, and she shivered. "I still can't believe I relaxed enough to sleep for nearly two hours," she said, stifling a yawn. "I must have passed out."

"You were exhausted," he said, opening the door of the black potbellied stove and shoving several small pieces of wood inside. "You and Annie both went out like a light."

Marcy looked again at Annie asleep on the cot. "Well, I hope she sleeps until morning. She could use the rest after the night we've had."

"So could you," Cruz said, crumpling newspaper from a stack near the wood box and cramming it inside the stove. "There's a feather bed in the loft—it's really comfortable—and there are a couple of heavy quilts, too." He pointed to the ladder on the far side of the room. "Just check them for critters."

"Critters?" Marcy repeated.

Cruz smiled, striking a match along the side of the stove and lighting the newspaper inside. "They get in sometimes through the vent in the roof."

"Critters," Marcy said again, eyeing the tiny open loft suspiciously.

"Don't look so worried. I'm just talking about squirrels. Or a chipmunk, maybe. No lions and tigers."

"Oh, my," she mumbled dryly, rubbing her hands up and down her arms. "I do feel better. Just squirrels and chipmunks."

"You can stay down here if you want. The sofa over there pulls out into a bed. It's not very comfortable, but…" His gaze shifted to Annie. "You know, maybe it would be better. Then if Annie wakes up she won't get scared seeing me there." He looked back at Marcy. "I wouldn't want to frighten her."

Marcy stopped rubbing and sat up. "Cruz, Annie isn't afraid of you."

"Oh, I know," he said, picking up another piece of wood and tossing it into the fire. "I just meant that…well, if she doesn't see you right away, she might get scared."

"She wouldn't be afraid," Marcy said, shaking her head. "You told her you would protect her and you have. She's not afraid of you, Cruz. She trusts you."

"What about you?" Cruz closed the door of the stove and slowly straightened. "You trust me?"

Another chill had Marcy shivering, but this time it had nothing to do with the cold night or the thin pajamas she wore. She looked at him from across the small cabin, seeing something flame in his eyes and feeling a burst of warmth deep in her heart.

"I'm here, aren't I?" she whispered.

He didn't answer. He merely stood there staring at her, until she grew uneasy under his steady gaze.

"It's warming up," he said after a long moment, gesturing to the stove. "You should pull your chair close—get warm." He walked over to the door and reached for the knob. "I'm going to get more wood from the pile around back."

Marcy watched as he stepped out into the darkness and closed the door behind him. Then she got up and dragged the chair across the rough plank floor. Heat had begun to radiate from the round belly of the black, cast-iron stove and felt wonderful against her frozen skin; it started a chain reaction in her body, causing her to shiver uncontrollably.

She pulled the chair close, resisting the urge to crawl up on the stove itself. Sitting back down on the chair, she brought her knees to her chest and hugged them tight.

The spell was broken. Whatever small moment of connection, whatever thin thread of rapport they had shared for just an instant, was gone now. He'd retreated again, had reined in his emotions and pulled down that visor of calm, unemotional detachment.

Another wave of shivering had her teeth chattering, and she hugged her knees even tighter. That mask didn't bother her anymore; that tight hold he kept on his emotions didn't seem so tight now that she knew it could be penetrated.

She glanced at the door, thinking about the chaos of the past several hours, how the tentative peace of their safe house had been shattered the way Brad Buck's bomb had ripped through wood and glass. Just like in Washington after the letter bomb had been delivered to her office, just like in the hospital when the package of explosives had arrived for Cruz, she'd been frightened for Annie's safety and for her own. She knew what it was to taste fear, to be paralyzed with panic and to have to endure in the face of danger.

She had been terrified when the blast had awakened her from a sound sleep, had frantically grabbed for Annie to make sure that she was all right. But as frightened as she'd been, as bitter and rank as the fear had tasted in her mouth, it was different somehow. From the beginning of all this, there had been those who had stepped forward, those who had offered their help, those she could turn to—her parents, Randall, FBI, police. They'd all been there to offer shelter and protection. And yet she'd felt so alone in her cause, alone in her campaign to protect herself and her child.

Over the snapping and popping of the burning wood inside the iron stove, she heard footsteps across the porch and felt her heart start to race. Cruz. Eleven days ago she'd struck out for Mesa Ridge with the intent of buying some time, with the idea of soliciting Cruz's help just long enough for Brad Buck to be caught and for her to restore her life once again. But oddly enough, something truly amazing had happened along the way. Amid the confusion and turbulence of gunshot wounds and hospital rooms, of safe houses and steeling through dark nights in broken-down pickup trucks, she had realized she didn't feel so alone any longer. Cruz was there to turn to, to help her…to protect her.

Coos will take care of us. 'Member, Mama?

As Cruz opened the door and stepped inside with an armload of wood, Marcy could hear Annie's whisper in her head, and she had to admit she'd come to believe that, too: he would take care of them. Despite the history between them, despite the hurt and the broken promises and everything that had happened in the past, she'd come to trust Cruz Martinez again.

"Feeling warmer?" he asked, kicking the door closed.

"Not yet," she said, rubbing her hands together. "But

I'm getting there." She pushed off the chair, peering first at the gaudy plaid sofa and then at the loft overhead. "Feather bed, huh? You say it's pretty comfortable?"

He dropped the armload of wood into the box beside the stove and followed her gaze to the loft. "What about the critters?"

She looked at him and shrugged, starting for the rough-hewn ladder along the wall. "If they're warm, they're welcome."

Chapter 9

Cruz couldn't breathe. His chest felt leaden, making each breath an effort. Then suddenly the pressure eased, and he gasped to replenish his depleted lungs with air. Except he was allowed only one quick breath before the pressure was back, worse than before.

"Are you sleeping?"

A piercing ray of light infiltrated the smoky darkness behind his eyelids, and he blinked to push it away.

"Are you sleeping?"

Once again a blast of light had him protesting, and he blinked again, opening his eyes to find himself looking into Annie's sweet little face.

"You awake?" she asked, straddling his chest as she bounced up and down.

"I am now," he said, realizing now why he hadn't been able to breathe. "When did you get up?"

"Just now," she said, bouncing up and down again. "What is this place? It's neat."

"It's a cabin. It belongs to Sheriff Mountain," Cruz said, rubbing at his scratchy eyes. He propped his head up on the pillow, quieting her bouncing with a hand on her leg. "You're not even a little bit curious where your mother is?"

Annie glanced around and then shook her head.

Cruz gazed at his little girl and felt the scratchiness in his eyes turn to a sting. "She's asleep up there," he said, pointing to the loft.

"She needs rest, huh," Annie said, looking up where he'd indicated.

"Yeah, she does," he said slowly. He paused a moment, watching her and marveling at how comfortable she seemed sitting there on his chest. "You know, I was afraid you'd wake up and be scared if you didn't see your mom right away."

"I'm not scared," Annie said, easing the chokehold she had on her teddy bear and giving him a smack on the mouth. She grinned down at Cruz. "Not with you here."

Cruz felt pressure building in his chest again, but it had nothing to do with Annie's bouncing this time. Marcy had said the little girl trusted him, but he hadn't really believed it—at least not until now. Clearing his throat, he shook off the grip of emotion. "You didn't mind sleeping on the cot?"

Annie shook her head, tossing her tangled curls. "But there wasn't much room for teddy. He fell on the floor."

"Oh, no," Cruz said, reaching for the bear. "Maybe we should give him a checkup." He made a play of taking the bear's pulse, moving his arms and legs, then handed him back to Annie. "He's okay. All he needs is a good breakfast."

"And rest," Annie added.

Cruz smiled. "And rest." He gave Annie's leg a pat.

"How about you and me finding something warm to put on and we go out and get some more wood for the fire?"

"Outside?" she asked, her eyes growing wide.

"Sure." He lifted her off his chest and onto the floor, then sat up.

"You mean it's okay? The bad man—he's gone?"

Cruz hesitated. He didn't want to lie to her, didn't want her to think it was okay to drop her guard, that everything was fine when it wasn't. But she was just a little girl, and she'd been through so much already.

"No, he's not gone," Cruz said, kneeling to her eye level. "But I don't think he can find us here."

"So I can go outside again?" she asked with an excited little hop. "Can I?"

"Well, not alone," he cautioned. "But if you're with me or your mom, I think it would be all right."

"Yea!" Annie said, giving her bear and then Cruz a hug.

"Now," he said when she finally released him, "let's go find some warm clothes to put on."

Marcy clutched at the heavy quilt and gingerly stepped off the ladder onto the floor. The rough wood felt like ice against her bare feet, and she gathered the quilt more closely around her shoulders.

"Anyone awake?" she called out in a loud whisper, making her way across the uneven floor. She stared at the empty cot in the corner, and the plaid sofa, and stopped in the middle of the room. "Where is everyone?"

But her voice was the only one she heard above the hiss of the fire. She stood there for a moment, struck by the fact that she wasn't panicking, that she wasn't screaming at the top of her lungs, frantically looking for Annie.

Giving her head a shake, she pushed the thought aside.

She didn't want to question too closely the feeling of calm she had, the sense of security that had nothing to do with the coziness of the cabin or the remoteness of its location. The fact was, something had changed for her, in the way she felt and the way she saw things, and she wasn't sure she was ready to face exactly why that was. Not just yet anyway, and definitely not this morning.

She walked over to the potbellied stove, opening the quilt like a coat and letting the heat sear her skin. There would be time later to figure out what was going on in her head and in her heart. Right now it was enough just to feel safe and warm. Cruz had been right about the feather bed. It had been toasty and comfortable, and she'd slept better than she had in weeks.

"Hey, where are you guys?" she asked in a louder voice, closing the quilt around her again and trapping a delicious cloud of warmth inside.

In the daylight, the cabin looked more spacious than it had in the night, with its bare floor and exposed beamed ceiling. The functional design and sparse furnishings had a no-nonsense, durable feel to them and spoke of a back-to-basics kind of lifestyle.

The kitchen was little more than an old-fashioned icebox, a row of small cupboards and a narrow counter with a sink in the middle. It was the sink that caught her attention. Something about it just didn't look right, didn't look normal.

"Faucets," she murmured, moving closer and staring at the vacant holes along the back of the sink. "There are no faucets." She ran a hand over the holes, noticing a pail on the counter for the first time. "There's no water. There's no—oh, no—" She spun around, shaking her head. "No, no, no, no, no."

The sudden thought had her scurrying into the middle

of the room, frantically looking about the cabin again. But even as she searched, even as she hoped, realization hit her just as the need did.

"There's no bathroom," she groaned.

She walked back to the sink and peered through the window above it. Outside, there was a small clearing; it sloped upward to a thick stand of pine trees. She groaned again. She had the uneasy feeling she was looking at the closest thing she was going to find to a bathroom.

"I can hold it," she muttered in a vain attempt to convince herself. She started to move away from the window, when she caught a glimpse of movement from around the corner of the cabin.

It must have taken her a full minute to actually recognize Annie. With a pointed stocking cap on her head, a huge jacket dragging along the ground and...

Marcy leaned closer to the window, squinting for a better look.

"What in the world does she have on her feet?" she wondered aloud, laughing. Annie resembled a chubby little gnome or one of Santa's errant elves more than her daughter.

She saw Annie wade through the snow up the slope, the "shoes" on her feet making her clumsy and off balance. She looked silly and must have felt silly, too, because even through the thick window glass Marcy could hear her giggling.

"I can do it. I can do it," Annie shrieked, falling back against the slope and moving her arms and legs. "I can make a snow angel."

"I'll say."

Hearing Cruz's voice, Marcy felt her heart trip in her chest. He stepped around from the corner of the cabin, dressed in jeans and a thick sheepskin jacket, and ran over to Annie.

Leaning across the sink, Marcy watched as he helped Annie up and they examined the image she'd made. He dusted the snow off her jacket, bending nearer and saying something to her that made her giggle again. Annie said something back, something that had him laughing, too, but their voices were too low for Marcy to hear.

With their heads together as they laughed and talked, they were like two peas in a pod—father and daughter—comfortable, familiar and at ease with each other. Seeing them now, it was hard to believe that a week ago they had been strangers.

A week. Marcy eased back from the window, pulling the quilt around her. It had been only a week since she and Annie had reached the outskirts of Mesa Ridge, and yet in the space of a week their whole lives had changed.

Marcy felt a strange, almost painful constriction around her heart. One week, and so many dramatic revelations. Cruz had discovered he was a father; Annie had someone new and special in her life whom she loved and adored. But it was what had happened to her herself, the revelation that had occurred in her heart, that was perhaps the most remarkable of all.

She watched Cruz as he took Annie's hand and they started down the slope, then rounded the corner of the cabin toward the porch. It was hard to believe he was the same man who had deserted her, the same man she had spent four years loathing, four years blaming for every lonely night, every empty relationship, every disappointment she'd had since then. She had never wanted to see him again, never wanted him to know about Annie or share in her life in any way. So why was it that when she'd found herself in trouble, when she'd really needed help, he'd been the first person she'd turned to?

"No," she said, shaking her head. She didn't dare open that door, not here and certainly not now. She didn't want to think about the cache of feelings and desires she'd allowed to escape, the needs and the emotions she'd ignored for so long. She had put her trust in a man she'd vowed she would never trust again, a man she'd told herself she hated, and she wasn't ready to consider the possibility that maybe she hadn't hated him quite as much as she'd thought.

"No," she said again, steeling herself against the emotions in her heart. She walked back across the cabin and opened the door. Hugging the quilt around her, she stepped out on the porch. Despite the morning sun filtering through the tall pines, the air was brisk and cold, and the wooden slats of the porch felt like ice on her bare feet.

"Mommy!" Annie gasped, coming up with Cruz. "Mommy, look—snow. It's just like the North Pole, Mommy, just like the North Pole."

Annie pulled away from Cruz. She did her best to run toward the porch, but the bulky coat made it difficult.

"Mommy, we made snow angels," she said, half climbing, half crawling up the step and onto the porch. "And a snowman, and lots and lots of snowballs. And we chopped wood and built a new fire in the stove and even saw a raccoon."

"My goodness," Marcy said, rushing over to help. "You've had quite a morning. And you've got a bundle of clothes on, too."

"It's the sheriff's coat," she said, grinning up at her mother. "I hadda wear it 'cause it's cold."

Marcy smiled, pulling the quilt tight. "You're right about that."

"See what I found?" Annie held up a huge pinecone. "We're gonna put it in the stove, and Coos says it'll make the fire burn real hot."

"Well, you look plenty warm." Marcy laughed, marveling at the child's resilience. Annie was adorable in the oversized coat and stocking cap. Her auburn curls framed her face, and her cheeks were rosy red from the cold. It seemed impossible that after the week they'd had, and the terrifying night, she could look so sweet, so content and so very happy. "Let me see what you've got on your feet."

"They're pelts," Annie announced, holding up the end of the jacket.

"Pelts?" Marcy repeated skeptically, taking a careful look.

"Yeah," Annie said, proudly displaying the animal skins wrapped neatly around each foot and secured with long leather tongs. "It's what the Indians did."

"Native Americans," Marcy corrected.

Annie eyed her mother. "Huh?"

Marcy shook her head, deciding there was a time to introduce political correctness to her daughter, but this probably wasn't it. "Never mind."

"Okay," Annie said agreeably. "Coos said the, uh, the...I don't know what he said, but they used to do it. The, um..."

"The Zuni."

They both looked at Cruz, who slowly climbed up the step.

"Good morning," he said to Marcy.

Despite the cold morning and her bare feet, she felt a flush of warmth move through her. "Good morning."

"Zoo-nee," Annie said with a giggle. "Yeah, them."

"Yeah, them," Cruz repeated, reaching out and giving

her small nose a plunk. "The Zuni would wrap the children's feet in coyote skins so they could run away fast from danger." He pointed to Marcy's bare feet popping out from beneath the quilt. "Seems we might have to find some coyote skins for you, too."

"Then Mommy and me can both run fast, huh?" Annie asked, smiling up at him.

"You bet," Cruz said. He turned to Marcy and gave her a helpless look. "And I couldn't think of anything else to put on her feet."

Marcy peered at the animal pelts again. "Sort of like instant moccasins."

"And they keep me warm, too," Annie added.

Cruz looked at Marcy and shrugged. "Of course the three pairs of wool socks might help there, but I guess necessity is still the mother of invention."

Or the father, she mused. "Uh, speaking of necessity," she began carefully, "I, uh, couldn't find the bathroom."

"Oh, right, okay," he said, turning for the door of the cabin and motioning for her to follow. "Come on."

Marcy's hopes soared. Could she have missed it? Was there a nook or a cranny in the cabin she'd overlooked? "You mean..." She gathered up the quilt and followed him across the porch. "Inside?"

"Sure," Cruz said, holding the door for her. "You'll need something on your feet."

Hope sank like a stone in water. She thought of the woods behind the cabin and groaned.

"Gotta go potty, Mommy?" Annie asked, her moccasins making her walk in a little marching step as she followed her mother into the cabin.

"Unfortunately, yes," Marcy mumbled, heading for the stove and warming up again.

"See if these fit," Cruz said, pulling a pair of blue flowered tennis shoes from a small wooden chest by the sofa. He handed them to Marcy and looked at the heavy quilt wrapped around her. "You'll need some kind of jacket, too."

Marcy held the shoes between her fingertips, eyeing them. "Aren't these women's tennis shoes?"

"Gee, how can you tell?" Cruz inquired dryly, turning back to the chest and searching through the contents. "Don't you think I'm the flower type? What about Joe?"

Marcy looked down at the shoes again and frowned, finding nothing funny in Cruz's joking.

"I could be wrong," Cruz continued, digging deep into the chest. "But I thought I remembered seeing—yea!" He pulled out a bulky, bright-pink sweatshirt with a zipper running down the front and a pointed hood. "It's not a jacket," he said, giving it a good shake before offering it to her. "And probably not as warm as the quilt, but likely more comfortable."

Marcy regarded the sweatshirt, then eyed the shoes once more. This was obviously women's clothing, and she felt a sudden tightness in her stomach. Imagining Cruz with other women had been something she'd tried very hard to avoid in the past four years, but images now loomed vivid and alive in her mind. He'd told her he came here to fish, but she hadn't seen any fishing poles or tackle boxes lying around anywhere. And the more she thought about it, the more this place looked like a cozy little hideaway, with its close quarters and feather bed high in the loft.

Suddenly a chill as cold as an arctic blast flowed through her system, turning her blood to ice. Had he offered her the bed he shared with other women?

"Thank you," she said in a tight voice, carrying the shoes and the sweatshirt with great distaste to the sofa and sitting down.

"How do they fit?" Cruz asked, watching as she slipped the tennis shoes on over her frozen feet.

"They're—" Her voice gave out on her and she cleared her throat loudly. "They're a little tight, but fine." She stood up. They were more than a little tight, but she didn't want to admit to it. Reaching for the sweatshirt, she let the quilt fall. "Besides, I'm not exactly in the position to be fussy," she said, slipping her arm through the sleeve and finding it about two inches too short. It was obvious the woman to whom these articles belonged was considerably smaller than her. She pulled up the zipper and looked up at him, feeling a little the way she had in sixth grade when she was a head taller than all the boys in her class. "Shall we go?"

"This way," he said, walking back to the front door and opening it for her in a gracious gesture. "After you." As she passed, he turned to Annie, who was peeling out of the huge coat. "Wait here and I'll be right back."

Marcy felt somewhat relieved when he led her past the woods to a small wooden structure hidden behind a huge pile of firewood.

"An outhouse."

He gave a curious look. "You sound almost relieved."

"If you knew what I'd been imagining, you'd understand why."

He held the door open for her. "Then I can only imagine how you're going to feel when you find out it's a two-seater. Annie thought it probably came in handy when you had company—you could bring a friend."

Marcy closed the door, but could hear him chuckling as he walked back up the path toward the front of the cabin. She turned and stared at the two porcelain toilet seats bolted to the bench. The primitive facilities were an improvement over the woods, but as she soon discovered only a small one. Holding her breath, she did what she'd come to do as quickly as she could, then stepped out into the cold morning sunshine and filled her lungs with clean, fresh air.

Starting back for the cabin, she tucked her hands into the pockets of the sweatshirt, trying to shrink her arms as much as possible so that none of her skin was exposed to the brisk air. Who was the woman who had left her clothing in that wooden box beside the couch? Was she his girlfriend? One of the nurses from the hospital who had taken care of her?

"Fishing," she muttered, her teeth clenched. What did he take her for, a fool? She was smarter than that. He and Joe Mountain probably both had girlfriends, and they probably all came up here and had high old times.

Marcy kicked at the snow, her foot wedged so tight against the side of the tennis shoe there wasn't even room for the tiny granules of ice to slip through. "It's none of my business," she muttered, grateful she'd found out now before she'd done something stupid, before she'd let her fear and frayed emotions make her believe she was feeling something she wasn't, before she'd thought anything had changed or anything ever would. "None of my business."

"What's none of your business?"

Marcy jumped as she rounded the cabin, startled to see Cruz leaning against the wall. "What are you doing here?"

"Waiting for you," he said innocently. "It's slippery and those shoes aren't meant for walking in snow. I thought you might need some help."

"Well I don't," she snapped, the snowy path with its steady incline, and the thin mountain air had her gasping for breath.

"You know you really should try and take it easy.

You're still pretty weak," he said, slipping a hand on her arm. "I could carry you to the door—"

"I don't need you to carry me anywhere," she snarled, cutting him off and yanking her hand away. "I'm just fine."

But her lungs suddenly felt as though they were going to explode, and the tennis shoes were pinching badly now, making her feel clumsy and awkward.

"At least take my hand," he said, offering it to her.

"Oh, all right," she muttered, feeling miserable. She could only imagine what kind of picture she made wearing pajamas with a sweatshirt two sizes too small and gaudy tennis shoes that pinched.

"Did you sleep okay?" he asked, holding her hand.

"I slept fine," she said, resisting the urge to let him pull her up the slope.

"What did you think of the feather bed?"

She stopped, yanking her arm free again. "Why?"

He stopped and turned around. "Just curious." He regarded her for a moment. "Is something wrong? You feeling all right?"

"I'm feeling fine," she said, pushing past him. "Would you stop asking me how I feel?"

"I can't help it," he said, catching up with her and taking her hand again. "I'm a doctor—your doctor, in fact—it's part of the job."

"Well, doctor, your patient is fine," she snapped, growing more agitated.

He seemed determined to be amiable and good natured—no matter what she said to him—and his kindness was killing her. She just wanted him to go away, wanted him to leave her alone and not look at her in the ridiculous get-up she had on. She didn't want him comparing her to the smaller woman who had left her clothes in the cabin.

Upset, she started up the steps, but weak legs, tight shoes and frayed emotions made her careless. She didn't even see the patch of ice until she felt herself start to fall.

"Gotcha," he said, catching her just as her feet went flying.

"Stupid shoes," she muttered as he helped her up the porch.

"You all right?"

She looked up at him, rubbing a hand along her tender abdomen and feeling her face flame red. "You're doing it again."

He grimaced. "Sorry." He shrugged, walking toward the door. "Old habits are hard to break," he said, pulling the door open. "Actually, I don't have any interest in how you're doing at all."

His smile belied his words, and his eyes danced with humor, and furiously Marcy found herself responding. She found him amusing and charming, and that only made her feel that much worse. She scowled—to stop herself from smiling—and hobbled across the porch toward him.

"I thought as much," she grumbled, walking past him and into the warm cabin. "Doctors."

"Lawyers," he replied, stepping inside after her.

"Want some more?"

With her mouth full, Annie slid back in the chair and shook her head. "Stuffed."

Cruz looked at her round, full cheeks and smiled, reaching for the cast-iron skillet from the top of the potbellied stove. "You look stuffed too," he said, wrapping a towel around the handle and gingerly picking up the pan. Turning to Marcy, he gestured with a nod. "How about you?"

Marcy looked at the corned beef hash in the skillet, then down at her empty plate. The makeshift breakfast he had thrown together from items he'd found in the pantry had been diverse—corned beef hash, canned peaches and apple sauce—but it had tasted like a feast.

"I don't know what it is about this mountain air," she said, lifting up her plate. She glanced down at Annie, who now had her teddy bear on her lap and was "feeding" him hash. "It seems to have boosted everyone's appetite."

"You should eat," Cruz said, scooping another generous portion of corned beef hash onto her plate. "You need the calories to build up your strength."

Marcy laughed, taking her fork and scooping it full of hash. "Oh right, tell a woman she needs more calories."

"What's wrong with that? It's the truth," he said, carrying the empty skillet to the sink. "You consume more calories, the body has more reserves to draw on, you get stronger, it's as simple as that."

"It might be simple," she said, taking another bite, "but women are conditioned since birth to watch their calories. You can cheat once in a while." She gestured to her plate. "But subconsciously, you're always keeping track."

He walked back to the table and sat down. "Are you telling me you count calories?"

"Always."

"Why?"

She paused and gave him a look. "If I ate a breakfast like this every morning, I'd have an even harder time fitting into these clothes you gave me than I do right now."

"Yeah, but those are Karen's things. She's at least four inches shorter than you are. That's why her clothes don't fit—weight has nothing to do with it."

Karen. Her appetite had suddenly vanished, and she pushed the plate away.

"Bear's full," Annie said, giving his mouth a swipe with her napkin. "You full too, Mommy?"

"Yes, sweetie, I'm full." Actually she felt like throwing up, but that was beside the point.

"I liked this breakfast," Annie said, scooting onto her knees and flipping the bear up on the table. She leaned on her elbows and smiled up at him. "You're a good cook."

"You think so?" Cruz said, reaching out and plucking her nose playfully. He turned to Marcy and grinned. "I was always pretty good at opening a can."

But Marcy didn't smile. She didn't even react to the affectionate interplay between him and Annie. She was too busy wondering what kinds of cans he opened for Karen. Did they sit and have breakfast here together too—or did he fix her a tray to share in that soft, feathery bed in the loft?

"I never had it before."

Cruz turned back to Annie, his smile fading just a little. "Hash? You've never had corned beef hash before?"

Annie giggled and shook her head. "Nope."

"And I'll bet you've never been fishing before either."

Annie shook her head again. "Nope, never."

He laughed, watching her curls fly crazily around her head. "Think you might want to come with me a little later?"

Annie turned to her mother. "Can I, Momma?"

At the moment, Marcy didn't feel too much like being generous with Cruz Martinez—especially with her daughter, but Annie looked so excited and so happy, she didn't have the heart to disappoint her.

"Sure," she mumbled. "As long as you stay bundled up."

"Can my bear come too?" Annie asked, turning back to Cruz.

"I don't know why not."

"Yipeeee," Annie whooped, tossing the stuffed animal in the air.

Cruz laughed, watching as she scrambled off the chair and danced joyfully across the room. He turned to Marcy. "Thanks."

"I didn't do anything."

"You said she could go."

Marcy shrugged, pushing herself away from the table. "You saw her—she wanted to."

"I know." He saw the line between her brow deepen and the rigid set of her shoulders, and the smile slowly faded from his lips. "The pantry—it's pretty well stocked. We'll be okay for a while, but it's all canned goods. I just thought some fresh fish might be nice—you know, for a change."

Marcy stood up, gathering up the paper plates. "It's no big deal."

"It is to me. Any time I can have with her is a big deal to me."

Marcy's hand paused momentarily as she reached for Annie's juice glass. "I, uh, I guess that's understandable."

"I suppose it is," he said, standing up and carrying his plate to the counter. "But there is something I don't understand."

"Oh? And what would that be?"

He held a trash bag open and helped her empty the soiled paper plates into it, then stopped her as she started to turn away. "I don't understand what I did to make you so angry at me again."

Chapter 10

"Angry," she said, feeling her face flush hot again. "What are you talking about? I'm not angry."

He gave her a skeptical look. "You sure about that?"

"Of course I'm sure," she insisted, the vehemence of her tone belying the denial of her words. She should have been more careful, should have been able to keep her feelings to herself. Frustrated, she took a deep breath, carefully controlling her words. "I'm not angry."

"Okay," he conceded. "Okay, you're not angry. But you do seem a little...tense."

"No, I'm not." She took another deep breath. "I mean, no more so than anyone would be who had a crazed killer after her."

He acknowledged her statement with a nod and a small grimace. "Okay, point made. I just thought if I'd done something or said something—"

"You haven't," she lied, cutting him off. What else could she have done? Tell him it made her sick to her stomach to think of him with someone else, to think of him with…Karen, whoever she was? "I'm…I'm still just a little tired, that's all."

"Well, that's understandable," he said, gathering the empty cans on the counter and stuffing them into the trash bag. "I can take care of the rest of this. Why don't you go sit down, or better yet, go lie down in the loft for a while. And don't worry about lunch. Annie and I will bring you a tray later."

Almost instantly, Marcy conjured up a picture of Cruz and Karen laughing and sharing an intimate snack in the soft feather bed.

"No," she said, shaking her head. It was ridiculous for her to feel jealous, and one way or another she was going to have to find some means of controlling her emotions—and her imagination. "No, thank you. I'm fine. I really am." She started backing up, pointing behind her. "I think I'll just…you know, go sit down for a while on the sofa."

"Okay," Cruz said, nodding as he watched her cross the room. "But if you need anything, let me know, okay?"

"Sure," she said, lowering herself onto the checkered cushions. "Yes, I will."

"Mommy?"

Marcy turned to Annie, who looked as sad and dejected as the teddy bear she dragged behind her. "What's the matter, baby?"

"Is he going to find me here?"

Marcy reached out and pulled her daughter close, thinking how their frantic night must have played out in a child's mind. "Oh, sweetheart, I don't want you to worry," she said, giving her a small squeeze. "You've got me and Cruz here to protect you. The bad person is not going to find you."

"Not the bad person," Annie insisted, shaking her head. "*Santa*. What if Santa can't find me?"

Marcy sat up straight, feeling a little as if she'd taken a snowball right in the face. Christmas. Good Lord, how could she have forgotten? With everything else going on, she'd lost all track of time and all sensation of its passing. She had a moment of panic that they might have missed it already.

"Uh, I, uh, I don't think you should worry about that," she said, faltering. She thought of the wrapped presents she'd hurriedly stuffed into the suitcase before leaving D.C. Unfortunately the suitcase had been in the trunk of the car, and she hadn't seen either of them since the accident. What was she going to do now? "He'll find you."

"But what if he doesn't?" Annie asked, her brown eyes filling with tears. "What if he forgets all about me?"

"Oh, sweetheart." Marcy sighed, hugging Annie again and shooting Cruz a helpless look.

"This is only December 23," he said, giving Marcy a small wink before turning to Annie. "Christmas isn't for two days yet." He tossed the dish towel onto the table and crossed the room. "And I'll bet you didn't know Santa Claus has a pretty special way of finding children no matter where they are."

"He does?" Annie asked in a tiny voice.

"Sure he does. Don't forget, he's been in the Santa business a long time," Cruz said, kneeling in front of her. "You ever hear of Rudolph?"

"He's got a shiny nose," she announced proudly.

"Well, there's something else about Rudolph that not a lot of people know," Cruz said in a conspiratorial tone, leaning close. "Most people just think he uses his shiny nose to lead Santa's sleigh on foggy nights, but that's not all it can do."

"It's not?" Annie inquired, her eyes wide with curiosity.

"Nope," Cruz said, shaking his head. "It can also sniff out hidden children."

"Huh?"

"Yeah," Cruz said with a nod. "That's the real reason Santa puts him right up there in front of all the other reindeer. If it looks like Santa might fly right over the top of some child's house without stopping, Rudolph's nose starting flashing, just like the light on the top of Sheriff Mountain's police car."

"It flashes?"

"It sure does," he said with a confident shrug. He slipped his hands under her arms and lifted her with him as he stood. "You know, Santa's been doing his job for a long, long time—even when your mom and I were little. You can be sure he knows what he's doing." He settled her on his hip. "So stop worrying and come help me with the dishes so your mom can rest."

"Cruz," Marcy said as he started to turn.

"Yeah?"

He was so handsome standing there with Annie clinging to him, so natural and comfortable in his new role as father. It had a pressure building in her chest, a painful tightness that came from feelings that had to remain hidden away.

"Thank you," she said, her voice barely above a whisper.

He looked at her for a moment and gave her a solemn nod.

"Come on, you," he said, turning to Annie and giving her a jostle. "I'll wash, you dry."

Marcy laid her head back against the cushion and watched them as they worked in the tiny kitchen area. Cruz poured water from the pail he'd filled at the pump out back and began washing up the few utensils and dishes that were left. He was being so nice to her—*really* nice, not just going through the motions as he had before—which only made her feel that much worse for acting like a jealous wife.

Wife. A chill had her shivering despite the heavy quilt that covered her. She'd almost been his wife. But almost didn't count when it came to loyalty and fidelity. The cold, hard fact was they weren't married; they weren't even engaged. They shared a child and a past—that was it. He didn't belong to her any longer and hadn't for a very long time. She had no right to be jealous, no right to be angry because he'd gone on with his life, and the sooner she got that straight, the sooner she'd stop making a fool of herself.

She thought of how he'd looked at her just now and felt her heart ram her rib cage. She could almost convince herself she'd seen something in his eyes just now, almost fool herself into believing there had been some emotion, some...affection.

"No," she muttered with a deep sigh, realizing how easy it would be to delude herself.

"Did you say something?"

She glanced up, surprised to see both Cruz and Annie looking across the room toward her. "Uh, no," she said, shaking her head. "No, no, I didn't say anything."

"Warm enough? I could put more wood on the fire."

"No," she mumbled, feeling color start to crawl up her cheeks. "I'm fine."

But she wasn't fine. She felt like a fool, and she was going to continue feeling like a fool until she finally got it through her head that there was no longer anything between them and never would be again. It wasn't his fault she'd spent four years duping herself and everyone else that she'd let go of the past, that she had let go of him. She knew the truth now; she knew that despite the brave words about going on with her life, about being over him and putting the past behind her, the reality was she still felt connected to Cruz—and not just because of Annie, but because of what she felt in her heart.

With eyelids drooping, she watched Cruz and Annie as they talked and laughed. If so many people hadn't been hurt by Brad Buck's cruel and vicious acts, she could almost believe all this was meant to happen, that somehow Cruz and Annie were meant to meet, were meant to be together.

They'd formed a bond between them already—father and daughter, parent and child. It was there in everything they did, everything they said. A link that wasn't going to just disappear. It was going to grow even stronger, regardless of what she herself did or what she wanted. They were father and daughter, and the unvarnished truth was that what went on between the two of them had nothing to do with her.

Suddenly the warm, comfortable drowsiness disappeared, and she pushed herself up into a sitting position. It had happened to her again. She'd been left behind, left out, first from Cruz's life and now from the relationship he shared with their daughter.

"Mommy? Want some tea?"

Marcy heard Annie's whisper float through her head like a little melody drifting on the breeze. Immediately the dark, unpleasant dream she'd been having about Cruz and a faceless beauty named Karen disappeared and she was transported to a field of flowers.

"Do you, Mama? Do you want some tea? It's simmanin."

Marcy felt a smile on her lips and was catapulted back to consciousness and reality with a small laugh. Cracking the lids of her eyes open just a fraction, she discovered she was nose to nose with Annie.

"Cinnamon," she corrected, her smile growing wider.

"Yeah." Annie nodded, her eyes round and serious. "And it smells real good, too."

Marcy opened her eyes wider, as Annie shoved a box of herbal tea bags under her nose. She reached up and gently guided the child's hand back just a little.

"It smells like cinnamon, all right," she said, pushing herself up against the arm of the sofa. She groaned as her muscles protested the move. "How long have I been asleep?"

"A little over three hours."

Marcy looked up at the sound of Cruz's voice, watching as he struggled with an armload of wood. "*Three hours?* I've been asleep three hours?"

He nodded, glancing down at the wood in his arms. "Like a log."

"No wonder I'm stiff," she mumbled.

He carried the wood from the door to the wood bin and dropped it inside. "You needed the rest."

"Mommy, know what?" Annie asked, impatiently tugging on the quilt to get her mother's attention. "Know what I did?"

Marcy glanced back at Annie. "What did you do?"

"I caught a fish."

"You—" Marcy turned to Cruz again. "You two went fishing and I didn't even wake up?"

"Just long enough to catch our dinner," he quickly assured her. "You weren't alone for more than thirty minutes tops."

"It's not that," she said, shaking her head. "I'm just surprised, that's all." She looked down at Annie. "And you caught a fish?"

Annie nodded, her eyes widening with excitement. "A trout. It was all wiggly, and I had to wind and wind really fast so it wouldn't get away." Annie delighted in having both her mother's and Cruz's attention, and she took the opportunity to enact the entire event, hamming it up and making them both laugh.

"Well, I don't see how I could have slept through that," Marcy commented. "So where is this monster you caught?"

"Cruz put him outside."

"I thought maybe I'd clean them later," he said in a low voice, giving Marcy a knowing look. "You know, while the two of you are busy somewhere else."

It took her a moment, but then she caught his drift, remembering the first time she'd seen a fish being cleaned. "Right," she said, nodding. "Good idea."

"You want me to cook you some tea, Mama? I know how."

Despite the quilt, Marcy shivered. "A cup of tea sounds wonderful—and warm. But first—" Steeling herself against the chill, she pushed back the covers and hauled herself up further. "First I'm going to have to make a trip to the facilities."

"Fa-sillies? What's that?"

Marcy glanced at Cruz and they both had to smile. Turning back to Annie, she leaned close and whispered, "I have to go potty."

"Oh." Annie giggled, covering her mouth with both hands. "Can I use the fa-sillies, too?"

"There's room for two," Marcy said, remembering the two porcelain seats. Swinging her feet to the floor, she carefully sat up. She felt stiff and clumsy, and the incision in her abdomen complained with a pinch.

"You okay?" Cruz asked, starting across the room toward her.

"Oh, sure," she said, stopping him with a wave of her hand. "Just a few stiff muscles." She raised her arms to stretch, but a cramp had her pulling back. "Actually, a lot of stiff muscles," she added in a wry voice, massaging a spot along her shoulder. "A few in places I didn't even know I had." She rubbed her hands together again. "Did it get colder in here?"

"Yeah, it did. The temperature's dropping, and the fire died down pretty low while we were gone. I brought in more firewood, though. It's burning good now. The place should warm up."

She pulled the small sweatshirt around herself tighter and looked around the room. "Do you know where I put those shoes you tortured me with earlier?"

Cruz laughed, walking to the wooden chest and opening the lid. "You'll be glad to know we can retire those now, and that sweatshirt. I found these in the back of the closet earlier." He bent down and pulled out a pair of faded blue overalls, a red flannel shirt and a pair of moccasins that rose midcalf, with long fringes around the upper rim, buckskin laces and hard leather soles. "I think the clothes might belong to one of Joe's nephews who was up here last summer, but the moccasins—I have no idea where they came from." He shrugged, shaking his head as he crossed the room toward her. "But they're bigger than the tennis shoes, and they'll be warmer, too."

"Maybe they're Karen's," Marcy suggested, taking the items from him. She thought she'd at least made an attempt to have her voice sound casual, but she realized she'd failed miserably when the words came out with a hard, sarcastic edge.

Cruz looked down at the moccasins in his hand again and shook his head. "Oh, I don't think so," he said dryly. "Karen Mountain wouldn't be caught dead in a pair of moccasins." He turned around and faced the wall, allowing her some privacy to dress. "Go ahead and change. I won't peek."

Marcy let the quilt drop, but not because she'd intended to start dressing. Frankly, she'd forgotten all about the clothes in her hand. Had he said what she thought he had? For a moment there it almost sounded as though he'd said...

"Karen?" Her voice sounded strange and foreign even to her own ears. "Karen *Mountain?*"

"Joe's wife," Cruz said with a nod. "She wouldn't have anything to do with anything remotely Native American."

"Karen is Joe Mountain's wife?" Marcy repeated, quickly pulling off her pajama top and sliding her arms into the soft flannel shirt. She felt breathless, even a little dizzy. She told herself it wasn't excitement she was feeling; it wasn't relief or exhilaration. But damn, it sure felt like that.

"Well, ex-wife," he corrected, shifting his weight from one foot to the other. "They've been divorced a couple of years. Can I turn around now?"

"Not yet," she said, stepping into the overalls and pulling them up. "Okay, the, uh, the coast is clear."

He turned around, giving her an approving nod. "Hey, not bad."

"They feel warmer," she said, uncomfortable with the way he was watching her. She didn't even want to think about how she might look in the baggy overalls, but vanity wasn't a luxury she could really afford at the moment. Besides, baggy or not, it just felt good to be out of the pajamas.

"Good," he said, walking toward her and taking her arm. "Now let's get something on those bare feet."

After helping as she gingerly sat back down on the sofa, he knelt in front of her. He slipped a moccasin on her foot, then laced it up.

"How does that feel?" he asked, rocking back on his haunches.

"Fine," she mumbled absently.

"Not too big?"

She looked down at him, trying for a moment to remember what it was they were talking about. "Oh, the shoe, er, moccasin. Yes, it's fine. Just fine."

"Better than tennis shoes two sizes too small, anyway," he said, reaching for her other foot.

"Right," she said, nodding as she felt sensation coming back in a strange tingling all over her body. "Yes, they're...they're great."

"Just like me," Annie said with a grin, hopping up on the sofa next to her mother and putting their feet together. "We both got mock-sins now."

"We sure do, baby," Marcy said, looking down at Annie and feeling herself grinning, too.

"Well, they'll keep you warm," Cruz said, lacing the second moccasin tight and standing. "And speaking of staying warm..." He walked to the rack beside the door. "There's a storm blowing in, which is why the temperature's started to drop. You'd better wear my jacket. Believe me, you'll need it."

Marcy sat and stared up at the sheepskin jacket, feeling a little as though she'd been dropped back into a dream.

Only, this dream wasn't dark or disturbing or filled with other women ready to snatch him up. This one had her head spinning and her heart hammering some sort of crazy rock sonata in her chest.

Karen, the woman who had shared the cabin, the woman who had slept in the feather bed in the loft and whose sweatshirt she had been wearing all day, was Karen Mountain, not some sultry mystery woman Marcy had been imagining in her mind, not the vamp she'd pictured in any number of romantic encounters with Cruz.

Marcy closed her eyes, feeling a rush of humiliation. Of course it had been stupid to feel jealous, and just because this Karen wasn't the love of Cruz's life, it didn't mean there wasn't someone somewhere who was. So why did she feel so ridiculously relieved? It was stupid and irrational, and simply made no sense.

Yet, as absurd as it was, that's exactly how she felt at the moment—relieved…and ridiculously happy.

"Give me your hand," he said, reaching for her. "I'll help you up. Let's get this around you."

It didn't occur to her to protest, to push him aside and inform him she could do it herself. Instead, she slipped her hand in his and let him pull her to her feet. Like a robot, Marcy did what she was told, sliding her arms into the wool-lined sleeves.

The leather smelled of wood and pine, the same scent that clung to him, and she breathed it deeply into her lungs.

"Okay, now you, young lady," Cruz said, walking back to the coatrack and reaching for the thick ski jacket she'd had on earlier.

"Can I hold the flashlight?" Annie asked as he buttoned the huge coat around her.

Cruz stood up and reached for the long black flashlight on the table beside the sofa. "It's all yours."

"It seems so silly," Marcy mumbled, helping Annie slip the stocking cap on over her curls. "All this trouble just to go to the bathroom."

"Maybe," Cruz admitted with a smile. "But think of the exercise we're all getting. You know, I'll bet if indoor bathrooms hadn't become fashionable, we'd all be a lot more physically fit."

In his huge coat, Marcy felt that she waddled across the room to the door more than walked. "Exercise," she muttered.

"Sure, and any doctor will tell you we could all use more exercise."

"Okay," she said, walking through the open doorway past him. "Then you won't mind when we wake you up in the middle of the night to get a little extra exercise escorting us to the potty."

Cruz's smile turned into a grimace. "Of course, there is something to be said for indoor plumbing."

Marcy laughed as she pushed up the sleeve on the jacket just long enough to let Annie find her hand.

"If you need some help coming back up the hill, just give me a holler."

Marcy stood for a moment, watching him disappear around the corner of the cabin. Her heart was actually fluttering in her chest, an honest-to-God flutter. What was happening to her? Everything was crazy; what she was feeling was crazy. Lines had suddenly blurred and memories were fading fast. She had to do something, had to hold herself in check before the emotion building in her heart erupted and had her doing something she would regret. She had to remember the reason they were there and what was going to happen when they left.

"I like Coos, Mommy."

Marcy glanced down at Annie, who stood looking up at her. "I'm glad, sweetheart."

"He says we hit it off pretty good."

She laughed hearing Annie use the phrase, knowing it had undoubtedly come from Cruz. "I kind of think you hit it off pretty good, too," she said, turning with Annie and starting down the path. "You two have become pretty good friends."

Annie nodded, sending the stocking cap bobbing up and down. "When we go home, can he come, too?"

Marcy hesitated, but only for a instant. Children had a way of cutting to the core of an issue, no beating around the bush, no playing games. "Honey, you just don't take someone home with you. Cruz is a grown-up. His home is in Mesa Ridge. It's where he works, where his friends are. I don't think he'd have any interest in going to Washington."

"But he said we were friends, that we'll always be friends."

"I'm sure that's true," Marcy said, finding it difficult to swallow because of the lump of emotion in her throat. "But friends don't have to live in the same town or even the same state. No matter where you are, I'm sure you and Cruz will still be friends."

Annie didn't say anything, and they made it the rest of the way down the slope in silence. Pushing her sleeve back again, Marcy reached for the door of the outhouse and pulled it open.

"Mommy?" Annie asked, looking up at her.

"Yes?"

"Is Coos your friend, too?"

Marcy stepped aside as Annie climbed up the steps and into the small enclosure, flipping on the flashlight. "Why do you ask that, sweetheart?"

"'Cause Coos says you were about the best friend he'd ever had."

"Forget something?"

Marcy stepped down from the ladder and turned around. Spotting Cruz propped up against the extended sofa bed, she stopped abruptly. "Oh, you're ready for bed. I'm sorry. I can go back up."

"No," he said, closing the dated sports magazine he'd been trying to read by the dim lantern light. "I'm not really." He tugged at the T-shirt and jeans he was wearing. "See? Still got my clothes on. Don't go."

Marcy's heart tripped in its steady rhythm, and she glanced back at him. "You sure?"

"Absolutely."

"Because if you get sleepy, I can go back up with Annie."

"I'm not sleepy," he insisted. "I just pulled the bed out now because I thought it might be too noisy later—you know, after she fell asleep." He glanced up at the loft. "I thought you two were going to tell stories."

"We were," Marcy said, walking to the stove and warming her hands.

"You weren't up there very long." He tossed the magazine onto the bed beside him. "Annie was so excited about sleeping in the loft I thought she'd be awake for hours."

"I know," Marcy said, smiling. She rubbed her hands together, as though spreading the warmth like lotion over her skin. "But she faded fast. She was asleep before the reindeer hooves even hit the roof."

Cruz smiled, sitting back against the cushions. "Ah, yes, good old Saint Nick. He sure gave us a few tense moments today, didn't he?"

Marcy thought of Annie's fears and the sweet story Cruz had told the little girl to make her feel better. "Well, *I* tensed up. You pretty much saved the day." She sighed, drawing in a deep breath. "I'm still not sure what I'm going to do come Christmas morning. How am I supposed to explain Santa delivered all her presents to the trunk of my car?"

Cruz shrugged casually. "We'll figure out something. Just not tonight. I don't think either one of us is in shape for that tonight."

"Well, not you, anyway," Marcy said, turning around to warm her backside. "You're forgetting I had a three-hour nap."

He tilted his head back, folding his arms across his chest, and looked at her through narrow lids. "As your doctor I can assure you that you needed the rest."

Marcy straightened. "Well, I don't care what you say. You look like you could use a little rest yourself right now. I'm getting out of here so you can get some rest."

"No," he said, leaning forward. "Please, don't go up just yet."

She didn't want to leave, didn't want to put an end to the quiet night and the comfortable feelings between them, but it was because she wanted to stay so much that she felt the ridiculous need to persevere in her protest, despite his attempts to reassure her. "But you've got to be exhausted. I don't think you've stopped all day."

"I'm used to it," he said with a casual wave of his hand. "Sit down, talk to me for a while, unless..."

"Unless what?"

He leaned back. "Unless we can't."

She stepped away from the stove and walked to the table. "What do you mean? Talking's not allowed?"

"That depends," he said with a tired shrug. "Not if

talking ends up to be arguing. That's been happening a lot with us lately."

She pulled out a chair and straddled the seat, facing the back's wooden slats. "I guess it has."

He watched as she draped her arms across the back of the chair, resting her chin on top. The pale light from the lamp had her skin looking satiny soft and her auburn hair like spun gold, and he felt the muscles in his stomach begin to knot. Maybe it would have been better if she had gone up to bed, to get her as far away as possible. She looked too beautiful, and he was feeling a little too comfortable and relaxed to remember to keep up his guard. "I think the past keeps getting in our way."

"That should stop," she said thoughtfully. "After all, what happened between us *happened*. It was a long time ago. It's over now. We've both moved on."

He narrowed his gaze, regarding her for a moment. "Can we do that?"

"I don't know," she said with a sigh. "But I think it would be good if we could."

His brow slowly rose. "Wow."

Marcy laughed at the honesty of his reaction. "You don't have to sound so surprised."

"But I am," he admitted, giving his head a small shake. "I never thought I'd hear anything like that from you." He hesitated a moment, taking a deep breath. "You realize that comes dangerously close to forgiveness."

Marcy sat up. He was right; she could try to deny it, but it would do little good. The days of telling herself she hated him, the days of blaming him for everything that was wrong or painful in her life, were over. She knew better now.

She lifted her gaze to his. "I guess maybe it does."

Silence hung around the edges of the room like the darkness, looming and thick. He carefully unfolded his arms and slowly sat up. "Does that mean you do?"

"I don't know," she said honestly. "I just know I don't want to argue any longer. I don't want any more secrets or bad feelings."

"I don't want that, either." He looked at the palm of his hand. "I know it maybe seems ridiculous now, after all this time, but I never meant to...I mean, I'm...I'm sorry I hurt you."

"Are you?"

He looked up at her. "More than you know."

The expression in his eyes had her heart ramming her rib cage. "I...I hope you know," she said hesitantly, feeling the heat of his gaze on her. "I mean, I really want you to know how much this has meant to me—everything you've done for Annie and for me. I'm not sure what I would have done if it hadn't been for you...." She forced herself to stop and shook her head. She wasn't saying what she wanted to. She was talking around it, hemming and hawing and rambling like an idiot. Drawing in a deep breath, she squared her shoulders. "What I'm trying to say is...thank you."

Whatever reaction she had expected from him, watching the smile fade from his lips and his eyes grow stone cold wasn't it. She felt a chill run the length of her spine, felt it penetrate right through to her heart. "I'm very grateful for everything," she quickly added, thinking he must have misunderstood somehow. "You've been so decent about all this, so wonderful about everything. It's meant so much and I'm very...I'm just very grateful."

"Grateful," he said after a long moment.

"Yes, very much so," she added quickly. "I want you to know how much I appreciate everything you've—"

"Okay, okay," he said, holding up a hand and cutting

her off. "You've done that. I get it now. I help you, you forgive me, we're even, you've met your obligation. You really don't have to be nice to me any longer."

"Nice to you," Marcy repeated, stunned. "Is that what you think I'm doing—being *nice* to you because I'm grateful?"

"I know it hasn't been easy for you," he said, running a hand through his long hair. "I could tell this morning you were having a tough time. Or didn't you think I noticed? But look, I'm telling you it's okay. There's no need to keep up the pretense any longer."

Marcy remembered all too well how angry and upset she'd been this morning and how ridiculously jealous. "Look, Cruz," she said in a reasonable voice. "If I seemed upset this morning, if I seemed angry—"

"You didn't *seem* angry," he said, interrupting her again. He stood up, walking across the cabin toward her. "You *were* angry, Marcy. You were angry."

"Yes, all right, you're right. Yes, I was angry," she conceded, looking up at him. "But not for the reasons you think."

"No? Then why don't you tell me what made you so angry?" He stared down at her, hands on his hips. "Why don't you just tell me?"

"Why don't I tell you," she mumbled, pushing herself off the chair. The expression on his face had something twisting deep in her chest. His anger couldn't hide the look of hurt and vulnerability. It would be embarrassing to tell him the truth, but she couldn't let him go on thinking what he was thinking. "I was upset because of...because of..."

"Because of what?"

She looked up at him, feeling helpless and completely frustrated. "I was angry because of the clothes."

Chapter 11

"Clothes?" Cruz narrowed his eyes. "What clothes?"

"You know, the clothes—the sweatshirt and the shoes," she said, twisting her hands nervously. "Look, I know this sounds stupid. It *is* stupid. But it's the truth. I was upset about the clothes."

"The sweatshirt?"

"And the shoes," she added.

He stared at her in disbelief. "This is crazy."

She took a deep breath, feeling more frustrated and more foolish by the moment. "I'm talking about the things you gave me this morning," she explained again in as calm a voice as she could muster. "You know, Karen's things."

He started to say something, then stopped, closing his mouth. Glaring down at her, he shook his head. "You're telling me you got angry because I gave you some of Karen Mountain's clothes to wear?"

"But I didn't know they were Karen *Mountain's*

clothes. If I'd known they were her clothes, I wouldn't have gotten upset.''

"So you were glad they were Karen's things?''

"Exactly,'' she said, smiling up at him as though he'd finally grasped the last clue to a crossword puzzle.

He shifted his weight from one foot to the other and gazed at her through eyes narrowed even more. "What do you take me for, some kind of idiot?''

Marcy's smile fell. "What?''

"What the hell kind of story is that?''

"It's no story,'' she insisted.

"I should have known there was no sense trying to talk to you,'' he said, giving his head a shake. "Nothing has changed. You're still pulling my chain about one thing or another and we're still arguing.''

"Look, I'm trying to explain. If you'd just give me a chance.''

"To do what? Try to make me believe some cock-and-bull story about Karen's *clothes?*''

"It's not a story, damn it,'' she said in a loud voice, tears stinging her eyes. "It's the tru—''

"Truth?'' he queried in a harsh voice, cutting her off. "What would you know about the truth?''

"Cruz, please.''

He stalked back toward the sofa bed. "No, no more. Go on up to bed. You can keep your gratitude and your ridiculous stories. I've had enough of both for one night.''

Marcy turned away, shaking her head. "You are such a jerk.''

"There, isn't that better?'' he asked sarcastically. He bent down, snatching up the magazine from the table beside the bed and glaring at her. "I knew it wouldn't take you long to start saying what you really feel.''

"What I really feel?'' she snapped, spinning back

around. "What would you know about what I really feel? You're so busy telling me how you *think* I feel you haven't bothered to listen to a word I've said."

He snorted a humorless laugh. "What do you mean I haven't listened? I heard every word you said about getting angry over...*clothes*," he told her, purposely making the word sound contemptible. "I just don't happen to be stupid enough to buy it."

"It wasn't just a few clothes, you big dumb jerk," she said, charging across the room toward him. "I was upset because they were...because I thought..."

"You thought what?" he demanded.

Marcy stared up into his cold black eyes and shook her head. "Oh, forget it," she muttered, shaking her head and turning away again. "Think whatever you want. I don't care anymore. I just don't care."

"That's probably the most honest thing you've said all night," he stated.

At the ladder, she stopped and looked back at him. "You know, you're right. Nothing has changed. You're just as cold, just as unfeeling, as you were four years ago. You wouldn't know the truth if it came flying in here on a snowball and hit you in the face."

"You don't think so?" he asked, tossing the magazine on the floor. He crossed the room toward her. "Then why don't you try me? Why don't you run a little truth by me?"

"I'm going to bed," she said, climbing up the first rung of the ladder.

"No," he said, stopping her as she got to the ladder's second rung and turning her around. "You wanted me to listen—I'm listening." He reached around and grabbed either side of the ladder, trapping her between his arms. "Hit me with your snowball, Marcy."

"I'm tired. I want to go to bed."

"I don't doubt that you do," he said in a caustic voice. "But first you're going to tell me the truth."

Marcy glowered at him. "You want the truth?"

"Please."

"I was jealous. I thought you'd been here with a woman. With lots of other women. And the thought of that made me jealous," she said through clenched teeth.

For a moment, Cruz did nothing. The ringing in his ears made it impossible for him to do anything other than stand and stare. "You were..."

"Jealous," she said, pushing against his arm again. "So there, now you know. Laugh all you want. Just let me go."

"Let you go," he murmured, leaning close and ignoring her struggle. "I did that once already, remember?"

Marcy glared at him. "I hate you."

"No," he said, shaking his head. "I don't think so."

Her position on the ladder brought her eye level with him, making it impossible for her to look away. In desperation, she squeezed her eyes tight, feeling hot tears stinging her lids, then searing her cheeks. She didn't want to look at him; she was too embarrassed, too humiliated. And she didn't want him looking at her. If only she could disappear; if only the floor would open up and swallow her whole. But that wasn't going to happen.

"Let me go," she said, opening her eyes and turning her head away.

"No," he said, leaning forward until his body made contact with hers. "Not this time."

Marcy stared into his eyes. The cold anger she'd seen in them only moments before was gone. They smoldered with heat now. "Cruz—"

"You don't hate me, Marcy," he said, cutting her off. "And I don't hate you."

"Cruz, please."

He leaned closer still, pressing her back against the slats of the ladder. "The truth is I want you. I always have."

Marcy felt her body ignite, burn at each place it made contact with his. "Don't do this."

"Don't what?" he asked, his mouth moving to within inches of hers. "Don't want you, or don't say it?"

"Cruz, please, this…this is crazy. This whole thing is crazy."

"You're right, it is crazy. You make me crazy."

"But it's been so long, so much has happened, so much has changed."

His lips brushed hers in a feathery touch. "I want you—you want me. That's never going to change."

"But—"

He stopped her with another feathery kiss against her lips. "Tell me I'm wrong. Tell me you don't want me. Tell me the thought of me with another woman made you as crazy as it did me when I thought you'd had another man's child. Tell me you don't still care, and I'll never bother you again."

Marcy stared into his smoldering eyes and felt her resistance dissolve. She'd given it her best, had fought hard to deny her feelings and weather the storm of her desires, but she couldn't lie—not to him, and not about this.

"I can't," she whispered. "I—"

If there had been more she had wanted to say, additional explanations she'd wanted to make, she forgot about them now. His mouth melded with hers in a bond that stole her breath, crushed her lips and erased all rational thought from her mind. She forgot about trying to hide her feelings and denying what was in her heart; she forgot about bombs in the mail, gunshot wounds and hospital rooms and the horror of the past several months spent afraid. She even forgot to breathe, her body finding subsistence and succor from his kiss and the desire that arced between them like fireworks on the Fourth of July.

To be with him, to be in his arms and have his lips on hers, was more than madness, more than impetuous; it was crazy and reckless—and what she wanted more than anything she'd wanted in her life. If she was making a mistake, if it was wrong, there would be time later to set things right again. For now it was enough to be in his arms and to accept her heart's desire.

Cruz felt desire sweep through him like a frenzied, maniacal fever, catching hold and ravaging his system. With the speed of a bullet, he was propelled from sanity to madness, from caution to recklessness. He couldn't seem to get enough of her, couldn't seem to get close enough, feel enough—taste, touch, relish, savor, stroke, think, dream or imagine enough. Her essence invaded him, hot, liquid and seductive, rejuvenating him, revitalizing him, making him whole again.

Only now, with her in his arms again, did he realize how barren his life had been without her. His spirit had become as parched as the vast Nevada desert. He'd been deficient, incomplete, half a man. But no longer. Now he had her. Now he could touch and taste her, and he found that he was whole again. She was like rain on the stagnant, arid ground of his soul, breathing new life into the emptiness inside him, making him come alive.

"Marcy," he murmured against her lips, struggling to pull her closer, even though it was impossible to do. She was practically a part of him now, their two bodies occupying the same space, their desperate lungs breathing in the same molten air.

"Marcy."

Her name rang in his ears, echoing through his system

until it had blotted out everything else. His entire being—mind, body, soul—focused in on her, making him
aware of every small trait, every minute detail. He heard
each tiny sigh, each helpless whimper, felt her heart in his
chest and her blood in his veins. She had become more
than need, more than desire; she'd become one with him.

He felt the metamorphosis occurring inside him, felt
aeons of civilization dissolve like dust in the wind. All the
trappings of culture and custom, all refinements, were
stripped away, forgotten, leaving only the barbaric, the
savage, the beast. At that moment he was Man, basic and
primal, and he wanted his woman.

"Mine," he growled against her lips, releasing his hold
on the ladder and sliding his arms around her waist.
"You're mine."

"Yes," she whispered in a breathless sigh. "Yours."

He looked into her face, the need in her eyes so clear
and so poignant he felt his control start to slip. "Do you
know how long I've wanted this, how long I've waited to
hold you again?"

"Too long," she murmured against his lips. "I never
thought…never dreamed it could ever be like this again."
She gazed at him, pressing her body closer to his. "I never
thought you would ever want me again."

Cruz groaned, not wanting to think of the pain he had
caused, not wanting to think of how alone and how vulnerable he had left her. "I wanted you the first time I saw
you, and every moment after that." He pressed soft,
soundless kisses onto her cheek, her eyelids, the bridge of
her nose. "I wanted you when you were screaming at me,
when you hated me, when you never wanted to see me
again." His lips trailed wet kisses along her jaw, to her
ear and down her neck. "I've wanted you for four long
years."

"Cruz," she whispered, her head falling back as his mouth ravished hers.

The kiss was powerful and intense and full of passion too long denied, too long held in check. When he finally lifted his mouth from hers, his depleted lungs left him gasping for air. He felt her body trembling, heard the raspy sounds of her breath in his ear. He wanted to remember everything about this night, wanted to imprint it in his memory, imprison it in his heart so it would never escape—because he knew that at any moment it all could change.

He'd learned the hard way the future came with no guarantees, and their future was tenuous at best. They could see the sun tomorrow, or their whole world could be shattered by the blast of one of Brad Buck's bombs. All they had, all he could be sure about, was here and now. And now, in this moment, in this one precious point in time, she belonged to him. She was life and love and all that he wanted. She was the sunshine and the warmth and all he ever hoped to have.

Desire pounded in his brain, making him crazy and turning the need clawing at his insides into an agony. Even as his mouth found hers again, he lifted her from the ladder and into the embrace of his arms. He carried her across the cabin, over the rough, creaking wooden slats to the open sofa bed. He wanted her with a desperation he'd never known, with a hunger that overtook him like darkness taking over the light.

At the edge of the bed he paused, struggling to calm his breath and grapple for a moment of sanity in the midst of madness. Stopping now would be like death; stopping now would be worse than death. But this was too important for there to be any mistake.

She looked up at him with huge, smoky eyes, and he

felt his body start to tremble. He was hurtling forward with
the speed of a rocket, trampling over finesse and disre-
garding delicacy and consideration. For four years he'd
never thought he would ever be with her like this again,
had never dared dream such a thing could ever happen. It
was too important to rush; *she* was too important for there
to be any misconceptions or misunderstandings.

"I can still stop," he said in a raw voice. "But once
we're there, once we're on the bed…"

"No," she said, halting him with a finger to his lips.
There wasn't so much as an instant of hesitation, not even
a shred of uncertainty in her response. Her reaction was
immediate and unmistakable. Looking up at him, she
slipped a hand between their bodies, letting it slide down
his belly and into the front of his jeans. "Don't stop," she
pleaded, finding him hard and ready for her. "Don't ever
stop wanting me."

Cruz groaned at her touch, and for a moment he didn't
move; for a moment he *couldn't* move. But that was only
a moment. The need in him was too savage, too urgent.
The fragile hold he'd maintained on caution snapped, and
with the last thread of reason gone, needs became cravings
and desire spun out of control.

"I never will," he groaned, lowering her to the bed and
following her down.

After that, the world lost all form, all order. There was
no past, no future, and the present had become a place of
sensation and feeling, of awareness and sensory percep-
tions. If there was a reason that things had happened the
way they had, he'd find it later. For now all he wanted
was the woman beneath him. She was his world, his
woman and his one, true love.

Marcy had no actual awareness of his undressing her,
of buttons being freed or zippers sliding open. She was

only vaguely aware of the gentle friction of cloth against her skin, only remotely conscious of the overalls falling away from her body or the flannel shirt sliding onto the floor. The only thing that mattered was that all those confining obstacles, all those cumbersome obstructions that hampered and hindered her from getting what she wanted, were being stripped away. She was being freed to touch and to move, to feel and to seek. Her world had become a place of heat and sensation and, in order to survive, she had to be free and unencumbered to experience all that she could.

She felt the cool rush of air against her bare skin, felt the smooth crispness of the sheets and the rough denim of his jeans. She was naked, exposed completely, and yet she felt anything but vulnerable, anything but defenseless. In fact, she'd never felt so invulnerable in her life—strong, invincible—and as sure of his need as she was of her ability to meet it.

Lying on the bed, she looked up at him as he sat above, watching as he pulled his T-shirt off and tossed it carelessly to the floor. The sight of his hard, lean body had longing choking at her throat, fire burning in her belly and her whole body growing restless and impatient. Desire coursed through her system, turning her blood to molten lava and moving in a wave of liquid fire.

He had been the yin and the yang of her life, giving her the best and the worst of all she had known. She had both loved and hated him, with no middle ground in between. He'd given her his child, and yet he'd deprived her of his love. Part of her wanted to worship him, and part of her wanted to kill him. There were times when she had never wanted to see him again, and others when she had thought she would die without him.

Good, bad—strong, weak—love, hate—Cruz, Marcy. They were wind and fire—volatile, unpredictable, yet explosive when together. Natural enemies, and yet indisputably linked by nature, by chemistry, by mutual need. It might not be perfect between them, their road might never be smooth, but it didn't have to be perfect to be right.

She couldn't look forward, the future was far too bleak. And she dared not look back. It was enough that he was with her now, that he wanted her, that they could soar with the angels and ride the clouds together. She knew all too well how quickly things could change, how hopes and dreams could vanish or be blown to smithereens by something as harmless as a letter in the mail. Tomorrow was uncertain, a dark hole in the future filled with pitfalls and risks. All could be well or their peace could be shattered. Brad Buck could find them and they'd be on the run again. There was only one thing certain, only one thing she knew for sure, and that was the love that swelled in her heart.

"Oh, Cruz," she whispered on a sigh, almost soundlessly into the night. The lamp had burned low, and its soft glow shone against his skin like moonlight against bronze. To her he was perfect—all she'd ever wanted; all she would ever need. "You are so beautiful. So beautiful."

"Beautiful?" He shook his head. "No, I'm not beautiful." He leaned closer, sliding his body over hers. "You're beautiful," he murmured, letting his hands drift over her torso. "This is beautiful." His hand moved over her breasts and down her belly and between her legs. "And what we do to each other is beautiful."

Marcy felt her body surge forward at his touch, felt her body shake and her blood ignite. "Cruz," she whispered again, reaching up for him. Her voice trembled with need and anticipation, and his name burned thick and hot in her throat.

"*You* are beautiful," he said, catching her hand and bringing it to his lips, pushing soft, wet kisses into her palm. "And what you do to me is beautiful."

The breath caught in Marcy's lungs as he lowered himself, sliding his hard, lean body over hers. It was as though nature had molded them for this purpose, her soft curves melding with his hard strength.

In one powerful thrust he entered her, and Marcy felt the Earth rock on its axis. This was what nature had intended, what aeons of evolution had decreed and the elements had predetermined. This is what she was put on this Earth to do: to love and be loved by this man. They had stopped being Cruz and Marcy. They had become Man and Woman; they had become Love.

"Look at me," he said, taking his hands and framing her face. His eyes searched her out, wanting her to listen, wanting her to understand. "Feel me inside you, Marcy. Feel what it is you do to me."

Marcy could barely hear him, could barely breathe or make herself understand, because of the torrent of feeling and sensation streaming through her system, assailing her with pure, raw emotion. Her body stretched to accommodate him, accepting all of him that she could. She felt the world beneath her slipping away, felt the Earth open up and a chasm appear where solid ground had once been.

"We were meant to be together," he whispered, moving his body deep within her. "Forever."

"Yes," she murmured, pushing the word out with her last conscious thought. "Forever."

They did belong together—she believed that in her heart and in her soul. He was a part of her, just as Annie was a part of them. She wanted to tell him, wanted him to know she understood and felt the same way. She had wanted him to know how she felt, what it meant to her to be with

him again, what *he* meant to her. But the time for words
had passed. She had been propelled too far forward, too
far into the chasm. She was beyond the point of rational
thought, beyond the point where words mattered and or
had a place.

His hands were moving now, wild and urgent, taking
her breath and sending her farther and farther into the void.
She was no longer a thinking, functioning human being,
no longer capable of putting thought to word or word to
action. She'd become solely a salacious creature, there
only to give and receive pleasure, to feel and experience
and perceive.

Cruz. He had become her world, her cosmos, her reason
for being. Cruz. He was in her and around her, all she
knew and all she ever wanted to be. Cruz. He took up the
middle and both ends of consciousness; he was the air she
breathed, the nourishment she craved and the object of all
she desired. Cruz.

The need in her took on a life of its own, growing,
flourishing, establishing predominance over everything
else. Control fell by the wayside; restraint became a thing
of the past. She was overwhelmed with hunger, overpow-
ered by urgency. With each brush of his lips, with every
stroke of his hand, the coil in her belly wound tighter. She
was slipping, falling, flying, soaring in a crazed, chaotic
course, until she thought she could take no more.

I...I love you, he thought. I always have.

In a brilliant burst, the void suddenly opened and swallowed her whole—the void where torment became bliss,
where pain became pleasure, where agony became ecstasy.

She clung to him, her journey taking her to the outmost
reaches, to where feeling met form, mind met matter,
where war met peace and found refuge. Pleasure became
an ocean, and she rode the crests, wave after wave, drown-

ing in a sea of yearning and desire until finally, in a tsu-
nami wave, she surged ashore, running aground in a place
where there was only one purpose, one mission, one man.

"Cruz. Cruz."

Cruz heard her call out his name, heard the raw desperation in her voice, and felt the madness starting to nip at
him. Her ecstasy was magnificent; the purity of gratification so powerful, so commanding, he was caught in its
wake. With her body convulsing around him, with her
breath harsh and ragged in his ear, he could fight the cur-
rent no longer. He did his best to fight, did his best to hold
on, to make the journey last as long as it could, but the
tide was too strong.

"Cruz. Cruz."

His name sounded like a carnal chant on her lips, calling
to him, beckoning him, propelling him forward. He had
put up a valiant struggle, but it was over now. He simply
couldn't hold out any longer. His body was trembling, and
his mind was a fever of want and need. Like a bomb det-
onating into a million pieces, he exploded, swept away in
the flow of her euphoria.

He gasped, following her through the void—past pleasure, past satisfaction. "Marcy—I—"

His body was not his own after that. It became mist,
vapor, floating through the atmosphere, surrounding her,
absorbing into her skin, combining him with her. He'd
moved beyond pleasure, beyond gratification; he'd left all
that behind in a world he was no longer a part of. He was
soaring with an angel now, and he never wanted to stop.

It was a long time before the world took shape again
and bodies took form, before the night sky had darkness
and the fire heat. It was as if they'd been adrift somewhere

in the cosmos, existing on a different plane, in some altered universe where time had no meaning and space held no pattern. But as it had to, the real world managed to crash through time and space, managed to find them and drag them back, landing them on terra firma again with a cold gust of wind.

"You're freezing," he murmured, feeling a shiver pass through her. He pulled the heavy quilt Marcy had used earlier from the back of the sofa and drew it over them. "Better?"

She nodded, but he felt her body trembling. She looked so beautiful lying there gazing up at him, so beautiful he felt his own body start to shake. It still seemed impossible that she was really with him, that he was holding her, touching her, feeling her warmth surrounding him. It had taken all he had to walk out of her life four years earlier, to step aside in order to give her the life he knew she deserved, instead of the one he had to offer.

"Wow," she murmured, reaching a hand to his cheek.

He smiled; turning into her hand, he pressed a kiss into her palm. "Wow?"

"Yeah," she said, smiling up at him. "Wow."

"No regrets?"

"Not one," she said. She felt his body stir beside her. "You?"

He brushed her lips with his. "Only that it's over."

She smiled, moving her body beneath his. "Nothing lasts forever."

He kissed her once, twice, feeling the waves of madness nipping at his feet. "Sometimes they do," he whispered, pushing into her and watching her eyes grow round. "Sometimes they do."

Chapter 12

"Mommy, Mommy, wake up."

Marcy heard Annie's breathy voice cut through the cozy warmth of her dream. "Shh, baby, shh," she mumbled, snuggling deeper into the covers. "Too early. Go back to sleep."

"But I'm not sleepy."

Marcy squeezed her lids tight, resisting wakefulness. She felt too comfortable, too content, to want to move. "Lie down."

"Mommy, I gotta tell you something."

"Shh, Annie, please," Marcy said again, nuzzling into the pillow.

"Coos, Coos, wake up. Wake up, Coos."

Marcy heard Annie whispering in the sleepy haze around her, and for a moment couldn't figure out why the child was calling her "Cruz." Silly goose, she wasn't Cruz: she was Mommy. Cruz would still be asleep downstairs on the sofa bed. He wouldn't be able to hear her whispering, he wouldn't—

Awareness hit her like a bomb blast in the face. Suddenly she remembered why she was so comfortable, why she felt so content and why Annie kept calling her "Cruz." Annie wasn't talking to her at all; she was talking to Cruz—who was lying right beside her in the bed!

Marcy's eyes flew open, and she lifted her head off the pillow. Only, her pillow wasn't a pillow at all. It was Cruz's arm, and he had the other one wrapped snugly around her waist.

"A-Ann—" She cleared her throat, reaching for the quilt and pulling it up tightly around her neck. "Sweetheart, what…what are you doing?"

"I want Coos to wake up," she said in a tiny voice, scrambling over the top of her mother and over the top of Cruz to the other side of the bed. "My teddy is stuck on the ladder and I can't get him off."

Marcy wanted to die, wanted to pull the covers over her head and shrink away into the darkness. What was Annie going to think, finding her in bed with Cruz? What explanation did she make? How could she have been so careless? How could she have let something like this happen?

"Uh, sweetie, uh, we can get your bear later," she stammered in a low voice. "Let's let Cruz sleep."

"Too late," Cruz mumbled in a stage whisper, the arm around her waist pulling her close and his lips nuzzling a soft spot along her neck. "He's awake."

"Yea, Coos is awake," Annie whooped, jumping up and straddling him like a pony. "You're awake."

"Oh, ouch," he groaned, slipping his arm from around Marcy and reaching up to halt Annie's jumping. "Calm down there a bit, wild girl."

Annie giggled, leaning down and putting her face in his. "I'm not a wild girl."

"Anyone up this early in the morning and as full of energy as you are is a wild girl," Cruz said, giving her a tickle under the chin. "You're Wild Annie."

"I'm not Wild Annie." Annie laughed with a shriek, pushing his hand away. "You're Wild Annie."

"I'm not Wild Annie," he said, playing her game. He caught her off guard, tickling her now under her arm. "You're Wild Annie."

Annie fell to one side, leaping from Cruz to her mother. "Mommy, tell him," she screamed, giggling with delight. "You tell him I'm not Wild Annie, that he's Wild Annie."

Annie landed on her with a thud, causing the quilt to slip, and Marcy struggled to hold it up. Her head was spinning, and she felt so awkward, so exposed, so…naked. It was bad enough that Annie had discovered them together, but now Cruz was awake and the situation had gotten completely out of control.

And yet, as if having her daughter discover her in bed with a man wasn't bad enough, the thing she found the most unnerving was Annie's reaction—or rather, Annie's lack of reaction. The child didn't appear frightened or upset. In fact, she looked to be having the time of her life.

Marcy was amazed at the interplay between Annie and Cruz. They were so comfortable with the situation, so at ease with each other, playing and teasing. It was as if they started every morning like this, as if it happened all the time. She had been ready to die of shame to think Annie had discovered her lying in bed with Cruz, but watching the two of them together, you would have thought it was the most natural thing in the world.

"Tell him," Annie shrieked again, reaching over her

mother and giving Cruz's chin a tickle. "Tell him I'm not Wild Annie. Tell him he's Wild Coos."

"Well, if I'm wild," Cruz said, reaching over Marcy to grab at Annie, "I must be going to get you."

Annie let out an ear-piercing scream and scrambled off the bed and across the cabin. "You can't get me," she said with a giggle as she climbed the ladder and disappeared into the loft.

Cruz looked down at Marcy. "Good morning."

Marcy felt herself blushing furiously. It had been one thing to make love with him in the dead of night with the darkness broken only by the dim light of an oil lamp, but this was the harsh light of day now. It was all out in the open now; there were no dark corners to run to, no shadows to hide behind. The night had been magic, filled with desire and passion, but the time to face the music had come.

"Good morning," she said, feeling her pulse throb in her throat.

Cruz leaned over, placing a kiss along her bare shoulder. "Talk about your rude awakenings."

Marcy felt her entire body react to the feel of his lips against her skin and shot a nervous glance toward the loft. "Uh, maybe we should, you know…"

Cruz followed her gaze, listening to Annie's laughter. "Did that make you uncomfortable—her seeing us like this?"

"Didn't it you?" she asked in a hushed voice.

Cruz slid down close, shifting the quilt just enough so that their bodies were touching beneath it again. "Nothing about being here with you is uncomfortable."

Marcy could feel him against her, could feel his body heating and growing hard, and she was helpless to stop herself from responding. "But what are we supposed to tell Annie? I mean…'' Her voice caught in her throat as his hand moved slowly over her. "What do we say if she asks…?"

But she trailed off, lost in a haze of awareness and sensation. "Oh, Cruz, please," she groaned, catching his hand and moving it away. "Don't, please, I—I can't think."

"Then don't," he murmured, brushing another kiss along her shoulder, and several more along her neck.

"But, Annie," she protested, feeling her body becoming swamped with heat. "I can't…we can't…"

Cruz stopped, raising up just enough to look down at her. "I know. You're right," he said, a shudder passing through him. "I was just—" he leaned down and kissed her lightly on the lips "—driving myself crazy."

"And me, too," she murmured against his lips.

"Good," he said, falling back against the mattress. Turning his head on the pillow, he nestled her into the crook of his arm. "I didn't want to make you uncomfortable, though—or Annie."

"Well, she didn't seem too upset," Marcy said with a wry laugh. "I mean, my daughter isn't exactly used to finding strange men in my bed."

He pulled back and looked down at her. "Are you calling me 'strange'?"

She rolled her eyes. "You know what I mean."

"Yeah, I do," he whispered, his smile slowly fading. "And you have no idea how happy that makes me feel."

"Oh, Cruz." She sighed as his lips covered hers for a gentle kiss. If he only knew. No man had ever been able to take his place in her heart or in her bed.

"Mommy. Coos."

Hearing Annie calling to them from the loft had them both looking up.

"What is it, sweetheart?" Marcy asked, spotting Annie peeking down from the loft's narrow opening.

"My bear's not stuck no more."

"That's good, baby."

"He likes jumping on the bed."

Marcy had to smile, suspecting it wasn't just the bear who liked jumping on the feather bed. "Well, you tell Mr. Bear he can jump, but he has to be very careful."

"Yea!" Annie shouted, disappearing back into the loft.

"I can't believe it," Marcy said, giving her head a shake. "She isn't the least bit surprised or uncomfortable."

Cruz glanced up at the loft, then back to Marcy. "She's three years old. What would she know to be uncomfortable with? She sleeps in Mommy's bed sometimes. Why would it seem unusual that I might sometimes, too?"

Marcy considered this. "I suppose you're right."

"But maybe it's not Annie you're concerned about. Maybe you're the one uncomfortable with my being here."

His words had a harsh edge, but she saw the uncertainty in his eyes, the vulnerability. "Is that what you think?"

"Maybe I don't know what to think."

She sat up, holding the quilt, and turned to face him. He was such a strong man, and so capable. He'd broken through social and cultural barriers, stormed the walls of prejudice and taken the whole world on in order to get what he wanted. She admired his strength, was in awe of his drive and determination. They were part and parcel of what attracted her, of what had drawn her to him in the first place.

Yet there was something about his vulnerability, something about his defenselessness and uncertainty, that had her falling in love all over again.

"Then I guess you're going to have to wait until tonight

so I can make it very clear to you how I feel about your being in my bed.''

"Marcy,'' he murmured in a hoarse whisper, reaching for her. "Marcy, I—''

"Coos. Mommy.''

Marcy heard Annie as she jumped down the last rung of the ladder and ran across the wooden floor toward the sofa bed, but her gaze was transfixed by Cruz's. His dark eyes smoldered. There was no sign of uncertainty in them now, only anticipation—the thought of which had her blood starting to heat.

"Mommy,'' Annie said again, crawling onto the bed and settling herself between them. "Coos.''

Reluctantly, Cruz tore his gaze from Marcy's and looked down at the little girl. "What is it, wild child?''

"I gotta use the fa-sillies.'' She wiggled against them, shifting her weight back and forth. "I gotta use the fa-sillies real bad.''

"You know,'' Marcy said, reaching for the flannel shirt beside the bed, "now that she mentions it...''

Cruz nodded. "Yeah, that's not a bad idea.''

Cruz heard the fire crackling, heard the chair moving and the floor creaking, but he didn't bother to open his eyes. He'd been awake for a while. The nap he'd taken after their long, leisurely morning had been short, but it had left him feeling refreshed. Still, he'd been enjoying just resting against the cushions of the sofa with his eyes closed, listening to Marcy and Annie as they sat at the table. They talked in whispers, Marcy patiently answering Annie's dozens of questions about Santa and what life must be like at the North Pole.

It seemed absurd, given the fact they were being hunted by Brad Buck, but the truth was he couldn't remember ever having felt so content. He had shelter and warmth and a full belly, and more important, he was with the two people on the planet who meant the most to him. It was only December 24, the day of Christmas Eve, yet he'd already been given his presents and opened every one. He had the woman he loved, and the child they had created together. Santa would have nothing in his big black bag of holiday delights that could compete with those gifts. After all, how much more could he ever want out of life, except maybe to have Marcy and Annie with him forever and for always?

Forever and for always. It was a concept he didn't even dare think about. It touched too close to hope, came too near to dreams. He was a man who dealt with cold, hard facts, with life and death, with believing in only what he could see and seeing only what was actually there. But when it came to Marcy and Annie, he could never be sure if he was seeing what was really there or just what his heart desperately wanted to be there.

Cold, hard facts. His mind shifted to last night, to Marcy and the long night of lovemaking. Stripping away emotion, tossing aside hopes and dreams, last night had been honest, uninhibited and brutally real. There had been no illusions between them, no coy manipulations or lame justifications. They had reached out to each other in a true expression of need. But the cold, hard fact was it had been much more for him. He was in love with the woman—heart, mind, body and soul.

"All finished."

Annie's stage whisper had him remembering the morning, had him thinking about what it had been like to wake up with Marcy in his arms and Annie hopping into the bed with them. Maybe he should have been more surprised at Annie's ease with the situation, at her lack of reaction at finding him there with her mother.

Of course, there might have been a time when it would have made him suspicious, when he would have gone off the deep end and let his jealousy start him imagining all sorts of reasons the child was accustomed to finding her mother in bed with a man. But no longer. If he'd learned one thing in the days they'd spent together, it was that there was a chemistry between the three of them, a chemistry that made their being together feel natural and right, a chemistry only a family could recognize and share.

Cold, hard facts, he reminded himself again. Another cold, hard fact was that if their lives had gone differently, if they had been different people, if he hadn't felt compelled to make the decisions he had, this might have been the way they would have started every morning—together.

"Can I show Coos, Mommy? Can I show him, please?"

"Let's let him rest a little longer, cupcake. You had everyone up so early this morning."

"But, Mommy—"

"Let him rest."

Cruz had to smile at Marcy's firm tone. There wasn't a kid in the world who didn't know that tone. It was the one every mother used, the one that meant there was no sense arguing, that her mind was made up and the case was closed.

Like a game of cat and mouse, he shifted his head against the cushion and yawned, making a play of stirring from his nap.

"Mommy, he's waking," Annie said immediately. "Can I show him now? Can I? Can I, huh?"

There was a pause, and Cruz yawned again just for good measure.

"Okay, but do it quietly."

He could hear the scrape of the chair, could hear Annie's moccasined feet along the floor. After a moment the cushion shifted, and he felt Annie's little hand on his arm and her curls dangling against his shoulder.

"Coos," she breathed into his ear.

He grunted, shifting against the cushion again.

"Coos," she said once more, bringing her mouth closer, until her breath blew loudly in his ear. "Me and Mommy have a surprise for you."

He slowly opened one eye, turning his head just enough to look at her. "A surprise?"

"Yeah." Annie nodded, her eyes wide with excitement. She scrambled back across the cabin to the table. "See what we made?"

Cruz opened both his eyes and rubbed at them, then slowly rose to his feet. Walking toward Marcy, he smiled. "Hi."

"Hi," she said. "Have a nice nap?"

"Yeah, I did." He stopped at her chair, running the back of his hand along her cheek. "I guess I didn't get enough sleep last night."

"I—I guess not," she said, brushing a kiss against the back of his hand as it passed her lips.

Cruz felt his body stir, and his mind was suddenly swamped with images and sensations from the night before.

"Look, Coos," Annie said insistently. "Look what me and Mommy made."

Reluctantly, Cruz turned away, his gaze shifting to the circle of pinecones in the center of the table.

"It's a Christmas reef," Annie announced proudly, standing on the seat of the chair and holding it up for him to see.

"Wreath," Marcy corrected. "A Christmas wreath."

"Yeah," Annie agreed. "A reef."

Marcy and Cruz exchanged a glance and laughed.

"Well, it's a pretty nice one," Cruz said, perusing the cluster of pinecones they had wired together in a circular design.

"We used a hanger," Annie explained, turning the wreath around. "And Mommy made the bow from some red socks she found in the trunk."

"Socks," Cruz said dryly, giving Marcy a sidelong glance. "Just don't get any ideas about stuffing the mattress."

Marcy gave him a playful swat. "I'm not making any promises."

"Isn't it pretty, Coos?" Annie asked, setting the wreath on the table. "Isn't it pretty?"

Cruz walked around the table and gave her a hug. "It sure is, baby. But you know what it needs?"

Annie looked up at him. "What?"

"A Christmas tree to go with it."

Annie's eyes turned to saucers. "A Christmas tree."

"Yeah, what do you think?" He looked over at Marcy. "Find a Christmas tree with me?"

"You mean it?"

"We're surrounded by a forest," he said with a shrug. "What do you think?"

She rushed around the table, hugging him even as he hugged Annie. "I think it's a terrific idea."

He wanted to kiss her. He wanted to haul her into his arms and ravage her mouth, then pull the bulky overalls and oversized shirt from her and ravage her beautiful body. But he couldn't do any of those things—not now, not yet.

"Okay," he said, clapping his hands. "Let's get going. Get bundled up. It's cold out there. And we probably should make another trip to the fa-sillies while we're at it."

He slowly walked to the door while they hurried off to

get ready. A Christmas tree. He didn't know why he hadn't thought of it before. Short of a miracle and circumstances changing dramatically in the next several hours, their Christmas was going to be spent together in the small cabin—not a very festive prospect for a three-year-old.

He shrugged on his coat and glanced back at the wreath on the table. It probably wasn't right, it was probably a very selfish thing, but he found himself hoping nothing did happen, that this one particular miracle would be the one overlooked. It was Christmas, and they were together. It was something that might never happen anymore once the real world found them again.

He looked across the room at the plaid sofa, desire stirring in his belly at the thought of Marcy in his bed. Last night had been unbelievable, literally a dream come true. But he couldn't fool himself into thinking it had solved all the problems between them. She needed him now; she and Annie both did. Yet all that could change once Brad Buck was behind bars and the danger had passed.

This might be all he would ever have with them. So much had changed since that day she'd been wheeled into the ER, and once they got their real lives back, it could all change again. Was it so wrong to want to make the most of it while he could? They were with him now—his woman, his child—and he wanted to fill the time he had with as much as he could.

"Too big. Way too big."

"No, it's not."

Cruz shifted the jagged-toothed saw from one shoulder to the other. "Marcy, that thing's got to be twelve feet tall. The ceiling in the cabin is barely about ten at the peak."

Marcy scrutinized the perfectly shaped Douglas fir.

"Twelve feet? You sure?" She turned back to him. "It doesn't look twelve feet to me."

"Believe me, it's twelve feet if it's an inch." Feeling a tug on the bottom of his coat, he looked down at Annie.

"It's pretty."

"I know it's pretty, sweetheart," he said, kneeling. "It's just a little too big. You know, I'll bet if we check out those smaller trees along the ridge over there we'll find another one just as—"

"But I like that one," she said, stopping him as he pointed to several small trees.

Cruz gazed into her big brown eyes, then up into Marcy's, and knew he was lost. He sighed heavily and slowly rose to his feet. Turning to Marcy, he raised an arched brow. "She's your daughter, all right."

Marcy smiled. "It's just so...perfect."

"Perfect," he muttered, slipping the saw from his shoulder and pushing the thick bows aside, trying to find the tree trunk. "You realize we're going to have to drag this thing back to the cabin."

Marcy walked over to him, then leaned down and gave his shoulders a playful massage through the heavy sheepskin jacket. "But you're so strong and have such big, broad shoulders."

He shot her a dirty look. "Oh, like that's going to work."

She laughed and gave his back a swat. "It was worth a try."

"Well, try making yourself useful and hold these branches out of the way," he said, getting down on all fours and peering through the tree's dense growth. "There's got to be a trunk in here somewhere."

"You gonna cut it down now, Coos? Are you, huh?"

Annie asked excitedly, jumping up and down. "You gonna cut our Christmas tree down now?"

"I'm going to try, baby," he said. He found the trunk and groaned loudly.

"What's the matter?" Marcy asked.

"This trunk has got to be a foot across." He pulled out of the tree, sitting back on his haunches and looking up at them. "You two sure it's got to be this tree? I couldn't talk you into something a little smaller?"

Marcy and Annie eyed each other, then him, and both nodded.

Cruz looked at them for a moment, the shrugged with a resigned sigh. "Okay, you two over there," he ordered, pointing with a tilt of his chin. "*Way* over there." He carefully positioned the saw's sharp, rough teeth against the tree's solid trunk. "This monster's going to cover some ground when it falls."

He groused and he groaned as he sawed at the tree trunk, but the truth was he really didn't mind. Granted, it took a considerable effort to fell the tree, and dragging it back to the cabin was going to be nothing short of Herculean, but it was Christmas, and Marcy and Annie were with him. That was all that mattered. Seeing them happy and excited made the strained body and sore muscles worth it.

"Timber," Marcy called out as the tree began to topple to the ground.

"Timber," Annie repeated, jumping up and down and clapping her hands. "Timber, timber."

The tree landed with a soft swoosh, sending snow billowing about in a cloud around it.

"Okay," Cruz said, brushing the snow and the pine needles from his arms and shoulders. "Everybody grab a limb. It's a long walk home."

Home. The small cabin had begun to feel like a home.

It didn't feel like "the boonies" any longer, didn't feel like the same cold, empty place he and Joe would come to. It had become a place of warmth and security, for he had his child and the woman he loved under one roof. In this tiny cabin they'd almost become a family—father, mother, child—and he wouldn't have missed it for the world.

By the time they reached the cabin, the wind had begun to howl through the treetops and the temperature had started to drop.

"We'd better hurry. There's another storm blowing in," Cruz puffed, his breath blowing out in long, white plumes. He dragged the tree to a stop at the steps of the porch and glanced up at the overcast sky. "Let's get this thing inside before it starts snowing." He turned to Marcy. "There are some two-by-fours around back I think might work for a tree stand. While I go get them, you bring me the hammer and nails. They're on the bottom shelf in the pantry."

Marcy and Annie were on the porch waiting for him when he rounded the corner of the cabin with the wood for the stand. Marcy held the hammer and Annie carried the box of nails with both hands. But they weren't looking at him as he walked up. They also weren't smiling any longer. They were standing in silence, staring down at the tree on the ground and frowning.

"What is it?" he asked, a cold shiver traveling through him, one that had nothing to do with the frosty wind buffeting them. "What is it? What's the matter?"

They turned their heads in unison.

"Uh-oh," Annie said, shaking her head.

"Uh-oh?" he repeated nervously.

Annie looked back at the tree. "Mama says it's too big."

"Oh, Cruz," Marcy said then, shaking her head. "It's never going to fit."

Chapter 13

"So, how much did you have to take off?"

Cruz slipped the wooden shim a little farther under the stand, tilting the tree a fraction of an inch toward the corner. After sliding out from under the tree on his belly, he looked up at Marcy, who was standing over him. "A couple of feet."

She took a step back and eyed the top of the tree, which brushed the ceiling beams. "I have a feeling it was more than a couple."

"Well, maybe it was more like four," he admitted, shifting onto his side. Pushing up on an elbow, he cradled his head in one hand and looked at her. "I think we wore her out."

Marcy turned to Annie, who was curled up asleep in a ball in the center of the sofa. "You know, if I had suggested she lie down for a nap, she never would have settled down," she said. "But you ask her to sit down and rest, and she's out like a light."

"Yeah, but you're her mom," he said simply. "Nobody likes doing what her mom tells her to do."

"Oh, is that right," she said, folding her arms across her chest. "Or maybe it's just that you two are simpatico."

"Simpatico?"

"Yeah, you know, in sync."

"Simpatico," he repeated, glancing across the room at Annie. "You think so?"

"Birds of a feather," she said. He laughed, making a dismissive gesture with his hand, but she saw the emotion in his eyes. He loved Annie; there wasn't a doubt in her mind about that.

"And what about us?" he asked, looking back at her. "You and me. Are we simpatico?"

Marcy felt her cheeks flush with warmth. "I don't know. Maybe."

He regarded her for a moment, then laughed again, pointing to the tree behind him. "So what do you think? Does it look straight?"

Marcy took another step back and appraised the tree. "It looks big " She sighed.

"Yeah, but is it straight?"

"Like an arrow," she said, glancing down at him as he lay stretched out in front of the tree. It had taken nothing short of pure strength to get the tree from the forest into the cabin, and she felt her body reacting at the thought of his strength. She slowly walked back across the cabin toward him, aware of how he watched her as she moved. He had determination and a will of iron. Nothing stopped him from getting what he wanted, whether it was a medical career or the Christmas tree his daughter had her heart set on.

Marcy stopped in front of him. Last night he had wanted her with the same strength, the same will and determination he'd gone after everything in his life, and that thought had the embers of desire stirring within her, making her hungry for him.

"It really is a beautiful tree," she said, feeling the pulse in her neck quicken.

He reached out a hand to wrap it around her moccasined ankle. "Like you."

"I'm not beautiful," she murmured, feeling heat start to spread through her body. She ran a hand through her tangled hair, trying to remember the last time she'd seen herself in a mirror or had been able to brush her hair. "I must look—"

"You look good," he said, cutting her off, slipping his hand beneath one leg of her overalls and reaching for bare skin. "*Very* good."

His words, the tone of his voice, the touch of his hand—everything about him had her reacting. It wasn't like her to become flustered and undone by the compliments of a man. She was too grounded, too down-to-earth to be coy or coquettish. But this hadn't been a mere compliment, and he wasn't just any man.

"I—I think you've been in the mountains too long," she murmured, feeling the air growing warm and thick around her.

"Oh, no, not long enough," he whispered, sliding his hand free of her pant leg and rising to his knees. Wrapping his arms around her legs, he pulled her close, pressing soft, warm kisses through her clothes, along her knees, across her thighs and over her abdomen. "Not nearly long enough with you."

"Cruz," Marcy murmured, feeling breathless and dizzy. Her legs had turned to water and her knees threatened to buckle beneath her, but his strong arms were around her now, supporting her, holding her close. He kissed the swell of her hip, her waist, the tops of her breasts—a slow, sensuous journey that brought him to his feet and her into his embrace. It didn't seem to matter that bulky clothes got in the way, that layers of fabric separated them from each other. She felt heat searing her skin, felt desire burn hot in her blood.

"All I've wanted to do," he whispered as his lips brushed hers. "All day, all I could think about was holding you." He pressed a light kiss against the corner of her mouth. "And touching you." Sliding his lips across hers, he kissed the opposite corner. "And tasting you." His mouth sank deep for a long, drowning kiss.

Her knees did buckle this time, and she fell against him, her whole world listing like a boat in stormy waters. She forgot about the Christmas tree, about Annie asleep nearby. In the space of a moment, she had gone from wanting to needing, from hunger to craving.

A shudder shook him, a deep, violent motion that rattled through him and straight into her. She felt the power, felt the strength it took to pull himself back, to wrestle with the need and regain control again. It took more strength, more will and determination than dragging a monster tree through the snow, and it was strong enough to help pull her back, as well.

"Whoa," he said, drawing in long, deep breaths. "Maybe we'd better slow down just a little."

She nodded, taking several deep breaths herself. "Yeah, maybe we should."

He set her back a few inches from him, his breathing coming in quick, shallow gasps. "You're dangerous, lady. You know that, don't you?"

"*I'm* dangerous," Marcy said with a shaky laugh. "I believe you were the one who started all this."

He smiled, pulling her close and placing a quick kiss on

the tip of her nose. "I can't help myself," he admitted, leaning his forehead against hers. "I go crazy when I'm around you."

"Oh, yeah?" she murmured. It was okay to tease now, okay to have fun and enjoy the delicious tension between them. The need was still there and so was the fire, but they were both in control now. "How crazy?"

"Pretty crazy," he said, his hands, which were on her upper arms, tightening a fraction. "So crazy that if it wasn't for that little girl asleep over there, I'd have taken you right here, right now, right under the Christmas tree."

He kissed her again, and Marcy felt another shudder, only this time she couldn't tell if it had come from him or from herself.

"You know," she whispered when he took his lips away. "Maybe we are."

He moved back and looked down at her. "Maybe we are what?"

She withdrew from his embrace, backing away from him. "Maybe we are simpatico."

He breathed out a quiet laugh. "Well, I can tell you one thing," he said, following her across the room. "If we aren't, we're certainly going to be after tonight."

"Oh, you think so?" she asked, turning and pulling out a chair from the table.

"Oh, yeah," he said, stepping behind the chair and holding it for her as she sat down. Leaning over, he brought his lips close to her ear. "I know so."

She groaned, his soft promise making her arms and legs feel weak and useless again. "Cruz, we have to stop," she warned as he pressed a kiss into the bend in her neck. "This is just asking for trouble."

"I like living dangerously," he murmured, dragging his

lips up to her ear again and pulling the lobe between his teeth.

"See, I told you it was gonna fit."

Marcy jumped so violently at the sound of Annie's voice from the other side of the cabin that she knocked her forehead painfully against Cruz's. She was still embarrassed about what had happened this morning. Annie's innocence might have saved her from having to answer a lot of awkward questions, but that didn't mean it was okay to push her luck. Annie might be too young to understand the significance of finding her mother in bed with a man, but she was old enough to understand hugs and kisses.

"It wasn't too big, mama," Annie said, sitting up on the cushion and pointing to the tree that more than filled the corner of the cabin. "It's just right. Our Christmas tree fits just right."

"You're right, baby," Marcy said, rubbing at the sore spot on her forehead. Looking up at Cruz, she mouthed an apology and reached up and rubbed the corresponding spot on his forehead, too. "It fits just great."

Annie jumped down from the sofa and scrambled across the floor toward Cruz. "Isn't it pretty, Coos? Isn't it perfect?"

"It is perfect," he said, catching her up in his arms and lifting her high.

"Me and Mommy were right, huh? It is the prettiest one, isn't it?"

Cruz settled her on one hip and looked at the tree. "You sure were."

"And it fit."

Cruz winked at Marcy. "And it fit," he said, glancing back at Annie. "Now all we have to do is decorate."

"Decorate?" Annie's eyes widened. "We can't decorate."

''What do you mean we can't decorate? Of course we can decorate,'' he said, giving her a little jostle. ''What would a Christmas tree be without a few ornaments?''

''But we don't have nothing,'' Annie said, punctuating her fractured grammar with a shrug. ''We got no sparkly lights or little Santas or candy canes or nothing.''

''Well, you're right. We don't have any of those things,'' he conceded. ''But we have lots of other things.'' He pointed to the wreath on the table. ''We have pine-cones. And there's a holly bush around back. We've got that. There's aluminum foil in the cupboard—we can make a star. I even know where we can find some mistletoe.''

''Mistletoe.'' She giggled. ''For kisses, huh?''

He tweaked her little nose, letting his gaze slide to Marcy. ''Especially for kisses.''

Marcy felt herself become hot all over, and she quickly looked away. ''And, uh, there's…there's a jar of popcorn in the pantry,'' she stammered, standing up on legs that felt like water again and trying to ignore the flush in her cheeks. ''We could string popcorn for the tree.''

''There you go,'' Cruz said, looking back at Annie. ''So you see, we've got lots of decorations.'' He lowered her carefully to the floor. ''And we've also got a lot of work to do, so we'd better get started. Ready?''

Annie clapped her hands with excitement, jumping up and down. ''Ready.''

Cruz straightened, reaching out and running a hand along Marcy cheek. ''Ready?''

Marcy gazed into his dark eyes and felt the flush in her cheeks turn into a comforting warmth. ''Ready.''

''One for the tree.'' Annie pierced a huge piece of pop-corn with the small needle, then slid it back, adding it to the others secured along the long length of fine fishing line.

"And one for me," she said, reaching into the bowl for another piece and popping it into her mouth.

"One for the tree," Marcy said, repeating Annie's actions on the opposite end of the fishing line. "And one for—" She looked down at the popcorn in her hand, then at the nearly empty bowl in front of her, and swallowed hard. They were on their third string and she had a feeling she'd eaten more than she'd gotten on the tree. "On second thought," she mumbled, slipping the needle through the popcorn in her hand, "I think I'm going to just concentrate on the tree for a while."

"Not me." Annie giggled, popping another piece into her mouth.

"You two aren't finished with that yet?" Cruz asked, coming through the front door with a gust of wind and snowflakes and an armload of wood.

"Almost," Annie said, slipping several more pieces of popcorn onto the string.

"Of course, you could always find another needle in that magic tackle box of yours and come help us," Marcy suggested dryly.

"No, no," he said, refilling the wood box. "I'm in no hurry." He shrugged out of his sheepskin jacket and hung it on the rack by the door. "And there's nothing magic about my tackle box. It's just well stocked."

"Well stocked?" Marcy echoed drolly. "You've got everything in there but the kitchen sink. I don't think a sewing kit is exactly what you'd call standard equipment for fishing."

"You've never lost a button or torn a sleeve?"

"Me or the fish?"

"Aren't we the funny one," he said, giving her a smile. He walked to the table where they sat working, rubbing his hands together. "We're going to want to keep the fire up tonight. There's another storm moving in and the temperature's really starting to drop.''

"Is it going to be too cold for Santa?" Annie asked.

"Oh, don't worry about Santa," Cruz assured her. "It never gets too cold for him." He reached across her into the nearly empty bowl of popcorn. "Hey, did you two manage to get any corn on the string?"

"Sure we did," Annie said with a laugh, missing the sarcasm in his voice. She pointed proudly to the long string spilled out on the table. "See?"

"I'm surprised," he said. Giving Marcy a sidelong glance, he arched a brow. "Given *some people's* fondness for popcorn."

"Now who's the funny one?" Marcy asked dryly, tossing a piece of popcorn back into the bowl and sitting back in the chair. "But I think even I have found my limit."

"Well, I should hope so," he said, grabbing up several pieces and popping them into his mouth. "So does that mean we don't have to worry about you sneaking around nibbling at the tree?"

"A funny man," she said again, picking up a piece and tossing it at him. "A very funny man."

He laughed, catching the popcorn in his mouth. "Good, I'm glad I could make you happy."

Happy. Marcy slowly sat up in her chair. She was aware that Cruz had turned away, that he was saying something to Annie and that Annie was saying something back, but she heard little of the exchange. She was too distracted, maybe even a little overwhelmed. He might have been joking just then, but it had struck at something very serious. He *could* make her happy, and had—happier than she could ever remember being. Despite the bombs and the danger, the primitive cabin and the uncertainties in their lives, the past and all the hurt there had been, she was happy. She was happy and it was all because of him—because he'd held her and kissed her and made her feel that nothing in the world was ever going to hurt her again—not even him.

"Shall we?"

She looked up into his dark, expectant eyes. "Hmm, what? Oh." She gave her head a small shake. "I'm sorry, what did you say?"

"The star for the tree. Should we put it on top now?"

She nodded. "Sure."

His smile faded. He put a finger under her chin, tilting her head up. "You were a million miles away just now. Everything okay?"

There was such concern in his face, such caring, it had a thick ball of emotion forming in her throat. Could this really be happening? Could what she was feeling in her heart be real? Had they really found each other again after all these years, after all that had happened between them? It seemed too good to be true, like something that happened in the movies or in a book, not to real people.

"Everything's fine," she whispered, feeling her eyes filling with tears. "Everything's perfect, in fact."

"But you're crying," he murmured, brushing a tear from her cheek.

She looked up at him and smiled. "Only because I'm so happy."

The hand on her cheek stopped suddenly. "You're happy?"

"Very happy."

He swallowed. "Honestly?"

For a moment there was nothing else in the world, just the two of them and a truth she had denied for far too long. "Honestly."

He pulled her close and kissed her, a long, deep kiss that blocked out everything and left her wanting for more.

"No," Annie shouted. "You're not supposed to do that yet."

The world came back in a crash, and Marcy felt herself turn cold all over. She pulled away from Cruz, turning just as Annie came storming across the cabin toward them.

"Annie, baby—" But she stopped when she felt Cruz's hand on her arm.

"Sweetheart," he said, stepping in front of Marcy and intercepting Annie as she ran across the cabin. "Does it bother you to see me kiss your mom?"

"You're not supposed to."

He bent down and lifted Annie up to them. "Because we're not married?"

Annie's eyes opened wide and she suddenly giggled, shaking her head. "No."

Marcy took a step forward. "Then why are you upset, baby?"

She reached around Cruz, pointing to the small mound of greenery stacked by the door. "'Cause we haven't hung up the mistletoe yet."

Marcy looked up at Cruz. He appeared as surprised as she felt. There was a brief moment of hesitation, and then they both burst out laughing. Pretty soon Annie was laughing, too, even though she wasn't exactly sure what it was she'd said that was so funny.

"Oh, baby." Marcy sighed, giving her daughter a hug. Tears stung her eyes again, from the laughter and from the happiness, then spilled down from her lids onto her cheeks.

This was how it could have been, she thought, feeling Cruz's arms move around her for a three-way hug. This was what their lives could have been like if the past hadn't tripped them up, if the hurt and the anger hadn't gotten in the way.

She closed her eyes, feeling emotion swell in her heart. She wasn't sure she believed in second chances. Besides, this didn't feel like a second try. It felt like a beginning—a new beginning—and she prayed they could get it right this time.

"Isn't it pre…pre—" Annie couldn't quite push the rest of the word out before a huge, full-mouth yawn caught hold.

Marcy glanced up at the Christmas tree and smiled, gathering Annie close. It did look beautiful, with its pine-cones, holly and popcorn garlands. The star at the top glimmered in the light of the lantern, appearing like the purest silver instead of aluminum foil.

The three of them had finished a Christmas Eve dinner of canned clam chowder and crackers hours ago. While she and Annie had cleaned up the dishes, Cruz had braved the cold and the snow to close shutters and restock the wood box. They'd all made one last trek to the outhouse for the night, and for the past hour had been sitting curled together on the sofa, singing Christmas carols, admiring their tree and listening to the storm howl outside.

"It's very pretty." Marcy sighed, remembering how Cruz had balanced Annie on his shoulders while she'd hung the star on the very crown of the tree. "But I think it's about time we got you into bed."

"No," Annie complained. She snuggled down deep between her parents and did her best to stifle another yawn. "I'm not sleepy."

"You know," Cruz said, running a hand along Annie's curls, "Santa Claus won't come until you're asleep."

Marcy put a hand on Cruz's arm, catching his eye. She

shook her head, hoping to stop him. She didn't want to
think about the morning, about how disappointed Annie
was going to be. She probably should have stopped Cruz
when he'd assured Annie again and again that Santa
wouldn't "lose" her, but she hadn't the heart. Annie's life
had been in enough upheaval. At the time it seemed a
harmless deception to give her the comfort of believing in
Santa, only now she wasn't so sure. The morning would
come, and she was going to have to find a way to make
Annie understand that Santa hadn't forgotten her; he'd just
left all her presents in the truck of their car somewhere in
the Mesa County sheriff's impound yard back in Mesa
Ridge.

"Come on," she said, sitting up. "Let's get you into
bed."

"No," Annie said, but her protest was more resigned
than rebellious this time.

"You heard your mom, squirt," Cruz said, rising to his
feet and bending to pick her up in his arms. Straightening,
he looked at Marcy. "I think it's time we all hit the hay."

Marcy felt herself flush all over. "Okay, cupcake," she
said, standing on legs that suddenly felt like water again.
"Up to the loft."

Cruz carried Annie to the ladder, and she rewarded him
with a hug around the neck that looked more like a stran-
glehold. "'Night, Coos."

"Good night, sweetheart," he said, giving her a kiss on
the cheek. "Felices Navidades."

Annie looked up at him and made a face. "What?"

Cruz laughed and lifted her onto the ladder. "That's
Spanish for Merry Christmas."

"Fallie—" Stumbling over the word, she stopped and
gave him a little smile. "Merry Christmas."

Marcy followed her up the ladder, then settled her into the feather bed beside her teddy.

"Mommy, will Santa be mad 'cause we don't have any cookies for him?"

"Oh, sweetheart." Marcy sighed, pushing Annie's curls back from her face. "I don't think he'll mind. This is a special Christmas, sort of unusual. He'll understand that we're doing things a little differently this year."

"'Cause of the bad person, huh?"

"Yes, baby," she said, running the backs of her fingers along Annie's cheek. "Because of the bad person. And that makes it an unusual Christmas for Santa, too. He may have to do things differently for us this year."

"Different?"

"Yes, you know, the way we made our Christmas wreath and our ornaments this year—that was different for us. Sometimes Santa has to do things differently, too."

"Different," Annie repeated with a yawn, thinking. "I know—like sometimes there's a fire in the fireplace and Santa has to come in the front door so he won't get burned. That's different, isn't it, Mommy?"

Marcy smiled. "Yes, sweetheart, that's different." She let the matter drop. Annie looked far too sleepy for much to sink in anyway. Marcy pulled the covers up and tucked her in. "Go to sleep, pumpkin. It's been a long day."

"Mommy?" Annie asked as Marcy leaned close. "How come Coos kisses you right here?" She pressed a finger against Marcy's lips. "And he kisses me right here?" She touched the spot on her own cheek where Cruz had kissed her good-night.

Marcy leaned back, looking down at her daughter. "Why don't we talk about this in the morning," she suggested, tucking the covers around Annie tight. "You need to go to sleep."

"That's the way mommys and daddys kiss on TV, isn't it?" Annie continued, not to be deterred.

"Some mommys and daddys kiss that way," Marcy conceded.

"Is Coos going to be my daddy now?"

Marcy's heart lurched. She'd had only a hint today of what their life could be like, what being a family would mean if she and Cruz were together. But they had a long way to go before any of that could happen, including telling Annie the truth.

"It's late, and I don't think this is the time to get into all this," she said. "We'll talk about it in the morning if you still want to."

"Coos doesn't have a wife, does he, Mommy?"

"I said we'd talk in the morning," Marcy repeated firmly.

"Do you like kissing Coos, Mommy?"

"Annie."

"Okay," she said in a small voice, recognizing the tone in her mother's voice. She grabbed her bear.

"Good night, baby," Marcy said with a smile, leaning down and giving her a kiss. Straightening up, she started for the ladder. "I'll be downstairs if you want me."

"'Night," Annie said, rolling onto her side. "Mommy?"

At the ladder Marcy stopped and turned around. "Yes?"

"I love you, Mommy."

Marcy smiled. "I love you, too, baby."

"And, Mommy?"

Marcy looked up as she began to climb down the ladder. "What is it?"

Annie hugged her bear to her, snuggling deep against her pillow. "Tell Coos I love him, too."

"I will, cupcake," she murmured in a voice barely above a whisper. "I will."

Marcy paused on the first step, a tremor making her legs feel unsteady beneath her. Annie did love Cruz, and he loved her, as well. There was no telling what was going to happen once they returned to their real lives, but that love was something that was never going to change.

Mommys and daddys. Today had been a fantasy, a fantasy mingled with enough fact that it created a distorted picture of the truth. She and Cruz were parents; they were a mommy and a daddy. But that hardly made the three of them a family.

Nothing that happened last night gave her any true insight into what he was feeling. They had shared needs and desires. He'd told her he wanted her; he'd even told her he loved her. But it would be foolish to hold on to anything said in the throes of passion. The truth was she didn't feel the same sense of certainty in his love for her as she did in his love for Annie. Last night had been a beautiful illusion and had started a beautiful dream in her mind—a beautiful dream where love conquered all and wishes really did come true.

She watched as Annie's eyelids began to droop and felt something painful twist in her heart. There was too much at stake for her to let her heart run away with her, and it was important she remember that. She was going to have to remind herself that none of this was real—not the situation, not the circumstances and maybe not even the feelings. This little cabin wasn't the real world, and she couldn't afford to let hopes and dreams and fantasies make her see things that simply weren't there.

"Good night, baby," she mumbled, starting slowly down the ladder.

Her dark thoughts had the warmth and good feelings

from the day slipping away, leaving her feeling lonely and
afraid. Cruz Martinez was an honorable man. He'd discovered he was a father, and nothing on this Earth was
going to make him deny his child. Was that what had him
turning to Marcy after all this time? Was it a sense of
obligation, a desire to do the right thing by his child, that
had him reaching out to the woman he'd deserted four
years before?

She'd gotten to the bottom of the ladder, feeling the cold
of the storm despite the heat radiating from the potbellied
stove. They needed to get some perspective on what was
happening, what was going on. Maybe they needed a
breather—maybe things were moving too fast. They
needed to iron things out, decide what it was that was
happening between them. Was it real, or was she reaching
for moonbeams and wishing on stars?

They needed to talk it all out before things went any
further, before they ended up in bed together again. She
stepped off the ladder onto the hard wooden floor, mulling
over what it was she wanted to tell him, what it was she
was going to say. But as she turned away from the ladder,
she found herself abruptly stopped and wrapped securely
in his arms.

"Kiss me," he whispered against her lips. "Right
now."

His mouth was fierce on hers, pushing her lips open
before she had a chance to breathe, before she had a
chance even to think. She forgot about the storm outside,
about being cold and afraid. Fire pulsed through her system, heating her blood and stirring the embers of need.

Somewhere in the back of her brain she knew she had
been worried about something, knew she had wanted to
talk to him, to tell him something, only she couldn't seem
to remember what it was at the moment. His lips were

moving on hers, starting a chain reaction and unleashing an ache and a longing that had her forgetting everything else. Whatever it was she'd wanted to say, whatever it was she'd wanted to discuss or straighten out, could wait until later.

"I want you," he growled against her lips.

She could feel his body grow hard, felt him tremble with the need. Everything else faded away—fear, anger, love, hate and doubt—everything but the hunger growing in her belly and the love that swelled her heart.

Chapter 14

"I'd wanted to talk."

Cruz turned his head on the pillow. The glow from the flame through the glass door of the stove caught the red in her hair, making it shine like gold. "Okay, let's talk."

She smiled just a little and shook her head. "It's a bit late now."

"You tired?"

She shook her head again. "I didn't mean it that way," she said, turning on her side. Cradling her head in her hand, she looked up at him. "I'd wanted to talk before we…" She shrugged, grimacing a little. "You know, *before*."

He raised a brow, nodding. "Oh." He paused for a moment, his eyes narrowing. "What did you want to talk about?"

"I thought maybe I should spend the night upstairs with Annie."

He turned then, too, moving his body to face hers. "You don't want to stay with me tonight?"

"It's not that, exactly."

"Then what, exactly?"

She shrugged, letting her gaze slide from his. They'd just made love—mindless, passionate love. And it wasn't as though she hadn't been a willing participant; she had been—more than willing, in fact. It seemed a little ridiculous talking about doubts and reservations now. "I thought maybe we need a little space."

He reached out, finding her beneath the heavy quilt and running his hand along the narrow inlet of her waist. "Space?"

"Yeah, you know, maybe get a little perspective on what's happening here."

He slid his hand from her waist over the swell of her hip. "What is happening here?"

She kept her eyes averted still. "I'm not sure." Then she looked up at him again. "Maybe you should tell me."

"What do you want me to tell you?"

"The truth." She drew in a shaky breath. "You're Annie's father. You're a part of her life now." She looked away, turning her entire body until she no longer faced him. "I don't want you to think that it's necessary...that you need to, you know..."

"Are you trying to say it's not necessary that you and I be together in order for me to have a relationship with my daughter?"

She nodded. Tears stung her eyes, and she didn't trust her voice to speak.

She felt him moving on the mattress, felt his arms around her waist and his body sliding behind her. He pulled her close, bringing his lips to her ear.

"Is that what you think this is about? My securing some kind of place in Annie's life by taking you to bed?"

Marcy felt the warmth of his body, felt the strength of his arms around her. "I don't know what to think."

"Then don't think at all," he said, turning her in his arms. "Just feel." He pressed a kiss against her chin, her jaw, her cheek, her lips. His body stirred and grew hard, and he held her tight against him. "Feel what you do to me, what we do to each other."

He kissed her again, and Marcy felt herself reacting, felt her blood heat and her loins begin to ache. Maybe he was right; maybe she was thinking too much, pushing and prodding, analyzing and scrutinizing, instead of just letting nature take its course. It hadn't been her intent to force him into a commitment.

"Cruz," she murmured against his lips.

"You want the truth," he said, holding her down against the mattress. "Are you sure you're ready for it?" But he gave her no time to answer, pushing her legs apart and settling himself between them. "I want you. But not because of Annie, not because I want a place in her life. Because I want a place in yours." He entered her in one powerful movement. "I want you because I love you. Is that honest enough?"

"You…love me," she whispered in a thick voice, heat rippling through her system like waves along the water.

"I love you, Marcy Fitzgerald," he said, his hands framing her face as his body took on a will of its own and began to move instinctively. "I always have and I always will."

"Oh, Cruz," she said, the motion of their bodies together creating a fever in her soul. "Cruz, I love you, too."

She couldn't remember much after that. The world faded into a haze of longing and sensation, of joy and fulfillment.

It was as if her own Christmas miracle had happened, as though all her prayers had been answered and her dreams had come true. She'd been given the most precious gift of all—the man she loved, loved her, too. She had his heart and his child. What more could she ever need out of life? The magic of Christmas had touched her in a very special way, and she would spend the rest of her life being grateful.

"I love you," he murmured into her ear after the fury had left them both sated and spent. His breath was ragged, and he held her to him tight. Like the storm outside, the frenzy of needs and desires had been stilled for a while, but the need to touch, the need to connect, the need to join, remained. "Don't ever doubt that. Don't ever doubt that."

"Where were you?" Marcy mumbled sleepily, feeling movement on the bed beside her.

"I just wanted to put another log on the fire," Cruz said, sliding beneath the quilt. "The storm has died down, but the temperature has dropped."

When his hands found her, she gasped and her whole body shivered. "You're freezing."

"Maybe because someone is wearing my shirt," he said, wrapping his arms around the soft cotton of his T-shirt that covered her body. He smiled, thinking how she'd insisted on wearing something so as not to be "surprised" by Annie again. "Warm me up."

Marcy turned and moved her arms up and around him. "It's like hugging an ice cube."

"Well, if there's one thing you can do, lady," he said, nuzzling his frigid nose into the crook of her neck, "it's melt ice." He kissed her neck, her shoulder, her chin.

"And rock and steel and..." He lifted his head, kissing her quickly on the mouth. "And me."

Marcy laughed, wide-awake now. "What time is it?"

"Around six, I think," he said, snuggling again. "It's starting to get light."

"Christmas morning," she said with a sigh.

He lifted his head again and looked down at her. "Yeah, Christmas morning," he said, trailing his hands over her body. "And just look at what Santa left for me." He kissed her again, longer this time. "This is just about the best Christmas morning I've ever had."

Marcy smiled up at him. He'd told her he loved her last night, and he'd shown her in all the ways that mattered that he meant what he said. It had changed everything for her—hopes, dreams, magic and miracles—and her life would never be the same.

"It's pretty special for me, too," she whispered, but after a moment her smile began to fade. "I just wish I could have found a way to make it special for Annie, as well. She's going to be so disappointed."

"We'll find a way to make it special," he assured her.

"I'm not sure that's possible," she said, breathing out a long sigh. "How do you explain to a three-year-old her Christmas had to be put on hold because of a nutcase like Brad Buck?" Marcy drew in a deep breath, staring up at the ceiling. "It's going to break her heart to find nothing under the tree. I should have tried to prepare her more, should have thought of some excuse to help cushion the blow."

Cruz slipped his arm beneath her to pillow her head. "Don't worry about it. Things have a way of working out. Besides, Christmas has its own sort of magic. Maybe Santa really will find a way."

She turned her head on his arm and looked up at him. "When did you become such a dreamer?"

He smiled and moved close, kissing her along her cheek. "When you came back into my life. I think I started believing in miracles then."

Marcy felt a thick lump of emotion in her throat. "Oh, Cruz, it really does feel like a miracle, doesn't it—you and me?"

"It feels pretty amazing," he agreed. He rolled onto his back, nestling her beside him. "And don't worry about Annie. We'll make her understand somehow."

Marcy settled against him, his body warm now and assuring. It was amazing; nothing really had been settled— she still didn't know what she was going to say to Annie, what kind of explanation she was going to make—and yet she felt assured. She had someone now, someone to share those parental burdens with, someone who loved Annie as she did. Cruz had said they would find a way to make Annie understand, and she believed what he said. He had a way of making her believe in the impossible—in miracles and magic, even Santa Claus.

"How do you do that?"

"How do I do what?"

"Manage to make me feel better, make me feel like everything's going to be okay?"

"Maybe everything *is* going to be okay."

"Maybe," she conceded. "But why do I feel better when you say it?"

He glanced down at her. "Is that what I do?"

"It's what you do to me."

"Oh, lady," he teased, lifting up on an elbow and nibbling at her neck. "If you only knew what you do to me."

"Cruz, don't. That tickles." She laughed, pushing at him. "I mean it—don't. Stop."

"What? Don't stop?" he asked devilishly, diving for her neck again. "Okay, if you insist."

"Cruz, please," she pleaded in a stage whisper. "You're going to wake up Annie. Now, stop. I'm trying to be serious."

"All right, all right," he said, letting her push him away. He collapsed against the mattress, turning his head to look at her. "I'll stop."

"Thank you," she said, maneuvering onto her side and resting her head on her hand. "I appreciate it,"

He gave a courteous nod. "I always do what I'm told."

"Oh, right," she scoffed, rolling her eyes. "You're a doctor."

"What does that have anything to do with it?" he wanted to know.

She gave him a caustic look, but inwardly she realized just how much she'd missed his presence in her life—his jokes, his teasing, his boyish smile. "A doctor never does what anyone tells him—ever. Everyone knows that."

"Oh? Everyone does, huh?"

"Yeah," she said, nodding. "Everyone."

"Is that right?" he queried thoughtfully. "And what is it they say about lawyers?"

"What?" she asked innocently. "That they're honest and hardworking, loyal and trustworthy?" She wound her leg around his. "It's all true."

"Oh, brother," he muttered, turning onto his side and bringing them face-to-face. "Did I ever happen to mention I dislike lawyers?"

"No, I don't think you happened to mention that," she said. "But it is quite a coincidence, what with me disliking doctors and all."

He edged closer, slipping a hand around her waist. "You know, I think we just might be the perfect couple."

She smiled, sliding her arms around his neck. "Is that what it is? Is that why I just feel better when I'm with you?"

"I think it's fate."

"No, really," she said, shaking her head. "I'm being serious."

His smile faded. "So am I." He pressed a gentle kiss against her lips, then looked into her eyes. "Maybe it feels good because it's right. Because we're where we're supposed to be." He brought his mouth to hers, moving against her lips. "Together."

His gentle kiss had her floating, had her drifting from the real world to that enchanted place that only existed for them. She had found her spot in the universe, her hidden nirvana, her own private Eden she shared only with him. They were together, mind and body, heart and soul. She was in the one place she truly was supposed to be—in the arms of the man she loved.

"Mommy! Mommy! Little dollies—he brought me little dollies. Santa, he found me and brought me little dollies."

Marcy jumped, snapping wide-awake. She glanced around the room, feeling dazed and confused, trying to put the world back on its axis again.

"Look," Annie said, climbing onto the bed and walking across the mattress. "Look what he brought. Look what Santa brought for me."

Marcy stared down at the small carved figures in Annie's hands, and gave her eyes a rub. She had no conscious memory of having drifted back to sleep in Cruz's arms after they'd talked in those quiet moments just before dawn, but obviously that was what she'd done. The sun was up now, pouring in bright from the window above the sink, and she scrambled to make her brain function again.

"Santa?" she mumbled, feeling stupid and thick. "Annie? Where did you get these?"

"From Santa," Annie said, pointing across the room. "And there's more, too. There's a horsey and a wagon, and a little baby." Annie stood up and teetered across the mattress, then jumped onto the floor and ran back across the room to the Christmas tree. "See?"

"I—I don't believe it," Marcy muttered, wrapping the sheet around herself and sitting up.

"See the horsey," Annie said, holding up another of the figures. "And the wagon."

"A horse and a wagon..." Marcy trailed off and ran a shaky hand through her hair.

"Actually, it's supposed to be a donkey and a cart," Cruz corrected, sitting up behind her and whispering in her ear. "But a horsey and a wagon is good enough."

Marcy reached down for the small figures on the bed and picked them up. A man and a woman. She turned to Cruz. "You did this."

He shrugged and smiled sheepishly. "Ho, ho, ho."

"But...how?" she asked, her voice cracking with emotion. "When?"

"I'd do a little here and there when I went out to chop wood," he said with a shrug. "The wood was soft—it didn't take very long. My grandfather taught all us kids how to whittle." He watched Annie as she gathered the rest of the figures up in her arms across the room. "I'm just glad she liked them—they're a far cry from Barbie and Ken."

"They're beautiful," Marcy said, feeling her eyes sting as she studied the figures in her hand. "I can't believe you did this."

Cruz turned his head and looked at her. "And I can't believe how lucky I am."

"Oh, Cruz." She sighed. "I love you."

"Merry Christmas, Marcy," he whispered, lowering his lips to hers.

Annie ran back to the bed and deposited the wooden toys on the mattress in front of her. "Can we check inside my stocking now?"

For a moment Marcy couldn't think of anything but Cruz's kiss and the intensity she saw in his dark eyes. But Annie wasn't to be deterred. She climbed up on the bed again and crawled between them, tugging on the sheet.

"Mommy. Coos. Can I see in my stocking now?"

Marcy looked down at Annie. "Stocking?"

"Yeah," Annie said, scooting back across the bed and sliding onto the floor. "That."

Marcy followed the direction in which Annie pointed, to the long, multicolored stocking hanging from the windowsill by the door. She looked back at Cruz. "Stocking?"

Cruz leaned close, whispering so that Annie couldn't hear. "I found a bunch in the back of Hattie's truck."

"Can I, Mommy? Can I see now?"

Marcy looked at Annie. "Sure, I—" she glanced up at Cruz, who gave a tiny nod "—I guess that would be okay." Then she watched as Annie darted back across the cabin, jumped up on tippy-toes and pulled the stocking down.

"You're wonderful," Marcy told Cruz with a sigh, leaning back against him. "Amazing and wonderful."

"Just a dad," he said, slipping an arm around her waist. "Thanks to you."

While Annie played with the beanbags she'd found in her stocking and her family of carved wooden toys, Marcy and Cruz dressed. The storm had passed during the night, leaving the air crisp and frigid and the sky crystal clear.

They made their way down to the small outhouse and back, and while Annie played with her new toys again, Marcy helped Cruz fix their Christmas breakfast of corned beef hash, canned bacon and pears, and crackers.

"This is the mommy," Annie said, putting down one of the wooden dolls and picking up another. "And this is the daddy." She held up the smallest figure. "And this one's the baby—her name is Annie." Then she gathered up all three dolls and put them into the cart. "All three together—just like us."

Cruz reached across the table to thread his fingers through Marcy's. "Just like us."

"Mommy? We're sorta like a family, huh?" Annie said, looking down at her toys. "You and me and Coos."

Marcy felt Cruz's hold on her hand tighten, and her heart stumbled. "Well, families are people who care about one another, and we care about one another."

"Yeah, 'cept I wish we had a horsey and a wagon instead of stupid old cars."

Cruz smiled at Annie's innocent remark and reluctantly tore his gaze from Marcy. He stood and rounded the table to where the little girl sat playing, then knelt down close. "You know, in the village in Mexico where my grandfather was born, the people were very poor and had to work very hard. Many times my grandfather would go to bed hungry because there weren't enough tortillas for all his brothers and sisters." He moved a glass and an empty can of pears so Annie could steer a path across the table. "One day, my grandfather came across a man on the road outside the village. The man—a stranger—had been tossed from his horse, and his clothes were torn and his hands and face were all dirty. He'd hurt his ankle and couldn't get back up on the saddle, so my grandfather helped him. The man was very grateful and thanked my grandfather and rode away, but several days later he returned, only this time he was dressed in the fine clothes of a don.''

"A don? What's a don?" Annie asked.

"A don is a nobleman, something like a prince," Cruz explained. "And this don had with him a *burro*." He reached around Annie and picked up the small wooden donkey. "And a *remolque*." He pointed to the cart. "The stranger gave them to my grandfather—a gift, a way for him to say thank-you to my grandfather for the help he had given him." Cruz set the figures back on to the table. "They were wonderful gifts, especially for a poor boy. With the *burro* and *remolque,* my grandfather was able to deliver cartloads of corn from the fields to the mills, and with the money he earned, he bought food for all his brothers and sisters. He used his gift for many years, and by the time the *burro* got too old to pull the cart, my grandfather had saved enough money to buy another *burro,* and then another one after that." He picked up the mommy and the daddy and the baby figure and put them inside the cart. "Many, many years later, when my grandfather came to the United States, he brought his *burro* and his *remolque* with him, and every Christmas he would give my brother and me and all my cousins a ride in the donkey cart."

"Just like this?" Annie asked, looking down at the dolls in the cart.

"Just like that," Cruz said, glancing across the table at Marcy. "He would tell us we should always remember how many good things could come from one small act of kindness."

Marcy felt emotion squeezing at her heart, and it was all she could do to keep the tears back. It had been a beautiful story, with far greater implications than Annie would be able to comprehend. It was a part of her heritage, a part of a history and a background she had yet to discover, and it wasn't until that moment that Marcy realized just how much she would be denying her daughter if she were to continue keeping the truth from her. This might not be the time and the place to tell Annie who Cruz really was and the part he would have in her life, but that had to happen soon—very soon.

"Your grandfather sounds like a very wise man," she said, her voice rough with emotion.

"He is," Cruz said, slowly rising to his feet and walking back around the table toward her. "I think you'd like him," he said, reaching for her hand and lifting her to her feet. "And I know he'd like you."

"Well, I hope—" Emotion had her voice catching in her throat. "I, uh, I hope to meet him someday."

"You know," he said in a low voice, pulling her close, "a wedding is a good place to get acquainted."

Marcy's heart skittered to a stop. "W-wedding?"

His hold around her tightened, and his voice grew serious. "Think about it."

"Cruz, are you asking me to—"

But Marcy's words were cut short when the door of the cabin burst open, sending a blast of light and frigid air inside.

"Merry Christmas," Joe Mountain said, his tall frame silhouetted against the sunlight. "And it is particularly merry now that Brad Buck is behind bars."

Chapter 15

"Socks," Cruz mumbled, leaning back against the seat and shaking his head slowly.

"Good old Hattie," Joe Mountain said with a laugh, turning the steering wheel hard and maneuvering his four-wheel-drive vehicle onto the shoulder of the road and around the tree limb lying across the blacktop. "Buck had managed to alter his appearance enough that he didn't even look like his mug shot. If Ryan hadn't spotted those socks in the back of the pickup he was driving, he would have sailed right through the roadblock."

"But how did socks get in the back of his pickup?" Marcy asked, turning as she looked up at Joe in the front seat beside her.

Joe's smile faded. "After...after you got out of there, the house went up."

"Oh, my God," Marcy gasped, covering her mouth with her hands. She turned farther and sent a shocked glance back at Annie and Cruz in the seat behind her.

Cruz leaned forward, putting a comforting hand on her shoulder, and spoke to Joe. "Varela?"

"He survived—barely—but only because he managed to crawl down into a root cellar Hattie had under the kitchen. It took us the better part of a day to dig him out." Joe slowed as they passed by several large boulders that had fallen onto the roadway from the cliffs above. "They found charred, burned socks for over a half mile—which is no doubt how some ended up in the back of the truck Buck had stolen."

"I can't believe it," Marcy murmured, looking from Joe to Cruz.

"Socks," Cruz said again, his mouth cracking with a small smile. "Unbelievable."

Joe started it, first with a smile, then a chuckle, but it worked like the first domino toppling in a long line. Soon they were all laughing, relief making the absurdity of the situation seem all the more comical.

"Damn, if the press only knew," Joe said finally, pulling in a deep breath. "They'd have a field day."

"Press?" Cruz asked. Suddenly there didn't seem to be anything to laugh about.

"Yeah, they began arriving once the FBI announced Buck had been captured," Joe said, glancing across the seat toward Marcy. "And once your boss arrived."

Marcy turned to him. "Randall's here?"

Joe nodded. "Wanted to be here to greet you himself," he said."

Marcy breathed out a small laugh and slowly shook her head. "And of course what better way to do that than in front of a horde of reporters." She looked back at Cruz. "Randall, always the politician."

"Yeah," Cruz mumbled with a feeble smile. "Always."

"Sheriff," Marcy said, turning to Joe again. "Do you know if anyone contacted my parents? Do they know we're all right?"

"They arrived with the big man himself last night," Joe said, tilting his head to look at Cruz through the rearview mirror. "I'd have been up to get you yesterday, but that storm front moved in and the roads have been a mess. Hang on—" He jerked the wheel hard again, slowing the car to a crawl to avoid another boulder that had fallen and left the blacktop cracked and broken. "See what I mean?"

"I'm beginning to," Cruz murmured, leaning forward slightly and peering out the front windshield at the littered roadway.

"It's fun," Annie said with a giggle as the broken pavement had the car jerking wildly.

With no car seat available, Annie sat in the back seat next to Cruz, clutching her little donkey and cart in one hand, her bear in the other, and bouncing wildly in the seat.

"Is your seat belt fastened tight?" Marcy asked, looking back. "Let Cruz check it. I don't want you bouncing out of there and getting hurt."

Cruz reached across the seat to test the restraints around Annie, then gave Marcy's arm a comforting pat. "She's tucked in tight."

Marcy looked at him and squeezed his hand. "Make sure you are, too."

Cruz felt something tighten in his chest as he watched her turn back around in her seat. The thought of what awaited them—the reporters, the "big man himself"—had a wave of dread rising up and washing over him. If only they could step back—back to that moment before Joe Mountain had arrived, before the world had come crashing in, to when he'd been holding Marcy and everything had seemed so right in his life.

He looked down at his hands, curling them into tight fists. He was relieved that Buck had been apprehended. Who in his right mind would want a madman like that on the loose? The man needed to be locked up, deserved it. *Of course* he was glad the creep was finally behind bars. Only…

The tension in his chest inched a degree higher, and Cruz shifted uneasily on the seat. The nightmare was over; they were free again. They'd been given back their lives—no more federal agents or police or safe houses, and no more hiding. Only…

Only why did it have to happen now?

All he'd wanted was a little more time, a few more hours, one more day. Was it so wrong to have wanted them all to himself for Christmas, to want to make snow angels in the snow with Annie and spend a long night with Marcy in his arms? Was wanting to be alone with his child, his woman, his family, too much to ask?

"Have they transferred Buck back to D.C. yet?" he asked Joe. "I don't want that guy anywhere near—"

"Don't worry, federal agents moved him out yesterday morning," Joe assured him, slowing the truck as they came to the end of the canyon and the narrow mountain road merged with the interstate highway. "This is more like it," he said, turning onto the smooth, wide highway. "We'll be back to civilization in no time now."

Cruz clenched his fists tighter. What was the matter with him? Why was he feeling so ridiculously let down? A wonderful thing had just happened: they'd been rescued, been given back their lives and their freedom. He should feel happy, encouraged, relieved.

So why was he acting as if he'd just lost his best friend—again.

He'd all but asked her to marry him—he *wanted* her to marry him. Nothing had happened; nothing had changed. They were still the same people, still Cruz and Marcy, still together and happy.

Cruz's entire body tensed. Whom was he kidding? Something had happened. The world had found them, had invaded their quiet haven, and everything had changed. It wasn't just about the three of them any longer, about Marcy and Annie and Cruz. There were other people to consider, other loyalties and responsibilities to consider, and the farther they got from the isolated mountain cabin, the more certain he was it would never be the same again.

"Hello, Dr. Martinez, welcome back."

Cruz glanced up at the student nurse behind the information counter as he walked through the hospital foyer toward the nurses' station. "Uh, thanks," he mumbled. "Thank you."

"Hey, Doc, saw you on TV last night. Lookin' good. Glad to see you back in one piece."

"Yeah, Rudy," Cruz said, nodding to the orderly, "Thanks."

His first twelve hours back in Mesa Ridge had been total chaos, and the second had turned into a nightmare, with Marcy tossing him out of her hotel room and slamming the door in his face. Not that he could blame her exactly. He'd managed to hurt her—again. Only this time there would be no chance for forgiveness.

They had arrived back in town yesterday afternoon to an even worse media frenzy than he'd expected. He'd had only a few moments with Annie and Marcy, a few moments alone, before all hell had broken out.

Andrew and Eleanor Fitzgerald had been there to greet their daughter and grandchild, and his own parents had driven the RV he'd given them last year for Christmas up from Los Angeles to see for themselves that he was safe and okay. But it wasn't the reunion of families the press had wanted to see; it was U.S. Attorney General Randall Crane.

In a hastily put-together press conference conducted from Joe Mountain's office, Randall Crane spoke with the eloquence of a polished professional. Before the glare of the cameras and with flashbulbs snapping furiously, he praised Marcy for the work she'd done, lauded the law enforcement agencies who had worked together to apprehend the fugitive and even managed to thank Cruz for having kept Marcy and Annie safe while Buck was on the loose.

Cruz had watched the drama unfold around him, feeling dissociated from all the confusion. He'd answered the reporters' questions, sat there and let the photographers take their pictures, but it was as though he'd been watching all this happen to someone else, as though he were no longer a part of the action. He'd felt alienated, out of place, as if they'd come a million miles through space from the tiny world of the cabin, from the world where Marcy loved Cruz and the three of them had been a family.

He had watched Marcy accept the acclaim from her famous boss with modesty and grace, had watched her handle the crush of reporters and the barrage of questions with poise and assurance. She was incredible—beautiful and smart, confident and elegant. She had so much to offer, was capable of doing so much.

He pushed through the door of the doctors' lounge, where he slipped off his sheepskin jacket and hung it on a hook inside his locker. He stared at the jacket for a moment, thinking about the morning before—Christmas morning. He'd had everything he'd wanted that morning—Marcy and Annie and a heart full of hope. Only…

Only so much had changed since then.

He slipped his hand into the pocket of the jacket, feeling around for the object at the bottom, then pulling it out. He looked down at the small wooden ring he had carved, the ring he'd made for Marcy, the ring he'd wanted to give to her in lieu of a diamond when she agreed to be his wife.

He tossed the ring back into the pocket and slammed the locker door closed. It had been a stupid idea, stupid and unrealistic. If he'd been thinking at all he would have realized that what had happened between them had been a result of the situation, of the solitude and the fear. She had turned to him because she had needed him, because she had been grateful and she could rely on him to help. She might have told him she loved him, but how could he hold her to that? Between Brad Buck, the car accident, being shot and being on the run, how would she possibly know how she was feeling? How could she know how she felt about him?

"Well, look what the cat dragged in."

Cruz turned at the sound of Carrie's voice. The sight of her solid frame swallowing up the doorway had emotion swelling in his throat, taking him by surprise.

"And here I thought you would have missed me," he said, hoping humor would cover the unexpected sentimentality.

"Miss you?" Carrie snorted, stepping inside and letting the door swing closed behind her. "You been gone?"

Cruz breathed out a small smile. "Just a little while, yeah."

"Just like you to go gallivanting off somewhere, having a high old time, while the rest of us are stuck here hard at work." She walked across the room and wrapped her arms around him in a bear hug. "Of course, I couldn't turn on the television last night without seeing your ugly mug there. Who do you think you are—Dirty Harry?"

"I guess," Cruz said, struggling with the lump of emotion.

Carrie pulled back and looked up at him, her face serious now and her eyes shimmering with tears. "You okay—really?"

"Fine," he said in a tight voice. "I'm fine."

She pushed him back and turned away, making a few impatient swipes at her eyes. "I suppose you're going to be all stuck-up now, expecting us to ask you for your autograph and all that."

Cruz smiled. "I suppose."

"So what about this Mrs. Fitzgerald and the little girl?" she asked, turning around and planting her hands squarely on her hips. "They okay?"

"It's…Miss," he murmured, walking quickly to the shelf beside the locker and reaching for a clean set of surgical greens. "And they're…fine." He didn't want to think about Marcy, about the look on her face or the tears in her eyes. He'd done the right thing; he had to believe that, despite how much it hurt. There could be no future for them, and someday she would realize that. "Getting ready to go back to D.C."

"Oh, really," Carrie said, giving a nod. "Well, I suppose when you're used to a place like Washington, D.C., Mesa Ridge must seem pretty dull."

"Yeah, I guess," he said, remembering the shock and the anger in Marcy's eyes when she'd kicked him out of her hotel room last night, remembering the sound of Annie's little voice calling after him. "She's been offered a job at the Supreme Court, clerking for one of the justices."

Carrie's eyes opened wide. "Wow."

"Yeah," he mumbled. He pulled the starched surgical shirt on over his head, thinking of how the reporters had gone wild when Crane had made the announcement at the press conference the other night, bringing a barrage of questions. He knew Marcy had been surprised by the prestigious offer and had insisted she would have to give it some thought, but what was there to decide? "It's the opportunity of a lifetime," he said, telling Carrie the same thing he'd said to Marcy last night at her hotel. "An offer she can't refuse."

"Of course not," Carrie agreed. "Not if that's the sort of thing she wants to do."

Cruz looked up, having been so lost in thought he'd forgotten all about Carrie standing there, all about the conversation he'd been having with her. "What did you say?"

Carrie shrugged. "I said, it's a wonderful opportunity if that's the sort of thing she wants to do."

"Of course she wants to do it," he insisted. "She'd have to—I mean, it's...it's an incredible opportunity."

"That's great, then," Carrie said simply.

"I mean, she'd be a fool to pass up something like that," he went on, tossing the surgical pants onto the floor in a heap. "It's the Supreme Court, for heaven's sake— the *Supreme Court*. How could she turn down the Supreme Court? How could she give that up just to..."

"Just to what?"

Cruz closed his eyes. How could she give that up just to be his wife? And how could he ask her to?

He glanced down at the neatly folded surgical trousers he held in his hands. He'd let things get way out of hand, allowed himself to forget for just a moment, and now he'd gone and hurt her again. He'd had no business asking her to marry him, had no right to expect her to give up everything just to be with him. He wasn't free. He still had an obligation to the people of Mesa County, but just because he was tied to this sparsely populated, out-of-the-way place it didn't mean he had the right to ask her to be.

"Just to what?" Carrie asked again.

Cruz looked into Carrie's kind face and shook his head. "Nothing, never mind."

"Well," Carrie said, "I think she's a terrific lady, and if that's what she wants, I hope things work out for her."

"Yeah, that's what she wants," Cruz mumbled as Carrie walked through the doorway and disappeared down the corridor. Of course she would want it—eventually—when she wasn't letting gratitude and appreciation get in the way of her thinking. Someday she would realize just what a life with him would cost her, how much she would have to give up. He'd made the right decision, and someday she would thank him. Someday...

He felt a cold sensation move through him, making him stagger back a step and turning his blood to ice. Dear Lord, he was doing it again. He was deciding for himself what he thought was best for them—what was best for her.

He reeled against the lock, causing the door to slam shut. Marcy had accused him of not listening, of trying to make her decisions for her. How could he have been so foolish, so arrogant—*again?*

He loved her; he always had. He'd only been trying to give her what she wanted, or rather...

He turned, hammering a fist into the locker. Or rather, what he *thought* she wanted. He hadn't trusted her to know her own mind or to love him. That was exactly the kind of thinking that had lost her once, and now he'd gone and done it again.

"Oh, Marcy," he whispered, moving away from the

locker and heading for the door. "What have I done? What have I done?"

Marcy pushed through the swinging doors, balancing Annie on her hip, and stormed to the information desk.

"I need to see Dr. Martinez," she said to the young woman behind the desk.

"Do you have an appointment?"

"An appointment?" She shook her head. "No, could you just call him and tell him—"

"Mrs. Fitzgerald?"

"It's Miss," Marcy murmured, then turned and spotted Carrie Burns coming down the corridor toward her.

"I thought it was you," Carrie said, stopping at the counter beside them. Reaching out, she tweaked Annie's nose. "Hi there, pumpkin, how's my favorite little helper?"

Annie smiled shyly and stuck two fingers in her mouth. "Fine."

"Mrs. Burns, we're looking for Cruz," Marcy said, lowering Annie to the ground. "Could you help us find him?"

"Sure," Carrie said, motioning them to follow. "He's in the doctors' lounge. Come on, I'll show you." She started back down the corridor. "I hear congratulations are in order."

Marcy looked up. "What?"

"The new job," Carrie said. "Cruz was telling me about it. The Supreme Court—that sounds pretty exciting."

"I suppose it does," Marcy said with a tired sigh.

"Coos! Coos!"

Both Marcy and Carrie looked over as Annie took off down the hallway.

"Well, I guess you've found him," Carrie said, nodding

to Cruz as he stepped from the doctors' lounge. "Goodbye, Mrs.—I mean, Miss Fitzgerald." She glanced back at Annie just as Cruz caught her and lifted her high in his arms, then at Marcy again. "And good luck."

Luck, Marcy thought as Carrie walked away. She was going to need more than that if she was going to get through this.

Starting down the hall toward Annie and Cruz, Marcy felt the pulse in her neck start to race. She'd been determined and ready when she'd arrived at the hospital; only now, seeing Cruz, she was just feeling nervous. But she'd come too far to let a case of nerves stop her. She'd allowed pride and hurt feelings to keep her from what she'd wanted once; she wasn't about to let it happen again.

"Mommy says I can stay with you," Annie said, bouncing with excitement on Cruz's hip. "I get to stay."

"Stay with me?" Cruz's gaze flew from Annie to Marcy then back.

"Just for a few days," Marcy said, pleased the shaking in her knees didn't reverberate in her voice. "While I take care of some details for the new job. Do you mind?"

"The new job," Cruz repeated, feeling as if he'd taken another shot in the stomach. He was too late. He'd lost her again. "You took the job?"

"It was time for a change," she said, the pale expression on his face bolstering her just a little. "I start the first of the year, which gives me only a few days to close things out at the attorney general's office."

"I was hoping I...we could talk about that."

"I thought we'd already done that last night."

"I know, but—"

"Besides, there's nothing left to talk about," she said, cutting him off. "I've made up my mind. I'll be heading for D.C. day after tomorrow and I'd like to leave Annie with you, if that's all right.''

"Of course. You know that," he said, looking at Annie and feeling himself die just a little inside. How cold and desolate his life was going to be, how empty and useless without the two people he loved the most. "And...and when you're ready, when you've gotten things settled, I'll fly her home to you."

Marcy squared her shoulders. "That won't be necessary."

Cruz's frown deepened. "What do you mean that won't be necessary?"

Marcy looked up at him. "I mean it won't be necessary."

"But..." Cruz gave his head a confused shake and started again. "I don't understand. You want to fly back and get her?"

"I mean Annie isn't leaving." Marcy's heart thudded so loudly in her chest she was certain he would hear. "I'm going to be gone for only a few days—to tie up some loose ends in D.C. and put the house up for sale."

Cruz slowly lowered Annie to the ground. "Your...your house for sale?"

"Well, it would be a little silly to keep it if we're living in Mesa Ridge."

"Mesa—" Cruz's voice gave out. He staggered back a step. "Mesa Ridge?"

"Of course Mesa Ridge," Marcy said, feeling her voice quivering with emotion, but it didn't matter this time. "Where else is a Mesa County Superior Court judge going to live but Mesa Ridge?"

"Superior Court jud—"

"The governor appointed me this afternoon," she added when his voice gave out again.

"Mommy said we're going to be a family," Annie declared, tugging on his pant leg. "For real this time."

Cruz felt his knees buckle, and he staggered back another step. He looked down at Annie, then at Marcy. "Do you...do you mean it?"

"Of course I mean it," Marcy said, stepping close and moving her hands up the front of his surgical shirt. "You asked me to think about a wedding, and I've thought about it and decided it's a pretty good idea. Of course, you can try to back out—again—but let me warn you we take breach of promise seriously in this county. I just might be forced to throw the book at you."

Cruz could barely hear because of the ringing in his ears. "When you told me you'd taken the job I thought..." He slipped his hands around her waist, pulling her close. "I thought...I thought I was too late."

"You were," she said simply, putting her arms around his neck. "Which is exactly why I decided to take matters into my own hands."

"Marcy," he whispered, his voice raw with emotion. "Marry me."

"Yes," she murmured without hesitation, surrendering to his kiss.

"Me, too," Annie said, pulling at them both.

They both looked down at Annie and laughed.

"You, too," Cruz said, bending down and bringing her up to them. He turned to Marcy, kissing her on the mouth again. "Thank you."

"For what? Saying yes?" She smiled. "Don't forget, it's what I want, too."

Cruz smiled, pulling her close for another kiss. "Yeah, it is, isn't it?"

"Does this mean you're the daddy now?" Annie asked impatiently, squeezed between the two adults.

"It sure does, baby," Cruz said, gazing at his daughter in his arms and feeling that he'd been given a second shot at Christmas.

"For real this time?" Annie asked.

"For real." Cruz smiled, turning to Marcy. "And forever."

Epilogue

"I do," Marcy whispered, feeling Cruz's hand tighten around hers.

"Then with the power vested in me by the people of Mesa County and the State of Nevada, I now pronounce you husband and wife." Retiring Judge Melvin Riley closed the book he held and turned to Cruz. "You may now kiss your bride."

His bride. Cruz heard those words and felt a calm, peaceful feeling settle over him. After having waited what seemed like a lifetime, it had finally happened—they were husband and wife; Marcy belonged to him now. He turned to her, carefully lifting the short, delicate veil that covered her face, and gathered her into his arms.

"I love you, Mrs. Martinez," he whispered, bringing his lips to her.

"Mrs. Martinez," Marcy repeated with a sigh, kissing him again. "She loves her husband very much."

"Congratulations," Joe Mountain said, stepping up

from his position as best man and placing a hand on Cruz's shoulder. "And I do believe it is my turn to kiss the bride." Leaning forward, he placed a gentle kiss on Marcy's cheek. "Cruz is one lucky man."

"Well, I wish I could say the same for this sweet girl you married." Carrie sighed dryly, shifting her matron-of-honor bouquet to one hand and giving Cruz a no-nonsense kiss on the jaw. "But I'm afraid your pretty wife is going to have her hands full with you."

Cruz felt himself grinning—a big, sappy, toothy, ear-to-ear grin—but he couldn't seem to help it. He was feeling pretty sappy at the moment.

"My wife," he repeated, turning to Marcy again. "I like the sound of that."

Marcy smiled. "I'm glad to hear my husband say that."

"Hey, wait a minute."

They both looked down, spotting Annie as she pushed her way through the cluster of adults that towered above her.

"What is it, baby?" Cruz asked, bending to scoop her up in his arms. He still wasn't sure she had understood everything they'd told her last night about how he'd been her daddy even before the marriage ceremony, but that was okay. There would be time later for reasons and explanations, when she was older and better able to comprehend the complications of the past. It was enough that she had accepted him into her life and they loved each other.

"When he asked if you wanted to be married," Annie said, pointing to Judge Riley, "you said, 'I do.'"

"That's right."

"And when he asked Mommy if she wanted to be married, she said, 'I do.'"

"That's right, I did," Marcy said, feeling a pang of guilt as she reached up and pushed a long auburn curl back from

Annie's face. The twenty-four hours that had passed since she'd stormed into Mesa County General Hospital had been frantic, frenzied and wonderful. Maybe it had been a little impulsive to want to get married right away—immediately, in fact—but hadn't they waited long enough already? Besides, their families were all still there in Mesa Ridge. Why wait? Still, putting a wedding together on a moment's notice hadn't been easy. But with everyone pitching in, it had gone off without a hitch. Only now, looking into Annie's sad little face, she was beginning to wonder if things were happening just a little too fast for the child. "Did that confuse you, sweetheart?"

Annie shook her head, her tiny mouth twisted in a frown. "Uh-uh."

Cruz tilted her head up with a finger under the chin. "Then why the sad face? I thought you wanted us to be married."

"He didn't ask me," Annie said, her eyes growing wide. "*I do, too.*"

Marcy and Cruz glanced at each other, and both breathed out a sigh of relief.

"Well, if you do," Cruz said, giving his daughter a squeeze, "and I do and your mom does—" he looked from his daughter to his wife and smiled broadly "—then I pronounce us a family...at last!"

* * * * *

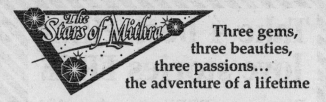

Take 4 bestselling love stories FREE

Plus get a FREE surprise gift!

Special Limited-time Offer

Mail to Silhouette Reader Service™

3010 Walden Avenue
P.O. Box 1867
Buffalo, N.Y. 14240-1867

YES! Please send me 4 free Silhouette Intimate Moments® novels and my free surprise gift. Then send me 6 brand-new novels every month, which I will receive months before they appear in bookstores. Bill me at the low price of $3.34 each plus 25¢ delivery and applicable sales tax, if any.* That's the complete price and a savings of over 10% off the cover prices—quite a bargain! I understand that accepting the books and gift places me under no obligation ever to buy any books. I can always return a shipment and cancel at any time. Even if I never buy another book from Silhouette, the 4 free books and the surprise gift are mine to keep forever.

245 BPA A3UW

Name	(PLEASE PRINT)	
Address	Apt. No.	
City	State	Zip

This offer is limited to one order per household and not valid to present Silhouette Intimate Moments® subscribers. *Terms and prices are subject to change without notice. Sales tax applicable in N.Y.

UMOM-696   ©1990 Harlequin Enterprises Limited

As seen on TV!
Free Gift Offer

With a Free Gift proof-of-purchase from any Silhouette® book,
you can receive a beautiful cubic zirconia pendant.

This gorgeous marquise-shaped stone is a genuine cubic
zirconia—accented by an 18" gold tone necklace.

(Approximate retail value $19.95)

Send for yours today...
compliments of *Silhouette*®

To receive your free gift, a cubic zirconia pendant, send us one original proof-of-
purchase, photocopies not accepted, from the back of any Silhouette Romance™,
Silhouette Desire®, Silhouette Special Edition®, Silhouette Intimate Moments®
or Silhouette Yours Truly™ title available at your favorite retail outlet, together with
the Free Gift Certificate, plus a check or money order for $1.65 U.S./$2.15 CAN. (do
not send cash) to cover postage and handling, payable to Silhouette Free Gift Offer.
We will send you the specified gift. Allow 6 to 8 weeks for delivery. Offer good until
December 31, 1997, or while quantities last. Offer valid in the U.S. and Canada only.

Free Gift Certificate

Name: _____

Address: _____

City: _____ State/Province: _____ Zip/Postal Code: _____

Mail this certificate, one proof-of-purchase and a check or money order for postage
and handling to: SILHOUETTE FREE GIFT OFFER 1997. In the U.S.: 3010 Walden
Avenue, P.O. Box 9077, Buffalo NY 14269-9077. In Canada: P.O. Box 613, Fort Erie,
Ontario L2Z 5X3.

FREE GIFT OFFER   084-KFD
ONE PROOF-OF-PURCHASE
To collect your fabulous FREE GIFT, a cubic zirconia pendant, you must include this
original proof-of-purchase for each gift with the properly completed Free Gift Certificate.

084-KFDR

Return to the Towers!

In March
New York Times bestselling author

NORA ROBERTS

brings us to the Calhouns' fabulous
Maine coast mansion and reveals the
tragic secrets hidden there for generations.

For all his degrees, Professor Max Quartermain has a
lot to learn about love—and luscious Lilah Calhoun is
just the woman to teach him. Ex-cop Holt Bradford is
as prickly as a thornbush—until Suzanna Calhoun's
special touch makes love blossom in his heart.
And all of them are caught in the race to solve
the generations-old mystery of a priceless
lost necklace…and a timeless love.

Lilah and Suzanna
THE
Calhoun Women

**A special 2-in-1 edition containing
FOR THE LOVE OF LILAH and
SUZANNA'S SURRENDER**

Available at your favorite retail outlet.

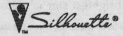

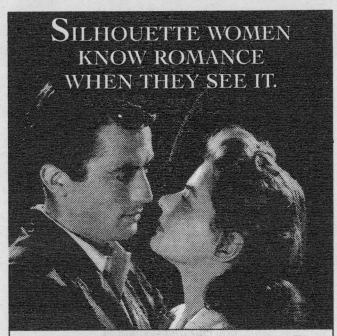